On
Dearborn
Street

On Dearborn Street

MILES FRANKLIN

with an introduction by Roy Duncan

University of Queensland Press
St Lucia · London · New York

© University of Queensland Press, St Lucia, Queensland 1981

Typeset by University of Queensland Press
Printed and bound by Hedges & Bell Pty Ltd, Melbourne

Distributed in the United Kingdom, Europe, the Middle East, Africa, and the Caribbean by Prentice-Hall International, International Book Distributors Ltd, 66 Wood Lane End, Hemel Hempstead, Herts., England.

National Library of Australia
Cataloguing-in-Publication data

Published with the assistance of the Literature Board of the Australia Council.

Franklin, Miles, 1879-1954.
    On Dearborn Street.

    ISBN 0 7022 1636 4.

    I. Title.

A823'.2

Library of Congress Cataloging in Publication Data

Franklin, Miles, 1879-1954.
    On Dearborn Street.

    Includes bibliographical references.
    1. World War, 1914-1918 — Fiction. I. Title.
PR9619.3.F6805   1982   823   81-11570
ISBN 0 7022 1636 4   AACR2

INTRODUCTION

Should a full-scale biography of Miles Franklin ever appear, it will probably show how she tried, with no leverage but *My Brilliant Career* and an aggressive personality, to influence and manipulate her publishers. Throughout the half-century of her writing life she niggled about contracts and advertising. In the late 1920s, when local speculation arose as to the identity of Brent of Bin Bin, renewed interest developed in *My Brilliant Career*. Miles steadily resisted all overtures to republish this book. Sensing a bargaining position in dangling it out of reach, she would proffer other manuscripts. In consequence, some novels have been published years out of their time sequence; some have done nothing to enhance their author's reputation, while others, worthy of publication in their day, have never seen the light. Among the last-mentioned are several manuscripts from the World War I era and, of these, *On Dearborn Street* is perhaps the most representative sampling from its author's American phase.

So far as that prolific period is concerned, nothing in the nature of an extended composition has found its way into print except *The Net of Circumstance* — and that would appear to have been still-born as it left the press in 1915, through its author's interference or wartime restrictions or both. The surviving five manuscripts from those years all show a fuller zest and competence than do certain published works from before and after. (Instances of interesting ideas embedded in artistic failure are *Some Everday Folk and Dawn* (1909) and *Prelude to Waking* (*circa* 1924, published 1950).

Hindsight suggests at least three reasons why we should feel it a matter of regret that *On Dearborn Street* was not published when written. In the first place it provides an American parallel to *My Brilliant Career,* which students of that first novel could fruitfully explore. Secondly it exemplifies a marked contrast in its dominant emotional tone to Miles's earlier and later "realism". Thirdly (for a minus which sociologocal interest now argues a plus), it escapes intermittently from its central theme to leave us some first-hand contemporary impressions of the outbreak of World War I. The vantage-point is specially interesting for being located in the then-neutral United States and for pointing to an American moral dilemma in that context.

Until the mid-1960s it had been generally supposed that after *My Brilliant Career* (1901) Miles had lost her creative drive and not recovered it until Brent of Ben Bin appeared with the chronicle novel a generation later.[1] The interval broadly corresponds with her expatriate life (U.S.A., 1906-15; England, 1916-27). The lapse in actual publications makes the supposition plausible, and it was tempting to infer that whatever her vision lacked was to be found exclusively in Australia. In fact the evidence is otherwise.

The shock of World War I, together with continuing irresolution about woman's position in society and marriage as an institution, stimulated five full-length manuscripts. One of the earliest, "Red Cross Nurse" (1914), is an impassioned piece. Digressing savagely on male responsibility for the War, it speaks of "this half-tamed yahoo, this ninety percent criminal which is known as civilized man". The script appears to contain a significant measure of autobiography. The late Bruce Sutherland, relying on diary entries, inferred particular friendships with several rich young Americans, one of whom was Demarest Lloyd.[2] "Demmie" seems to have inspired the dangerous playboy of "Red Cross Nurse". Part of him also appears in Dearborn Street's Bobby Hoyne, where the moral deficiencies are distanced by humor. To the same period belongs the above-mentioned

Net of Circumstance. This novel, with its focus on the plight of an American woman whose life-style and feminist discernment are remarkably parallel to those of the author, has remained a mystery book — unsold, uncirculated, and therefore unread.[3] Rather different in structure and emphasis is "Love Letters of a Superfluous Woman" — a monologue of grief for a soldier killed in the War. It appears to have been written in 1919, after Miles had completed her stint of duty with a unit from the Scottish Women's Hospitals in Serbia. Finally, in 1921, "Sam Price from Chicago" was completed. It alludes to several of the Dearborn Street characters. Plotting follows the familiar pattern of a girl and two different men, but, unlike Dearborn Street, the tone is seriously adapted to war-time tension. Ultimately the lover, blinded in battle, becomes completely dependent upon the woman who has given herself to him. Here is an endorsement of the idea which accounts for Miles Franklin's interest in *Jane Eyre* — that the marriage works when circumstances give mastery to the wife. It is reminiscent of a reference to Harold Beecham in *My Brilliant Career*: "He offered me everything — but control".

On Dearborn Street commenced as "the Sybyl story" in 1913. At this time, and over the next year or two, negotiations were proceeding in an intermittent way for the publication of *The Net of Circumstance*. It was August 1915 before a further diary reference was made to working on the Dearborn Street manuscript.

By then Miles had become thoroughly acclimatized. She had been in the United States for almost a decade. For most of that time she had worked in secretarial and editorial positions in the National Women's Trade Union League of America, and had taken a special interest in the American woman. She saw the latter as generally belonging to one of two categories — working women struggling for social justice and independence (whose cause was her own), and privileged women who had purchased power by marrying into wealth (whom she despised). Local color and American colloquialisms had become second nature. Words such as "dudeling", "stand-patting", "yawping" in *On Dearborn Street* are used in a completely unselfconscious way, and the only concession to Australian origin appears in a single echo from Paterson ("and all the veterans had gathered to the fray"). In her preface she identifies fully with the supposed characteristics of the "United Stateser". It must be remembered that, in her American period, Miles's executive position in a women's organization of forty thousand gave her a voice and an identity which she had never enjoyed in Australia. It both gratified and exhausted her. Despite her eventual strained relationship with the overbearing Mrs. Robins, she adopted the "Murkans" very naturally. With them she came to maturity.

That being so, it may seem a little surprising to find anything in the nature of a parallel to *My Brilliant Career* emerging from this maturity. *My Brilliant Career* had been a spontaneous phenomenon — a naive expression from a twenty-year-old Australian bush girl, based in the up-country environment which limited her entire experience. The first obvious difference between this and *On Dearborn Street* is that the latter is a sophisticated city novel, written when its author was well into her thirties. Yet each is essentially an exploration of courtship and an attempt to come to terms with the idea of marriage. Each stems from a sense of the woman's disadvantage and of society's evident acquiescence in that disadvantage. The Australian "universal" which A. G. Stephens discerned in *My Brilliant Career* went only part of the way. Stephens wrote:

> All over this country, brooding on squatters' verandahs or mooning in selectors' huts, there are scattered here and there hundreds of lively, dreamy Australian girls whose queer, uncomprehended ambitions are the despair of the household. They yearn, they aspire for what they know not; but it is essentially a yearning for a fuller, stronger life . . . . (*The Bulletin*, 28 September 1901).

But while Sybylla Melvyn yearned she was specific about the central difficulty. She perceived a social injustice about the status of the sexes which even went so far as to impugn the traditional conception of God ("He was no gentleman!"). The perception became the shaping force in the novel. It differentiated her from most of those other girls longing for they knew not what. As the voice of Miles herself, Sybylla expressed a developed feminist consciousness, derived intuitively. It owed nothing at that time to the considerable feminist activities of Australia in the 1880s and '90s.[4]

On Dearborn Street is a product of the same consciousness. But in several respects it takes a different tack. It takes a light-hearted approach to a serious subject — which contrasts with the mood of dejection recurring through *My Brilliant Career*. The approach enables the male narrator to speak with serious undertones of "the frowsy sentimentality with which men regard matters of sex" and to appeal for simplification of the feminist cause ("just women, fellow beings with men"). His difficulties in sustaining that objectivity are so consistently understated that the whole unlikely device of putting the narrative voice into a too-perfect male suitor works like a fairy-tale for most of the time. The fantasy is held at the right distance to sustain suspension of disbelief.

The indulgence of sentimentality, under an ostensible appeal for its opposite, allowed Miles to steer the plot more closely in the direction of eventual marriage than she permitted herself to do in *My Brilliant Career*. The preface excuses this indulgence as the American mode of consciousness. This at least suggests that the author knew what she was about in bending the universe to bring honest Sybyl Penelo to the point of saying: "I want you to hold me tighter . . . and closer . . . and never let me go". That she manages this convincingly is no mean achievement in view of the prevailing philosophy. Equally adroit is the way in which Sybyl subsequently procrastinates and distances herself from the bondage implied in that wish. She is altogether a more experienced manipulator of love's occasions than was her near-namesake, Sybylla Penelope Melvyn. Nevertheless she reflects the original Sybylla in her coquetry, her potent wit, and ultimately in sexual fastidiousness and an instinctive baulking at marriage. The dominant traits are identical.

What can be said of the pursuing lover? Here the technique of making Cavarley the first-person narrator reflects a bold decision. The difficulty is greater than Miles was ever willing to acknowledge. It is not simply the problem of the ultra-feminine author's grasp of the male sensibility. Super-added is the need to make that male extraordinarily ethical and self-controlled. Cavarley has to emerge as something more than the author's mask and something less than a god. In *On Dearborn Street,* Miles almost succeeds. By comparison with her other attempts to impersonate the male, she succeeds admirably. The libido and its control in the first-person narrator of *Prelude to Waking* are as mechanical as a wind-up toy. Cavarley, however, is sufficiently human at the level of comedy at which the novel operates. His much-professed desire carries no punch, but his virginity is believable. It is much less credible that he remains un-contaminated by his wealth. But, over-riding the credibility of personal quirks, the novel eludes major difficulties by its remarkable consistency of tone — a quality which hints that the intention is not so far removed from melodrama that characters and events cannot be allowed exaggeration in pursuit of an over-riding idea.

A factor which invites comparison with *My Brilliant Career* is the presence and importance of Aunt Pattie. She is to both Sybyl and Cavarley what the Caddagat grandmother was to Sybylla Melvyn. Here we find a familiar ingredient in Miles Franklin's plotting — the elderly woman as security-figure and catalyst. Such characters are not replicas of each other but all are dominant, all are sympathetic and eminently acceptable. Aunt Pattie's decisions, arbitrary and high-handed and more concerned with ends than means, produce the desired effects. Without her, the plot remains at an impasse, and the lovers remain as eternally separated as the pair on the Grecian urn. Her type appears in the early Miles Franklin juvenilia and matures as Mrs. Mazere in the Brent of Bin Bin series. "My grandmother", wrote Miles in the *persona* of "Red Cross Nurse", "stands out as the supreme love of my life, the one individual who never sold me out".

Here, again, autobiographical experience contributes to plot-making, and we recognize this author's need for the reinforcing data of her actual world. Her consciousness of this need inclined her to a somewhat defensive endorsement of realism. That consideration gives *On Dearborn Street* a paradoxical importance for it could hardly be called a realistic novel. It safely eludes objectivity in much the same way as a fairy-tale does, by establishing its frame of reference as fantasy. The Chicago Loop is distinctly more "actual" than the Caboodle and the eventual pirate ship is the extreme end of a wish-fulfilling development away from the real.

The novel stands then in opposition to Miles's earlier and later commitment to things-as-they-really-are. Her general reputation is that of one who called a spade a spade and who consciously strove to tell uncomfortable truths. Admittedly in *On Dearborn Street* we find the disparagement of civilized society in relation to the War as forthrightly uttered as in any of her writing. But this appears as an excrescence upon the prevailing feeling. Generally the work reflects a romanticism which succeeds only on that basis, and then only through good management of dramatic arrangement rather than the ring of truth. Mystical affirmation is made to sound valid. This is the other side of the Miles Franklin coin. It can be traced in most of her work affirming wishes which, at a more objective level, she was forced to deny — that marriage is not a cage, that a man is not a beast. But it is doubtful whether any other of her novels gives the romantic indulgence as wide a rein as it is given here.

By contrast, the Brent of Bin Bin books, with their stable-mate, *All That Swagger,* represent a conscious attempt at objectivity. There the principles of naturalism are fully endorsed. Plotting gives way to "possuming" and Miles's actual family history provides the skeletal framework. Outwardly there is a marked difference of approach when we compare these with *On Dearborn Street*. Nevertheless the same basic quest is discernible, with the same need to create idealistic males, such as Dick Mazere and Peter Poole — all of them unconvincing when brought in from the periphery and given the centre of the stage. The factor of mystical affirmation, validated by sentiment, remains in a much larger measure than Miles, in her "realism", would have liked to admit. The need for the fantasy life endorsing marriage and an heroic view of family life led her intuitively to certain literary devices. One of these was the "larger than life" expansion of situation, in terms of which we find extended generations, heroic dimensions of character, and mystical significance in mountains and rivers. The chronicle novels of Brent of Bin Bin developed these aspects. To recognize them is to understand more fully the author's need for the closing phase of *On Dearborn Street*. It stands in marked contrast to the ending of *My Brilliant Career*. In the final analysis it might express her bulwark against despair.

As a novel of ideas, *On Dearborn Street* is limited by the very factors which enable it to succeed artistically. Its comic spirit, tightly reined, governs the extent to which the characters can function as inhabitants of a war-shocked world. We are encouraged to enjoy their posturing, knowing it to be just that. They begin to crumble when we are pressed to accept them as serious spokespersons for social values.

Therein lies Miles Franklin's perennial difficulty in a structural sense. She sought to develop this composition as an exploration of an honest female response to an acceptable male. This was part of the larger proposition — which can be seen in terms of her total output — that man is a destructive animal and that woman must save him by leading him to a renunciation of the flesh. It is a difficult idea which demands a dual apotheosis — first hers and then his. I doubt that Miles ever thought out the implications of this demand. Some of her characters reach "renunciation" (as in *Prelude to*

Waking); but the positive influences which might be expected to follow this negative condition are never explored. Respect for the other person's liberty tended to deny that route.

The five works of the cluster to which *On Dearborn Street* belongs, hidden away and virtually unknown over sixty years, reflect Miles Franklin at her most fluent and uninhibited. In this respect they stand above the nostalgic novels which sprang from her re-discovery of Australia in the mid-1920s. By then she was nearly fifty, looking backward. Literary-critical prejudices in favor of "Australianism" were about to limit her range. But virtually all her work from this period onwards was destined to be printed eventually.

That consideration makes it the more significant that *On Dearborn Street* is at last being published. It helps to correct an imbalance. It provides a taste of the vitality of Miles's middle period.

As such it carries a sociological interest, expressing its author's first-hand response to the outbreak of World War I. The shock is great enough to disturb the narrative point of view, and we find Miles Franklin's own personal perspective taking over from Cavarley. There is an intensification of disgust and horror in the recollection of a woman shouting: "War, Glorious War! I hope it comes to America too! We need its quickening influence!" The capturing of that stark moment from "the last week of July 1914" is itself a useful thing. Despite — or perhaps because of — her limitations in the imaginative field, Miles Franklin's books are full of such moments. Her dependence upon visibly authentic incidents from the actual world has left a legacy of little cameos which capture human attitudes at particular times. The years enhance rather than diminish this factor. It assists *On Dearborn Street* to reflect in some measure the objective of the classic: to sustain a nexus between the fixed "then" and the ever-moving "now".

Roy Duncan
Toorak State College
April 1981

NOTES

1. See for example, Marjorie Barnard, *Miles Franklin* (Melbourne, 1967), p. 69.
2. Bruce Sutherland in *Meanjin Quarterly*, IV/1965, pp. 439-53.
3. See Jill Roe, "The Significant Silence: Miles Franklin's Middle Years", *Meanjin*, 1/1980, pp. 49-59.
4. Miles Franklin eventually came to know Rose Scott and, through her, Vida Goldstein with whom she formed a close and lasting friendship. But these contacts did not begin until after the publication of *My Brilliant Career*. Miles was never enthused by the organizational aspects of social reform. She devoted herself to the fictional exploration of feminist ideas with characteristic independence.

EDITOR'S NOTE

The Editor's hand has necessarily dealt lightly with this manuscript, making nothing more than one or two corrections in the name of consistency, and some slight alteration to punctuation in the interests of clarity.

To
A., B., D., E., F., L., and M.
Happy-go-luckily inscribed

NOTE BY HERO

Memoirs of an infatuate, satirically and gleefully offered
for what they are worth, and without shame.

If in thus running amok in the vernacular I should
be accused of sentimentality, then unabashed I claim
the right to my national adjective. The United Stateser
has as much right to his characteristics or characteristic
defects as the next fellow. If he is sentimental, then
sentimental he is. Let it go at that.

The Russians are pessimistic and tragic, the English
wooden and conceited, the Germans sequacious and
stolid — so they say. Other epithets of irritation are as
generally applied to the Japanese, the French, the
Chinese, the Scandanavians; so, if sentimental falls to
me and my compatriots, I guess we have earned it as
honestly, or as little deserve it as the others deserve
their share of abuse. Doubtless sentimentality is the
result of an environment as desirable as that which has
produced the volatile, the conceited, the patient, the
unreliable, or the pessimistic, and I for one, am quite
unabashed in diving into story-telling, which might, in
this instance, more accurately be classified as tale-
bearing, under such a national tag.

The Hero

A BACHELOR OF MEANS

My graduation as a bachelor of means took place after I had reached maturity. This maybe is why my vision has fewer scales than that of the average rich man. I can see lots of things that the regular prosperous business man fails to discern.

I was adopted before my eyes were opened by Mrs. Pattie Cavarley, wife of the Honorable George Cavarley, once Governor and many times Senator for the State. The adoption was not legal so far as I knew, and my foster mother taught me to call her aunt instead of the more intimate title. I was kept in such sedulous ignorance about my origin, that as I grew towards manhood I surmised that it had been a tragedy to some foolish young woman betrayed by a bachelor or husband who ran life according to the Loop, as distinguished from Sir Galahad's standards.

In time I decided that the Honorable George was my sire, a suspicion that was deepened by his inviting me to call him "Dadda" or "Popper" occasionally when we were alone. It had been a secret between us, one of those which little boys consider a grand adventure and which they will guard like the deck of Casibianca. Sometimes I had been curious as to whose little boy I was, and the Honorable George had followed time-honored precedent in sending me to the woman. She had assured me that I was here just the same as if she were my really-real mother. This had sufficed while I was very young but later I had grown more insistent, when Aunt Pattie had efficiently discouraged helpful confidence by assuring me that if it did not matter to her whose boy I was, it should not matter to me; and surmise took root as certainty.

In those days I had not been oppressed by gratitude to Aunt Pattie, but as I grew old enough to explore life, a settled reserve overcame me towards her. I calculated that at one time if not now, she must have regarded me as an object of sorrow and humiliation. I felt more at home with the old geezer. I thought I had something on him.

I was educated to be an architect, combining the profession with that comprehensive and inclusive calling entitled "real estate". I chose this business because I had to do something. Aunt Pattie was too wise a bird, and so was the Honorable George to raise me as an idle, glass-cage ornament. I consorted with rich young men and maids but was not myself allowed to cultivate the proclivities of a dudeling. The mothers of the latter, I knew from results, sometimes commissioned my familiars to sound me as to whether I was to come in for the Cavarley money, which would have off-set the lack of data on my parentage. I was given clearly to understand that I never should, and so very special young ladies for whom I showed predilection were generally taken on a trip to Japan or Europe.

Perhaps the competent nipping in the bud of such affairs was the reason that I never fell pell-mell in love, and that there grew up in me an unobtrusive but persistent sensitiveness about the fogginess surrounding my birth.

For two years after the old man cashed in, I continued to live with Aunt Pattie in the big house on the North Side, and watched more and more houses in our rank sink from their estate and become infested with mere boarders, while vulgar money-making factories reared their clamorous and soot-belching heads right on our street.

I was not a brilliant architect. The self-advertisement necessary repelled me and I was afflicted with boresome honesty. It is more profitable to be spectacular. I was not glib, I did not imbide, nor did I have affinities. I did not design houses that looked like the cities of the Hopis and Piutes. I had no zest for the scurrying and grabbing necessary to get away with the big loot. I did not play trumpet solos with myself as motif, and, as says my friend Edna Maguire, to whom I shall introduce you anon, to blow one's horn continually, at least draws attention to the fact that one has a horn. I was among

3

those not even credited with a horn, so I expected to go plodding along year after year, neither adventurous nor gifted to the degree which would jolt me out of the rut I saw deepening along my way. But one night Aunt Pattie surprised me.

I was sitting with her before a big grate fire in our deteriorating mansion when she asked, "Supposing you had a million dollars, what would you do with it?"

I was able to detail without hesitation a scheme which had been long in my head. "I'd build the kind of shebang I've had in mind since the year one, and I'd live there and run the whole toot myself. There is a great call for suites of rooms for thriving bachelors, with garage, gym, and optional café attachments. I like to potter around among folks. They're lots funny if you take them the right way. They're so full of the same stuff as one's self and so unexpected that a fellow cannot help but be right at home and highly entertained among them. And that would be a business that would run after me. I shouldn't have to chase around as I do in the real estate graft. People have to eat and sleep somewhere even during a war or an earthquake."

"Bully for you! You take after me in that!" exclaimed Aunt Pattie. That I took after her was one of our standing jokes founded on our general congeniality.

"I have wanted to go to the Amphitheatre Annex for some time," she continued. "It is going down hill fast and I'm sure I could do a great deal to yank it up again, besides I'd like to live there where there's lots going on instead of in this lonely old barracks."

Not long after that Aunt Pattie nearly gave me heart failure by announcing that she had levied on her property so that I could build myself a little caboodle, as she called it. She drew a good hunk of her income from one of the big down-town hotels and was interested in my venture.

"I think you are old enough now to be trusted with a little pocket money," she said in her ironic way.

So I built myself a baby skyscraper after my own heart and called it The Caboodle out of compliment to

4

Aunt Pattie's sobriquet. I was my own architect and when the hotel was finished I was my own steward and manager and several other things. Work for me assumed a zest. I was tarred with the brush of industry (or is restless activity the truer phrase?) in any case, but now work to me became what creation is to the artist and I could arrange it so that I had leisure to become acquainted with myself and a number of other people in the most diverting way. Leisure in Chicago's Loop! Think of that! There are oceans of idleness and wasted time in this prime hunting ground of business, but Simon Pure leisure there is an unknown art.

Six months after The Caboodle had been ready for occupancy it was evident that it was going to be a highly paying as well as an entertaining concern, so Aunt Pattie made it over to me by deed of gift — a tidy fortune. The one fly in the ointment of the convenience of the place was the prairie-waggon kind of transportation for which our prodigious village is celebrated, but to worry about that was to rail against what was stronger than God in our civilization.

Aunt Pattie let it be known gradually that should I prove to be more of a man than a milksop, when the time came, I was to inherit the bulk of her fortune.

This made a great change. Fortunately I was a very ordinary man, I did not have Titian hair, nor an Apollo physique, nor soulful eyes, nor did I indulge in *vers libre,* nor have a desire to play act, nor possess any social graces which would have brought upon me a prominence likely to turn my head. Thus I stuck close to earth where I had always been.

There were some changes of course, even to me. Where I had ploughed, I now ran among people of surplus means. My fellow men treated my ideas with alarming deference compared with what they had been wont to do; but it was among women that I felt the most intoxicating difference of attitude. "He is rich" I found almost equivalent to the possession of Aladdin's lamp, and the realisation that the whole world was a treasure trove of things mental and material spread out

5

for purchase was enough to induce spiritual palsy.

I was thankful I had not begun life as a man of possessions or I do not see how I could have escaped being fat-headedly enchanted with myself as a veritable god, wonderful as anything in Greek mythology, irresistible as the heroes in sentimental fiction. Millionaires went up in my estimation. I marvelled that more of them were not even more completely blithering idiots than many of them are.

CHAPTER 2
"WOMAN" AND WOMEN

The most desirable of all purchasable wares, of course, was WOMAN. Through the ages she has ever been the most tempting morsel on the mountain of loot, whether it is that which goes to the victors in an armed camp of existence such as Chicago's Loop, or on the more primitive battlefields where commercial supremacy is contested inch by inch in blood.

I did not consider myself abnormal in any way in regard to women, though perhaps I may have been unusual as a specimen of the unfair sex, in that I was not sex-obsessed. Women had not entered unduly into my consciousness hitherto. In fact some of my associates, more gifted in dalliance, less circumspect in action, delighted to call me an old maid. Women passed me up as something of an anchorite until I became a bachelor of means, when immediately they fell into my line of notice to the extent of a popular commodity which is advertised *ad nauseum.*

To the man with money to buy and leisure and inclination to learn, I found that women may be divided into various classes; or to be true, women to the bachelor of means are perhaps all of one class, but of varying degree. They are all parasites — the parasites which the driving genius of masculine organization has so impregnably made of them. Theirs it is to adapt themselves to circumstances as any other beast or bird or insect must do to survive, and to provide themselves with food and covering, and if possible, luxuries and high positions, through the lure of sex, the much or little they are able to procure depending on their opportunities and their business acumen. And let me be frank at the outset, I am not setting myself up as their critic but as their student, perhaps as their champion.

A fortune enabled me to adopt the unprofitable in art, and as women were thrust upon me to a suffocating extent I took the course of least resistance and espoused the woman movement as my hobby. Nothing original or ahead of the times in that when every booby who could hold a pen was writing a book or an essay or bleating a lecture on WOMAN or women!

I had always been sure of Aunt Pattie as a strong-willed and self-reliant being who lived her life on her own plan, but my eyes were opened after her husband's death when she went to live in a big hotel, drifted out of the circle of her husband's associates, the stand-patters, and, plunging into some of the most advanced movements of her day, became well known to all people skilled in social enterprises for the further extension of civilization to man in Chicago. To her I owe the taste for adventures through the scientific looking glass of feminism which shows what a grotesque is the institution of unbridled masculinism.

About the first thing I learned in her new circle was to quit yawping about WOMAN, as that left me back in the class of paleolithic antiques. I found that no such institution as WOMAN existed except in the frowsy sentimentality with which men regard matters of sex. I was taught that in the realm of feminism — Aunt Pattie's feminism — there were just women, fellow beings with men.

Through Aunt Pattie I met many independent professional and business women who were most stimulating. From these I dissembled the fact of being the

Cavarley heir and by hesitation and indefiniteness when asked my profession managed to convey that I was some sort of a factotum in the new bachelor apartments which Aunt Pattie had erected. Thus I was able to meet happily as a working equal, not as a waster.

It was in this new groove that I stumbled upon Sybyl, who stands clean outside of classified groups, and whom, praise be to the missionary work of certain Boadiceas, my up-to-the-day-after-tomorrow headlights have enabled me to discern without dismay. This tale, whereby shall hang many remarks, deals largely with Sybyl.

CHAPTER 3
A SUNDAY AFTERNOON CALL

I have defective sight and the most helpful oculist I have ever known was a woman unearthed by Aunt Pattie. This prejudiced me in favor of women physicians so when a stubborn cold reduces me to snivelling and snorting I seek out Dr. Margaret Hengist who drags out my tongue nearly to my waist and navigates unimagined expanses of subways in my head with just as much assurance and certainty of discomfort and with just as satisfactory after results as one of the divinely appointed male practitioners.

I was calling on Dr. Margaret one Sunday afternoon. A comfortable and attractive individual she is to call upon because we can like each other without growing feverish on account of it. I do not have to provide a chum nor she a chaperone, as a witness against the possibilities of a breach of promise case which I find is the haunting fear of some bachelors of means. Dr. Margaret always tires of me despite our sincere mutual regard, for I am not of the temperament effervescent which enthrals the average member of the medical profession, so we were discussing things in a rather yawny way. Dr. Margaret had left her door ajar and presently we were galvanised into attention by a clear voice of low pitch which should have been an asset to a public lecturer or histrionic star.

"Dear me," it exclaimed with vivacity and emphasis, "look at this bathroom! Mrs. Hallinan, is your flock responsible for this?"

Mrs. Hallinan could be heard appearing.

"Looks like their work," said she in unruffled tones. "That's the way with men folks. You can't get them to be careful like women."

"Yes, and that's how the poor uncivilized things will remain if you don't educate them."

"If you have a husband and two big boys you have to put up with them." This in a tone of complacency.

"Perhaps," conceded the merry voice, "but *I* don't have to submit to that sort of thing."

"If you don't have to, I don't blame you for kicking," said Mrs. Hallinan, "you unmarried women certainly have the best of things."

"Now Mrs. Hallinan, you're not consistent. You can't have your cake and eat it."

The spinster laughed outright. Dr. Margaret was also convulsed with mirth.

"She's dead right. That bathroom is a scandal, but no one could complain about it but Sybyl. When she says a thing it seems funny and no one gets ruffled about it."

Dr. Margaret accepted my suggestion that she should take me to call upon her neighbor with an alacrity that showed she was finding me very slow. She returned in a minute with the news that her friend had embarked on the chore of washing her head and could not receive me. Dr. Margaret explained that this young lady was a partner in the best stenographic business in town. I took the name, as I have many embroglios with superior young pounders of the machine which has supplanted the quill, and as I nearly always come off among the also rans, I determined to see what might happen me in an encounter with a lady who was particular about the state of bathrooms.

As I was reaching for my hat a boy's fresh voice called across the hall, "Miss Penelo, I've done the bathroom. Come and see if you like it."

There ensued the opening of a door and a light step, "Why, that's fine! Just tip-top!"

"I'm sorry we left the place in such a mess," the boy apologised in gratified tones, "but you see Mommer lets us do it at home as Popper doesn't like to be called down about anything."

"A little mere strap oil when Popper was little, I guess would have turned the trick."

"I guess so," grinned Popper's offspring.

CHAPTER 4
INVESTIGATION

Having learned of an excellent stenographic business, I did not let the week's soot accumulate very deeply till I set out to test the truth of the report. Good stenographers do not grow on gooseberry bushes, nor too many of them in the Loop. They are made by grafting energy and experience on to natural intelligence, though many of them seem to think they have only to be born, attend business college, and complete the process by arranging their hair in some wonderful pattern. Many are content with a vocabulary limited to two hundred words and the inability to spell some of these according to standard. They let the subjunctive mood remain a dark continent and consider quotation marks applied with the pepper pot covering for a multitude of literary deficiencies.

I repaired to the address named by Dr. Hengist, there to be more precisely directed by the official presiding over the elevators rising from the vestibule. It was not an up-to-date building. It abounded in small separate businesses, many struggling and not a few shyster lawyers, a consul or two of negligible states, two or more obscure magazines, and other "concerns". The status of the structure could be gauged unerringly by the attitude of the tenants using the elevators. They did not take off their hats unless a very well dressed woman, who was patently a bird of passage, entered one of the cages; and in spite of the notice: NO SMOKING ALLOWED IN THESE CARS, got no further than a feeble pretence of taking their cigars out of their faces if a very pretty girl happened to appear.

I shall say that the location was on Dearborn Street, partly because that is where it was not, and more because I think Dearborn one of the most fascinating streets in the Loop, and this not intended as a snub to our ambitious Boul. Mich., because though of the sacred Loop district, the latter is not in it at all.

I ascended to the fourteenth floor and found a glass door neatly lettered as follows:

Edna Maguire) Law Reporters, Public Steno-
Sybyl Penelo) graphers, General Letter Makers
& Co.) and Compilers of Commercial
Advertisements

All branches of the Business,
Public and Private
Teaching by Special Method
Office open from 7.30 A.M. to 6.30 P.M..
Night Service at Advanced Rates

I entered where a glass partition separated a handsome matronly woman from a large workroom with big windows wherein a number of young people were clicking on machines at a tremendous rate and where folding, enveloping, and mimeographing were proceeding. Off this were doors, one lettered MISS MAGUIRE, another MISS PENELO, and so on.

"Good afternoon," said the lady.

"Good afternoon! Miss Penelo?" said I.

"Did you wish to see her personally or on business?"

11

"On business, if you please."

"Will you kindly state your business to me," said she, opening a book and taking up a pen.

"My business is with Miss Penelo," I persisted.

"Pardon me, have you an appointment?"

"No."

"Then I shall be glad to make one for you." She took a small book with Penelo on the back of it.

"I want to see her without delay if possible," I said, sparring for time and trying to think of some arresting letters I could dictate at once, letters of secret and urgent business: but my life was not run on those lines. Bother the woman, putting on such airs when I had happened along casually out of curiosity.

"I'll see," said the lady disappearing down a passage. Presently she re-appeared. "Will you step this way?"

I would. I followed her into the room marked Miss Maguire and found myself beside one slender young lady who was dictating to two others from a bulky note book. She wore a little black silk apron and black silk sleeve-protectors over her blue silk dress. She was very neat and Priscilla Alden maidenly in appearance. Her eyes were as blue as the skies in summer. There was nothing of the vanity of some stenographers nor the dowdiness of others in her hair dress.

"Miss Penelo?"

"My name is Maguire."

"It was Miss Penelo I wished to see," I said with great distinctness.

"Excuse me, has some one recommended you to her?"

"I wanted some work done," I said as stiffly as I could attempt to such blue eyes and such a gentle, timid manner.

"Miss Penelo does only very special work."

"My work is very special," I insisted.

"I'll take you to Miss Penelo," she said so softly that I had to bend forward to hear it. This was almost an offense. A low voice may be an excellent thing in a woman if she is a debutante or affinity and some

Johnny has her in the conservatory or on the stairs, and by reason of the low voice has an excuse to bend so near to hear what she says that he can rub noses or cheeks or lips, but it would be much more convenient if business women in Chigago's Loop would fit themselves to their environment and bawl so that they could be heard above the roar of the traffic.

Miss Maguire indicated in a hesitant appealing way that I was to follow her. She knocked almost inaudibly on a door and ushered me into a small corner office, airy and light, well heated and generally cosy.

"Miss Penelo, this gentleman wishes to state his business to *you*," and with that Miss Maguire disappeared like a shadow.

Miss Penelo offered a chair. "Just a minute," she chimed in a voice which gave a hint of great open spaces. There was no difficulty in hearing her. I sat down promptly. Miss Penelo was an extraordinary person when regarded from the conventional idea of business efficiency. She was what one might expect in a comic opera star or an ingénue in comedy. She was interesting, entertaining. There could be no mistake about that, even at a first glance.

"Nine sevens are sixty-three," she hummed while I took stock of her. A big blue pinafore covered her dress giving a childish appearance. A pair of tiny, very non-common-sense slippers were in plain sight under a trim skirt, and there was a wedding ring on each of her third fingers. An old-fashioned silver locket on a band of blue velvet was at her throat.

Nothing business like in such a uniform, and on her head was a dunce's cap of crepe paper which fitted like a pudding bowl and gave a ridiculous appearance. Presently she swung around towards me.

"Please excuse me, but I was just at the end of some figures, and if I had stopped an hour's work would have slipped at the last notch. Figures are beastly things aren't they?"

I heartily agreed. There was an indescribable friendliness and freedom from affectation or self-consciousness

13

in her manner. I might have been some old friend.

"Did you want some work done?"

"I had rather an important letter I wished you to write for me."

"Yes." She looked at me with alert intelligence but did not take up pencil or note book.

"Shall I dictate it right away?"

"Oh, I don't take ordinary dictation. I shall hand you over to one of our expert stenographers."

"I specially wanted your work, but —"

"And I shall be glad to let you have my work," she replied charmingly, "but you see, I specialize."

"Then may I ask what is your specialty?"

"Well—er—I write special letters and other things —"

Miss Penelo seemed to have difficulty or modesty in explaining her speciality, but at this moment she caught sight of her reflection in the glass door of a book shelf and snatched off the paper cap exposing a head of the glossiest hair I have ever seen, glinting copper and brown as the sun from the western window fell upon it.

"Well I never!" she ejaculated. "These young people think my head is a receptacle for everything. I forgot to take this thing off." She emitted a musical peal of laughter. "I beg your pardon. You must have thought you had got into a circus by mistake." Her infectiously merry manner invited me to feel that formality is affectation. In the matter of friendships she had the faculty for plunging direct into song without lenghty preludes.

"I mustn't delay you any longer," she murmured.

I hastened to make known that I had all the time there was. I was curious to see as much as possible of the comedy upon which I had stumbled in the idea that I was to discover feminine business efficiency.

"I should like you to talk to Miss Maguire, the head of our firm," she said, "and then you will know definitely whether we can do your work or not."

Miss Maguire promptly reappeared after Miss Penelo had pushed a button. My second observation proved my first inventory correct. Her eyes were as sweet as fringed gentians, their glances timid and maidenly, her cheeks as pink as an infant's, but I was too wily to be deceived. Ah, ha, Miss Maguire! you did not deceive this invincible if not infallible student of woman kind! I knew that I trembled in the presence of the supreme head of the firm. Sybyl Penelo would be an easy mark, but if I desired the entertainment her acquaintance promised I should need to ingratiate myself with Miss Edna Mary Maguire.

Before she had said a word there was a tap on the door followed by one of those haughty blonde young goddesses before whom a fellow has to deport himself with ceremony and cunning indicative that he is aware of his inferiority so that time may not be wasted in putting him in his place. She did not seem to be aware of my presence. I did not expect her to. She approached Miss Penelo with a look of benevolent indulgence and affection, straightened the locket which was moving towards the wearer's ear and whispered something about a Rosemary Bray who seemed to be running away and who was "cutting up terribly" and "just crazy" to see Miss Penelo.

"All right. Thank you Lieutenant Yellow-Hair, I'll be with you in a few minutes," she whispered in return.

CHAPTER 5
WHILE ROSEMARY RAN AWAY

When the door closed again Miss Maguire bowed to me a second time and put the slender points of her fingers into the pockets of her little frilly black apron. She began in a hesitant little voice which seemed on the verge of tears, and hesitant little blushes came and went with her breath entrancingly. Sybyl looked at her with the abandon of a mother with a precocious child. It was palpable that she was very proud of her business partner.

15

"You see," she murmured, "we requisition Miss Penelo's great literary gift in a little different way —"

Miss Penelo made deprecatory murmurs.

"You know you have exceptional gifts," persisted Miss Maguire, and the one to gainsay her seemed brutal. Upon further acquaintance I found that Miss Maguire had trouble with her business partner's very unbusiness-like habit of self-depreciation. Miss Maguire knew that it takes all that genuinely efficient people can do to keep themselves in sight above the herd of mere horn-blowers.

"If you'll excuse me for a few moments," said Sybyl bowing to me and disappearing.

"It's this way," repeated Miss Maguire to me. "Miss Penelo has a very remarkable literary gift which would be wasted at straight stenography so I have started a new business for her. All sorts of businessmen with no gift for writing used to come here and mumble around, and then she'd express what they wanted to say — sometimes they would have the nerve to ask her to make up high-priced advertisements that would cost them dollars and dollars anywhere else — and expect it for the price of ordinary dictated work. And some would come here with a dead story and get her to put the punch into it and expect that for the price of copying a manuscript. I don't think it business efficiency to put such ability to ordinary shorthand work."

"I should say not!" Under my agreement Miss Maguire gained courage.

"You know how stenographers are expected to supply the brains and literary quality for their masters. A great deal of the business in the Loop really depends upon the character and discretion of stenographers who never got any credit."

"It is a shame!" I observed. Five minutes of the stenographers' case by Miss Maguire and I was ready to champion the down-trodden, exploited angels.

"But why does not Miss Penelo make use of her literary talent independently?" I enquired, when I had recovered.

16

"She does, and will, but she despises mere story telling and likes to be connected with some solid business."

"Yes," I said, "We are allowing ourselves to be deceived as to the true place of story telling and all other arts today. Every author has become a dull pamphleteer and every painter a stodgy propagandist. I don't know where we shall wind up."

"Yes," said Miss Maguire, "will you look at this?"

She handed me a neat little card inscribed with the name of the firm and bearing the information:

A specialty is made of copying, correcting, revising and re-arranging literary MSS.

"Who was it recommended you to come to Miss Penelo?"

"One of my friends on the North Side."

"What had Miss Penelo done for him, if I may ask?" went on the gentle little voice.

"He made a great secret of it," I hazarded.

"Yes," said Miss Maguire, "quite a bunch of society people claim credit for books and articles that would have been terrible only for Miss Penelo. She edited one of the big biographies that is the journalistic event of the season, and really re-wrote a book on Spanish art that has been reviewed up to the skies."

Ha! Ha! Now I had discovered something. I was sure I knew that book on Spanish art. The author was my old school fellow Swinbank Dummer Dummer-Jones. Many of us had suspected that Swinbank had either bribed the reviewers or retained some ghost.

"If you have any of that sort of work we treat it as strictly confidential," pursued Miss Maguire, "and in all branches of our work we guarantee satisfaction. Of course if you think of getting Miss Penelo to write a book for you, you would have to arrange the time to suit her. I have to protect her from too much of a steady grind."

Here I perceived something above and beyond more business, for which Miss Maguire had many qualifi-

17

cations. Miss Penelo was her treasure, and I had not a doubt but that Miss Penelo paid similar tribute to the differing characteristics of her partner, and that was why they throve so well together.

I told Miss Maguire that I was having a folder prepared to advertise certain hotels and that I had hoped Miss Penelo might write the story for me. I wanted to give the impression that I was the advertising manager.

Sybyl Penelo returned while we were still talking.

"You tell her what you want, she can do it," murmured Miss Maguire and then she went out leaving us alone.

"I guess I've had my money's worth for one day," I said with the audacity which a bachelor of means may exercise with impunity, and which a joyousness of bearing in this Penelo girl provoked in me. I felt already on terms of cousinly intimacy with her. She had unusual facility in beginning with people as if she had known them for always.

"Have you got something very interesting for me to tackle?" she inquired.

"I hope so. I'm a hotel man and I've been telling your partner that I want some advertising copy. I'll call again as soon as I have it ready."

"Thank you," said she, with unconscious courtesy escorting me to the outer door and giving me her hand with a mischievous smile.

I went up Dearborn Street pondering that smile. Did it mean that she took me for a Swinbank Dummer Dummer-Jones, bitten by the desire to astonish the natives as a *littérateur* at the expense of my pocket and her brain, or what?

CHAPTER 6
THE PURSUIT OF ROSEMARY

Safe in my own lair that night, I found that Sybyl Penelo's appearance and personality lingered vividly in my memory, and I lay awake floundering for the right word to describe her.

I finally decided that it was her familiar aloofness or aloof familiarity which provoked. She had the unconscious, God-given impudence of the independent woman richly dowered with sexual attractiveness, and who is utterly indifferent regarding this ingredient of her personality, taking it as inconsequently as her white skin or long hair, because she has never known anything else, while her interest centres in other aspects of life. Her manner captivated because it had nothing of either the timidity or bitterness of the women whom men do not desire. And what was the bewitchment of the indescribable little face? There was such a tang to it that I arose next morning with that delightful sensation of something pleasant to be recalled to consciousness — something rosy, as when one is very young and has an iron stomach and elastic muscles and stirs with the birds to remember that the apples are sufficiently formed to eat, or that the day is bringing a pic-nic in the woods.

I went to my tub with the realisation that I had been to Dearborn Street and had met there a little girl with greeny-grey-blue-brown eyes, with an impertinent twist to her chin, who looked as if she would think it no end of a lark to stick out her tongue at a bishop. And before I got thru' shaving I remembered that Miss Maguire's voice was soft and sweet and her eyes as blue as the King's own color, that she had the daintiest taper fingers I have ever seen on a young woman, and that I had been invited to call soon again on business. Considering it was strictly on business I made *soon* two days later. Business waits for no man.

This time I was shown into as nice a little parlor as a conventional fellow who believes in women remaining womanly ever walked into. There was a lounge, a big mirror, and a deep easy chair; several good pictures and photographs adorned the walls; books and magazines lay about. Lord save us, there were dainty curtains on the window with frills on them, and plants in pots, like a real home! I found out later that Miss Maguire was responsible for the installation of this drawing-room and Miss Penelo keen on its enjoyment.

"What a dandy little den," I remarked to Miss Penelo. "Not many like it in the Loop."

"Oh, this is part of our scheme of efficiency. We want to have a little joy as we go along. I think Miss Maguire lists this room under the heading of happiness."

"And is happiness in your scheme of business efficiency?"

"Rather!" she said eagerly, "You see, a human being is an animal, not a machine, and by getting on the inside and understanding him or her, and loving them both — why, it makes a whole world of difference. It creates an easier atmosphere, and you know, the right to happiness is fundamental."

"The constitution recognises that in arranging for its pursuit, but it falls short in not guaranteeing its capture," I said, and the atmosphere about me having been made exceedingly easy and good humoured, I was just about to state my business expansively when we were again interrupted by the young yellow-haired lieutenant of yesterday, who whispered this time that Popper and Mommer were in pursuit of the Rosemary who had run away on the day of my advent. This pursuit proved noisy and excited and took Sybyl Penelo away from me to deal with it. As I was able to hear all, and as it was one of the most dashing comedies I have ever witnessed, I enjoyed the delay, though the delay was all I had time for, before keeping a date, so I rose as Sybyl Penelo returned.

"I'm so sorry," said she, "you fell upon a most emergent emergency, but if you are game to, come again —"

20

"You couldn't keep me away," I said, and meant it, and this was a genuine tribute to their efficiency.

CHAPTER 7
BUSINESS FIRST AND FRIENDSHIP AFTER

I awoke next morning with the desirable green apple and pic-nic sensation still unabated, and so that I might enjoy more of the comedies on Dearborn Street I set about scaring up letter making for the firm of Maguire and Penelo. Upon the instigation of Miss Maguire, and before I knew what had happened, I found myself displaying her business card in the offices of The Caboodle and Amphitheatre Annex. Others whom I found to be laboring with similar devotion in Miss Maguire's Vineyard were the elevator men in the Concord Building, for did I show any tendency to consult the board for the room number, one of them would hasten to inquire if I wanted a stenographer and to volunteer the information that Miss Maguire and Co. on the fourteenth floor, did the best work in town.

I so thoroughly enjoyed the access I had to the chief members of the firm, that my wish was to be received on the basis of a friend as well as client so that I might have their society after hours under more leisurely conditions. But when I ran out of grist for their mill, I found it unexpectedly difficult to promote any but a business familiarity with them. I invited them both to dinner and the theatre and when I was consistently refused on the grounds of other engagements, I became suspicious. I then tried Miss Maguire alone and flamboyantly plagued her into acceptance.

When I had her corralled at the Blackstone, I polished up my glasses and locked her straight in the eyes, "Why did you never accept my invitations? I suppose you think I'm the sort of geezer, that to be seen with would ruin your reputation."

"I would not have accepted your invitation tonight if I had thought that."

"Then are you afraid I'll fall in love with you?"

"Such a fear never entered my head."

Overcome with engaging confusion, she blushed rosily, which has always been irresistible to my sentimental sex. Would Sybyl have blushed under such badgering? I rather think she would have delighted to act so that prelates or grand-dams who have always wondered what the world was coming to, would feel sure that it had come.

"Well I know what's the matter," I pursued. "You're afraid that I'm such a blithering billy goat that I'll imagine you're in love with me."

"Men think that about most women who see them once or twice," she retorted so quietly that I could not be sure if my hearing were all right. I always suspected that my hearing was becoming impaired after conversing with Miss Maguire. Her quiet composure discouraged in me the desire for further levity so I left her to re-open the chat.

She assured me that many years since she had found it advisable to keep her friends and her business customers separate. But she urged me to entertain Sybyl, as the child had no home life and no one to take care of her. Miss Maguire often pretended to have business down town just to keep her company for dinner. Miss Maguire thought it would be a good plan if I did the same.

Altogether I found it an evening well spent.

CHAPTER 8
SYBYL AND SYLVIA

I had learned from Miss Maguire that Sybyl usually dined at a cafeteria on Wabash Avenue, so I prepared myself for the adventure of eating there. I had never been to the cafeterias, but knew them to be patronised by people who could not afford to eat the midday meal at first class restaurants. It is significant that the measure of business success estimated as so high for women that it is worthy of a "feature" article in the Sunday press, is not such as to warrant the chief figures eating at restaurants patronised regularly by men not considered at all prosperous.

Arriving at Dearborn Street just after hours next day I remarked to Sybyl that I had to stay down town for dinner and that she would be conferring a great pleasure on me if she would eat with me. She refused.

"But I want you. I am willing to pay for your dinner for the pleasure of your company."

"I hire out my brains by day but not my company by night," said she, chin in air, and with the most tantalising laughter.

"Well pay for your own doggoned dinner," I said, considerably amused, "but let me eat at the same place."

"Couldn't afford to eat with you and I prefer a cheap dinner in peace to a grand one that I have to sing for. I used to do that sort of thing once, but now I wonder why shouldn't women be able to command men to entertain them at dinner instead of it being the other way about."

"Well, goldarn it all," said I, "you have to eat somewhere. Will you permit me to eat at the same place if I pay for myself and don't attempt to pay for you?"

"But I eat at a cafeteria."

"Lots of people tell me that the chances for escaping a stomach ache at a cafeteria are better than at A1 hotels. Me for the cafeteria."

23

"Would you really come?"

I assured her that I was willing to pay heavily for the privilege of going with her, and whether she liked it or not, I should tag along and to get rid of me she would have to call the police.

The contrary puss will not let people extend hospitality to her, but when the boot is on the other foot, hospitality becomes a religious rite as binding as it was on the ancient Greeks. As a subject of hers I became an object of special regard. She was enthusiasm personified and so winsome and entertaining that I was dazzled. She even reversed ancient procedure and towed me across the streets like a vivacious motor boat conducting a freighter. Presently we climbed to a second floor where all proper, pioneer, sure-enough cafeterias abounded before the greedy eyes of big business had fallen upon them, and arrived within the Fireside.

My hostess took my hat and coat, secured a table by depositing her gloves and tilting a chair, and with bewildering celerity supplied me with a tray, napkin, silver, and plate.

"The only way to learn is to plunge in. Here, we begin with the breads."

I have never seen such a tempting and endless exhibition of food in my life. I started out in a field of breads, then came pies, cakes, sauces, salads and cold meats, raw fruits, followed by the hot vegetables, meats, and puddings. Here the display relapsed again into ice creams and cold drinks but anon rose to tea, coffee, and innumerable relishes.

I wanted everything I saw, which Sybyl said was the regular symptom of a beginner in a cafeteria. One apparently had to learn control and discrimination by the practice of some sort of Frouble or Montessori system. By the time I had seized breads and salads my tray was full and I thought I had better put it down and take another, but just at hand was a tempting soup, a bowl of which was thrust towards me while I was merely enquiring. Then came an array of sweet pastries which I never could resist. It was like being let loose in

24

the pantry at last. My tray was soon overflowing and I clasped it under my arm in a way that inclined people towards giving me the berth of a pariah.

Sybyl had tripped in and out, received with smiles and jokes by the attendants. "You just stand still where you are," said she, "and I'll depsit my wares and come back for you."

Alas, I didn't know enough to remain stationary and balance that infernal tray. Something began to slip. I tried to right it with a jerk, then lo, people were skipping from me and I was covered with ice cream washed on to the middle of my star spangled banner by a thick creamed tomato soup. Bread rolled hither and yon, and mayonnaise and salads mingled with apple sauce completed one of the messiest messes I have seen on well-scrubbed boards. An attendant ran to the rescue with towels and napkins.

Sybyl with great promptitude and without any affectation or humbug prescribed the insertion of a table napkin so that I should not be scalded. A nice old lady scraped the ice cream and soup off me with a knife. Sybyl did wonders with a soup bowl of water and a handkerchief. I was covered with confusion as well as salad and soup and ice cream and apple sauce and mashed potatoes, and was the cynosure of all eyes, as real writers express it. We were very early and I was thankful that the place was comparatively empty. No one laughed. People sympathized with me instead of my having to apologise. I thought cafeteria manners remarkably good.

The first aid extended the tenderfoot had been so swift and efficient that the soup had not penetrated my clothes far enough to be uncomfortable, and a lovely young girl came to remove the debris. I should have liked to offer her five dollars but I did not know what to do and then Sybyl, finding I was uninjured, recovered her sense of humor and led me away.

"You poor thing, I'm so sorry," she cood, and took me to a heater to dry a little while she flitted away like a ballet dancer and presently returned with a tray laden with all the things I had chosen, and some more. She set out the table and put me in my place like a little girl playing dollies. Making sure that we were behind a pillar in a corner, and safe from observation, she smacked me and put one napkin around my neck like a baby's bib and another across my knees. She called me a booby and an entrancing blunderbuss — every such epithet from her lips a term of endearment to stir a man's blood. Desire quickening in mine like a strange new spiritual elixir inspired me to great deeds, foremost, the winning of the right to return those adorable smacks with kisses.

The proprietor, a lady of considerable charm and beauty, came over and was introduced.

"What do you think of the infant?" inquired Sybyl.

Mrs. Laddy expressed herself as delighted and in her soothing way apologised for the mess I had made, till I felt quite puffed up with magnanimity in being the victim of fortuitous circumstances.

"Now," said I, when Mrs. Laddy had moved away, "you have accused society of placing women in the position of having to charm for their supper, but as I am now in that enviable situation, what can I do to recompense you for your expense?"

"I love people to let me dig into their souls," she said promptly. "To understand my fellow beings is the one unbridled desire of my life. Aren't you awfully sorry you are only a man instead of a girl?"

"I think I could manage to put up with being a man if only I could find the right counterpart," and feeling gay, I added, "and I think I've found her tonight."

"Don't be silly," said she, as matter of fact as a pat of butter, and with no attempt to further the opening for a flirtation or something more serious. "You don't have to charm for your dinner to that extent. I am interested in your *life*. What do you do all day? What did you do last night?"

"I ate with a young lady — well, a young lady who charmed for her dinner," and then, lest that might not sound nice, I added; "she charmed because it was her natural state and she could not do otherwise."

The charming for her dinner business analysed so patly by Sybyl was a flashing revelation as my thoughts reverted to Miss Sylvia, beside whom I had sat on the previous evening. She was a young woman frankly without yearnings to set the Mississippi on fire in any way but through matrimony. She was no beginner and had every manoeuvre of the luring business consciously calculated. She had even a little black cresent on her heavy chin, and her simulated vivacity had bored me. It was "old stuff", as the vaudeville devotees express it. It had been an expensive dinner compiled by some caterer and paid for by Sylvia's dad, the packing house magnate. It had been followed by a box at the theatre, but all suddenly the cafeteria meal, paid for by little Sybyl became a banquet of honor.

I gazed with growing tenderness at the fragile form opposite me. The cotton shirt waist was crumpled from Loop vicissitudes, the eager face was dead white as if the strain of the day had been almost too much, but it was guiltless of paint or powder or any of those black spots — dirtily licked on, which are supposed to be so fetching, but which remind me of a plaster to cover a pimple. Sybyl's delicacy touched me and the charms of Sylvia's robust physique right away palled. Her accomplishments, though honestly the result of her environment, were so obvious. They had been cultivated to supply the demand of the tired business man who seeks diversion on the lines of New York's Broadway, or Chicago's Loop — the "good time" compounded of an expensive dinner in a glaring restaurant with cow bells being rung in the orchestra; half undressed women cabaretting and every one conspiring to increase the sense of rush and bellowing. The average man's taste in women is as uncultivated as his idea of a good time, and he expects to secure a woman in exactly the same way.

He will hustle and lie and strain all day and half the night to get ahead of the game in wresting a bully share of loot, but for nothing else will he put forth effort.

27

Perhaps he has no more. Everything else, including women and one woman, he expects to procure by handing out the dollar. He gets the dollar, the dollar must get everything else.

When the average business man occasionally meets a woman who is impatient with the idea of procuration by purchase, and who waxes capricious, if not irritable, under his big bargain advances, the formula is to excuse her as "nervous", and to make the real estate considerations heavier.

It is, I believe, readily conceded as a scientific fact by foreigners, that the American man is a lamentable specimen of arrested development. Even many American women, who have undergone the advantages of European travel and society, agree that he cannot make love or converse about non-essentials like a human being; but they readily admit that he is primarily and finally a business man.

Ah, ha! He has had the business ingenuity and the enterprise to produce the most wonderful women in the whole of creation. That is what saves the nation. His bailiwick abounds in so many peerless women that he does not have to be a lover, a swashbuckler, a dude, and a dilettante. His feminine compatriots average so much higher than the mere male of any nationality that the American would-be husband and father does not need discrimination. The women of America have to take him or leave their children in the land of dreams, for there are not enough impoverished European noblemen and poets to go around. So it goes. But there are just about five of us to the hundred who are repelled rather than attracted by the tired-business-man, good-time brand of lure. We like to be compelled to use a little more art in annexing a partner. We are conceited enough to think we have it to use, and the qualities to grow in companionship after the contract is signed. We also want some of our wonderful women to recognise and appreciate that there is an indigenous male or two able to put more than the tired business man's value upon them.

I leant across the table to my little friend and said, "Now confess, aren't you tired of this grind? Wouldn't —"

"I know what you are going to ask — wouldn't I like to settle down in a dear little home? No! I would *not*! Sometimes I am lonely, but then I sniff the air of freedom and prefer it to companionship and fetters. Each morning when I wake to find the far quietude replaced by the roar of the traffic, I arise with fresh joy and relief. The thunder of the Loop is sweetest music to me. It tells me that the day is to be full of motion and people, that I am going to work among others, that there will be common confidences, jokes, and arguments. I love every minute of it!"

The Fireside closed at eight o'clock. With pride I watched my hostess pay for me. She permitted me to walk home with her. I hoped she would invite me in, but no.

I hurried back to The Caboodle and as the waiters had not all left the dining room I commanded expert instruction in carrying a tray. I traipsed up and down for twenty minutes till I could conduct myself respectably. The waiter, entering into the spirit of the thing, asked me was I doing it for a bet. I accepted the explanation. I was neither brilliant nor spectacular, but not for nothing did the good Lord make me persistent.

I was going to appear at that cafeteria many times. I saw a whole winter of business which should necessitate my dining down town, and The Fireside, where I should presently be able to carry my tray like a gentleman and a waiter, was to have the benefit of my patronage.

And if this should not procure the desired result, why then like Swinbank Dummer Dummer-Jones, I should produce a volume — on something, it mattered little whether art, open-air schools, the milk supply, or fly swatting — into which I should engage Miss Penelo to put the breath of life. Tempting thought, perhaps I should even dictate a romance with myself for hero and for heroine — well, how could I have the editress for

heroine without giving the show away? Well, perhaps —
ah, ha! here was quite an idea.

CHAPTER 9
THE GARDEN OF DELIGHT

It did not take long to become addicted to a cafeteria
patronised by Sybyl Penelo, who did not question the
explanation that my work had changed from one end of
the day to the other so that I was off duty after three
o'clock in the afternoon and had to forage for myself
for the evening meal.

In this way I saw her sometimes three nights a week
and the necessity for composing a romance or a
brochure on fly swatting was postponed. I must confess
that at first I felt ashamed that she would not let me
pay for her food. It seemed cowardly when I had money
to burn to let a little thing who worked so hard, pay for
herself.

It was always with a lifting sense of delight, that I
went to The Fireside to meet her and I liked to imagine
that she was growing dependent upon my society as I
was on hers. In this way we drifted through several
months, or rather glode down the days in a magic
barque which gave no warning of its speed.

I cannot portray Sybyl. I shall attempt only to give
an impression of her innate unconscious coquetry, her
delightful whims, her merry outbreaks of mischief and
sensitive emotion — the surface glimmerings under
which she hid her inmost lights of existence; and the
husk of her being, I trow, was more entertaining and
replete with good things than the innermost depths of a
large number of people.

She was alluring from the word go. Her every quick
motion, her delicate vigor and her irrepressible merriment had their characteristic charm. Then too, I must

admit her preponderating sex attraction. She was if any-thing, over-feminised. She betrayed it in her clothes, in the glances of her eyes, in her pranks in leading the unwary male into discussion, deriving intense amuse-ment from the "workings of his massive brain" as she expressed it, and then to leave him floundering in the syrt of logic, across which she flitted like a Will-o'-the-Wisp provokingly indifferent to his conclusions. Ridiculous to her were the cumbersome digressions and superfluous gymnastics of the masculine brain when the goal could be reached in a flash of intuition.

She had no illusions about men and that made her so restful. She might inspire a man to live up to the best that was in him but he had few pretenses to maintain in her presence. She was as accustomed to me cluttered under her feet as she was to the daylight, and as the daylight she accepted them. She may have pined if deprived of their company, but while they abounded in plenty and variety, they were a component part of exis-tence — nothing more, nothing less.

It was useless of a man trying to be a hero in her eyes just because he was a man, for she pitied us for the poor creatures we insisted upon being, choosing to grovel in the mire, slaves to appetite, inconsequent loons held down by superstitions about the demands of nature, we who might walk as gods upon the earth. These facts she stated with bewitching certainty and accepted as a mighty Niagara which could never be diverted from its course, nor drained for the next million years or so. She did not fret about it nor make it a grievance. She held that a person that way afflicted was as obnoxious as an agitator with a green umbrella.

She was inimitably unique. When accused of it she laid the blame, or I prefer the credit, on her early environment, to which she occasionally alluded but never described, though had she been raised on Fifth Avenue or on Lake Shore Drive in tightest orthodoxy, she still would have differed from her sisters.

But it was the flights of spirit on which she could take a man that really set her apart. Of these I cannot speak. They lie too close to some other world that is obscured through our coarse blundering. This part of our companionship, like a butterfly's wing, I should fear to spoil by handling or to blur by explanation. The book of dreams into which she permitted me to peep was so intangible, though illuminating, that it must remain unexpressed except in the effect that it had on my life. Its texture was interwoven with an all-abiding love for every living creature from an elephant to a grass hopper, from a sequoia to a violet, and to a man, who was meant to be a god if the morasses of ignorance could only be drained and his potentialities freed.

Thus it went from day to day. I brought other men to her attention just to see what she would make of them. There was something proprietary in this and I began to feel myself her discoverer. I felt I ought to take her to Aunt Pattie, who could introduce her to some of the nice girls in our old sets, and see that she had a little more of society than grubbing in a Loop office afforded, but the situation was too heavenly to be disturbed.

CHAPTER 10
CUPID

That winged sensation that the day holds a promise of joyous adventure continued and my idea of adventure presently crystallised into the act of penetrating the jungles of the Loop in order to arrive on the fourteenth floor of a building on Dearborn Street when the happy time of after hours had struck. I sought the cause of an intoxication which, as an after effect, but increased in enchantment and came to the conclusion that Cupid must have an ambush somewhere near.

At last! Think of that!

The symptoms increased and multiplied. I found

myself breaking into snatches of guttural song in my bath and feeling a new interest in windows full of colored socks and ties and gold-headed canes which were beginning to be worn by some of the lady-killers.

Good heavens! Could I really be in love! I!

In love! At last!

Was I abashed? No! I was as the undefiled in the garden of Eden.

Did I feel like wearing sack cloth and ashes? Did I seek to dissemble my state? Did I attempt to stifle my emotions? Not on your tin type! I was consumed with joy. I went forth to meet the greatest thing that had ever happened to me with full realisation of the splendor of my good fortune.

Whoop ye little hills! Skip ye little billy goats and lambs! Bend down and bow ye trees! Make a garden and a seat therein for me and my love! Oh muses with shins and knees, cast me an epithet of joy! Go into the four A.M. of the world and compose an alaba!

I felt impelled to celebrate in the language of the psalmist and modern *vers libre*, only I had forgotten the style of the one and had not yet mastered that of the other. To celebrate in some way seemed imperative.

After the way of excessively young men, I had been contemptuous of the strange affliction which at intervals smote the members of my species and rendered them *non compos mentis* for a time, but as I grew older and remained impervious I came to envy them their excursions in the great illusion. I envied the very cheapest of them the most ephemeral of their tawdry love affairs.

But here at last, the little idiot god had struck me with his shaft and I was ardent to worship at the shrine of some god: perhaps this was but a foolish god, but foolish gods are preferable to false or an existence enriched by none.

My heart was not always to remain a desert! I awoke one morning to find it a glowing garden with singing streams and young men and maidens playing on stringed instruments or chasing butterflies of gorgeous hue and beckoning me to join the merry throng. And among the maidens the sweetest of them all was welcoming me! Glory allelujah!

I was approaching forty, but I do not think that age has anything to do with it unless a man has dissipated the springs of his youth or is actually an octogenarian. I do not know how the sleek twenty-year-olds feel when overcome by puppy pangs, they look considerably mushy, but no matter how they feel, they could not be any more transported than was I.

I became whole-heartedly aware of my state. When I awaited her voice on the telephone in its moving contralto key and with its teasing note of laughter my heart fluttered like a boy's of ten. Delicious disturbance!

Then I was gloriously sure of the worth of my love. It was evident to a booby that she had never known the soil of intrigues or entanglements such as strangle that pride without which a high spiritual love can neither root deeply nor flourish.

I did not seek primitively to possess her that she might give me carnal joy and flatter my vanity and sustain my pride. As a far more rare and unique adventure I desired to open the way to mutual understanding and to know what was her thought, her pain, her joy, her soul's reaction as a free thing upon all of life's experiences.

This was the high adventure for which I spread my sails.

In love! IN LOVE!

Give thanks, oh, my soul, for the joy of life!

CHAPTER 11
SWEET DAYS FOR EVER GONE

There was no doubt in my mind who was the one woman of my life, and I wanted her with no ifs or buts or ands, but all approach to a declaration was parried with the skill of an expert fencer dealing with a man who has never handled a foil. She met me without a blush or anything in the way of prudery or humbug so that progress along lover's lane was difficult. She seemed to proceed on the thesis that unevolved men had to act this way with every girl where propinquity was an element, because they were so sex-conscious and sex-obsessed that they had no other plane on which to meet women. Her plan was seemingly to indulge them, to ridicule them playfully, to tolerate them as one does semi-lunatics, to divert their minds and attempt by association to make them feel that she was a human being as well as a WOMAN, so that they could meet her on a common-sense basis of human fellowship.

I discovered in those precious months that she was very fond of men, highly inured to them as she expressed it. She had been reared almost entirely away from women, with men in many offices of life which women fill in older communities. She made me say *reared*, insisting that she not a vegetable or a cow, and only such were raised. She came from the far edges of civilization, but she never stated where. I did not press for information lest she might turn the tables. I made a special policy of ignoring the question of origin. No matter what hers was it could make no difference to my desire and determination, and by never expressing curiosity, and by changing the subject when she voluntarily approached it, I hoped to build up a brief in my favor should she some day deplore my hazy nativity.

I guessed she must have grown up in Canada, though sometimes, owing to her contempt for our climate, I thought it more likely to have been South Africa or Australasia. She spoke English as the educated Londoners, very strong on the letter A and very weak on the letter R. She would have considered it an unspeakable hoi-polloi-ism to say *Noo York* or *absolootely*, but she said "Oh deah!" and "How queah!" with all the assurance of a Southerner. It was that cold delicious accent, which has always been music to me and which would

35

permit a woman to traverse segregated districts unharmed. Such a woman has only to open her mouth the world around where English is spoken, and if there is intelligence behind the accent, men give ear and put their best foot forward, for this is the female of the arrogant human tribes known for some reason as Anglo-Saxons, and they who would dishonor her had better beware.

I was gloriously in love. There was no doubt about it. I had all the symptoms and then some. I lacked however, a definite plan of conquest. Sybyl did not push me towards one. The way along which we strayed ended in a nebulous haze as enchanting as love itself. Life in the present had become a triumphant measure. Why hurry!

After all, in most cases it takes the woman, if not by concrete statement, at least by tactful suggestion to focus the results of love to a head, and Sybyl was careless in that respect. She asserted as an academic fact that men rarely loved anything but themselves, and let it go at that.

Thus we dawdled along undisturbed to any extent until Bobby appeared. Bobby's case needs explanation.

CHAPTER 12
WHEN BOBBY GOT RELIGION

Robert Hoyne was the brother of Nancy Hoyne, who married Hastings Howe, and this made him a cousin by courtesy of Tony Hastings, heir to the department store millions of that name. Bobby had not a tithe of Tony's spondulix, but he had all the money he wanted to spend on himself since he had been twenty-one, and it does not take a follower of the feminists to know what sort of a trail a young man so fixed is likely to leave in this world.

The reason he so long escaped the early death of

matrimony in a society where ninety-five per cent of women are frantically if not frankly, concerned in the pursuit of men as the most lucrative and congenial method of support open to them, was his predilection for numbers. He fell in love so often that it would have been difficult for the preliminary arrangements to be pulled off before he fell out again. It was an every-day affair with him like taking a bath.

Also, when he came into his patrimony, the first salute he had received from the sex antagonistic was a suit for breach of promise brought by a waitress with whom he had trifled while at college. She made it a conspicuous "college widow" case and had given him a run for his money. His elder brother Jim and Hastings Howe and all the clans had gathered. They had sat up nights and had detectives running about, and used bad language and even talked of getting Bobby declared a legal spend thrift. They moved his domicile and eventually sent him to south America with a nice young German professor as keeper, who was about as gay as a Sunday school pic-nic. Altogether they had a high old time besides having spent thousands of dollars in defeating the enterprising peroxide. This had taught Bobby caution. He kept his flirtations inside the danger line after that and abjured originality.

Thus, when he was on the border line of thirty and the rumor of his sure enough engagement continued with more than usual persistance, we began to bet mildly on one of half a dozen debutantes in Chicago, whom we thought might have had a look in. Bobby generally came west for a few weeks each winter and was seen around with his sister Nancy, who was a general favorite.

After his scare with the waitress, it was always débutantes with Bobby. He discarded last year's offerings as scornfully, and followed the new crop as religiously as the woman of fashion takes up the new style of Easter bonnets each season. He trifled with little greenies, while the sophisticated types, married or divorced, trifled with him, as far as his once-bitten-

37

twice-shy caution would permit. He did not seem to have enough depth to engineer an affair to interest the seasoned old blackguards who abounded in our back yard.

But when he eventually contracted an engagement that held water, the woman was not a little greeny at all. We were all way off in our prognostications. It was a real grown up woman, who said she was twenty-five, though some of the fellows who had seen her with Bobby reported that she was more likely to be forty. She was a New Yorker, and it goes without saying, the daughter of a clergyman. How we all howled with glee over that; for Bobby, owing to his parents' views, had never even been christened. She was no insipid maiden but a genuine sod widow. La Pointe had been the dear one's name. How Bobby met her, he knew, we all did not. One of The Caboodle denizens who brought home the news, shrugged his shoulders when questioned, but he said Bobby was a moving mass of enthusiasm.

She was a *real* woman, Bobby had told him, no young doll with a mind like callow spring asparagus. She had a brain and a great soul. This sounded more like something which might have originated with Mrs. La Pointe than with Bobby. Of her husband, she did not like to speak. She had been persuaded to elope when sixteen, such an innocent little dove that she had not realised what she was doing. It had been a disastrous marriage but death had released her. She felt ennobled by her sad experience. She was now ready to appreciate a priceless jewel like Bobby's iridescent love.

"The fonder a man is of women," observed Harold Brubaker, "the more of a flirt and a lady killer, the bigger rube he always is in choosing one for keeps. He is mostly caught away from base either by some numskull or adventuress so patent that the crows would know her for what she was."

However, we considered Bobby well able to take care of himself. There was no need to sit up nights worrying that he would not be able to protect his money or his person. None of us could approach his prowess in the dancing room, and besides, in the rush of Chicago life one can give no more than casual attention, and multiple divided interest to how, when, or why, his neighbors are born, buried, or married — especially married, as a man may be married today and tomorrow not.

So we forgot Bobby's engagement till Harold Brubaker, one of the most expert quidnuncs of three cities, took a trip east and returned with the first hand news that Bobby's peerless bride-to-be, the sweet widow La Pointe, was "one of 'em".

We gathered from Brubaker that the widow had verified the shrugs of Bobby's acquaintances rather than the rhapsodies of Bobby himself. This was not surprising in an age when women try out equality in more ways than either men or women realise. Bobby's noise about his wife-to-be being his moral equal did not bring forth any logic in our crowd. They were conventionally minded and juggled to cheat the science of mathematics in sexual morality.

As Brubaker had the story, it appeared that Bobby had been passing the abode of his beloved at two o'clock one morning, on the way home from a dance. Brubaker had inferred there were many dances at which Mrs. La Pointe was not due to appear until she became Mrs. Bobby. Bobby stopped on the sidewalk opposite with the intention of shrilling their private whistle and surprising his love by his presence, should she be awake. He found the apartment lighted.

She must be still up. O curiosity!

Yes, there was her shadow. O rapture!

But there was another shadow with it. O suspicion!

It was a bulky short-haired shadow. O hell!

He repaired to the apartment and knocked. No reply. Sudden darkness and complete silence. He disguised his voice as that of a boy and announced a telegram. Presently the door was opened cautiously and an arm thrust out for the missive. Bobby rushed in, turned on the lights and whooped through the apartment finding one of his college mates hiding in a closet. He was a married man with a pretty wife and two small daughters of his own.

It was such a clean bowl out that the lovers, as I shall call them, did not attempt anything but to jeer Bobby off the boards. The widow La Pointe had been a luxury which Bobby's friend enjoyed over and above legal specifications until business reverses had necessitated retrenchment, when it was decided between the lovers that Bobby should be the fatted calf, whom the widow was to marry as a means of support, and, presumably, continue to entertain the model husband and father as a hobby, or a soul mate, or a contribution to the art of living, as it is developing in these days.

Bobby, as becoming an outraged lover, had tried to kill them with a chair or syphon, but they had made their escape, it was in the story, dressed as refugees from a house on fire in the middle of the night.

There the incident might have ended if Bobby had shut his head. There are too many similar for it to create a sensation, but Bobby for a wonder took it hard. He had been mentally and materially fixed so as to escape all encounters with disciplinary influences such as sorrow or struggle on his own behalf or others. This blow to his vanity was his first taste of discomfort and it punished him like frost on a tropic plant.

The conventionally virile course seemed to be to take to drink. To have shut his mouth or to have forgiven his bride-to-be as a boon companion was not to be contemplated. So drink and the blues and going to blow his brains out it had to be, and there was nothing left in life — just the prescribed emotional jag. He had many to uphold him in the tragedy idea and the family clans met once more and wished something could be done to save him. But his brother Jim said it seemed impossible to save a fellow who had so little in him to take hold of, and who was loaded up with all that money. He was too big to be soundly thrashed, which might have made a man of him, and he had not the supreme gift of a mother like Aunt Pattie. She would have put the come-hither on him in less time than it takes to tell.

40

But God save the President, and the star spangled banner, and the tax collectors, the next time I heard of Bobby Hoyne, I'll be dinged if he hadn't been and gone and got religion! Ye gods and lil' fishes! He had been to Paris of all places, to contract such a germ! He had been inoculated by Tony Hastings, of all people to teach religion!

Tony was over there studying to shine upon us natives as a combination of Strauss, Caruso, and Campanini, while incidentally trying to recover from a broken heart because some remote little girl he had loved had up and died at the time when she should have lived.

At any rate that was the story, though not a mother's son of us, nor even a cub reporter, had ever known who the girl was, or what. Tony, with all his money and good looks and the swarms of charmers who waited with many wiles to console him, would not be comforted. He was the exception to prove the rule of the arrant infidelity of men. One never can tell what kinks the human mind conceals nor which way the cat of human nature will jump.

Bobby, who heretofore had had nothing but family connection in common with his dapper and high-brow cousin Tony, went to Paris to tell him how much worse was his case, because Tony still had the beautiful dream of his love, while Bobby's had turned to gall. He had gone to Tony for comfort and Tony had given him religion.

We discredited the news when it got to us. The most phlegmatic of Bobby's acquaintances used expletives of derision. It was sure some phenomenon.

I didn't give it credence till informed by the family. They had heard direct from Bobby. They were very happy about it and said it would be the making of him. His brother Jim said Bobby had a hell of a lot in him and only needed something to bring it out.

CHAPTER 13
OLD SAKE'S SAKE

I had a real warm spot in my heart for Bobby. When I was at high school and college in the east, his older brother Jim used to take me home with him for week ends and holidays, and Bobby, who was a little chap, adored me as only a small boy can adore an older one, and no older boy ever gets a sweeter kind of homage. He had not been glib and there always remained with me the memory of his eyes darkening and softening with the intensity of his efforts towards self expression as he followed me around Roz, Rozzing continually to be sure of my undivided attention.

I could not credit that he had turned sanctimonious. It made me feel unsafe myself. On his return to New York I wrote asking if the good news were true, and if so, suggesting out of politeness, that he should come on to Chicago, put up at The Caboodle for a spell and convert the heathen.

He wired in reply that he was coming. He was in such a hurry that he could not wait for the mails. His trouble was to get any one to listen to him, for he was at that stage when he had to proclaim the Lord or burst. When I encountered him I wondered how the good Lord had managed previously to this latest and greatest conversion.

His degree of evangelical fervour is not infrequently associated with soiled linen, bad grammar, and noisy exhortation. It was odd to see it manifested by a plutocrat, a dandy — for that's just how Bobby had developed, and no mistake. He was not the dilettante, manicured, light-grey-suited, picturesque-hatted, thin-nicked kind of swell who faints if some one mixes a metaphor or fails to respond to references to Verhaeren, Gogol, Dostoevsky, Tchekov, Garshin, or Krupin. He was far from these affectations, the other kind who can wear grand clothes without looking foppish and who give orders to underlings in terse slang instead of in cynical epigrams.

He was suffering that heat which drove him to wear his religion on week-days as well as Sundays and to take it with him when he went calling and to announce to people that their souls needed saving. It may have been more owing to my lack of interest than to Bobby's failure in lucidity that I never really grasped what was his special brand of creed. His references to "the key to the scriptures" made me think it was Mrs. Eddy's faith with which Tony had jugged him, and I further inclined to this idea because it is the only religion that can be made to comfort the rich. They have no need of the others.

He made a dead set at the heathen as soon as he got to town and never slackened his pace. At the end of a week the unregenerate inmates of The Caboodle were consigning me further for the pest I had brought upon the place, while the real Christian Scientists would have liked to repudiate him by putting up a notice that this was a spurious brand of the water of life, but as that would have been contrary to procedure, there was nothing left but to slough him off by a demonstration of mind over matter.

I had to do some thinking to account for him for he had been in no way mentally defective at Yale. I remembered he had never consorted with fellows who philosophised. His only reading had been a detective story or some sporting record and he never read these unless stalled by the weather. At thirty he was as unsophisticated as a boy of ten with his first bicycle. Incredible though it may seem, this was his very first essay in spiritual realms. He had nothing whatever behind as ballast, or to correct, nothing out of the store house or junk pile of philosophy or religion to clog his progress or muddle his belief. He was therefore cocksure that he had discovered the world's one best bet, that no one had ever seen such a light before.

To have him loose at The Caboodle, considering the theories and dogmas, the creeds and credences we had played with, was like a bunch of Edisons or Marconis being compelled to listen to the raptures of one who has just made the discovery that there exists an invention equivalent to a wheelbarrow.

Bobby could keep his end up in all the manoeuvres of hospitality because he had the wherewithal to do so without effort or self-sacrifice and had been trained in a great tradition of open house. As a roaring young blood telling of riotous adventures, he could be quite enlivening; as the entrepreneur of outings comprising expensive girls and delectable viands he knew the ropes. His vivid health furnished him with physical magnetism, he was good to look upon and not irritatingly obtrusive, so that socially, despite his boyishness, he had his attractions and uses, but as a Christian-Mental-Scientist he was a plague and a bore, a freak and a phenomenon.

If people are endowed with unwavering self confidence there is little to balk them in their career of getting what they want for themselves and in believing that they are manifesting God by the process. With concentration back of it this species of egotism can move mountains, which are much easier to move towards unselfishness than are chronic millionaires.

The Christian Scientists repudiated Bobby because he put unhealthy meanings into one of the most lovely of the interpretations of the Bible. All softness, humbleness, or suspicion that he was not of the super-elect of the earth, and which had endeared the young Bobby to me, had been hardened out of him by his understanding of his new, or I should say, his first religion. His interpretation of man upon the planet resulted in that brand of optimism held by the man who does not give a whoop what happens so long as it does not happen to him. He used it to shut his heart to every pang of sympathy for any one or thing. If people were not as strong, as rich, as young, as handsome as himself, he had ruthless contempt for them that they would not listen to him and immediately thereafter make a demonstration of being anything they wished from a John D. to a gryphen.

I had a curiosity to see him dissected by Sybyl Penelo. His earnestness and old sake's sake forbade my being rude or openly amused, so when he got beyond endurance I decided to unload him on Dearborn Street and see what would happen him there. She would be good for what ailed him. I was not sure what that was, but I looked upon her as a general panacea, and I knew it would be good for what ailed me, to have some one capable of permeating the invincibility of Robert.

CHAPTER 14
BOBBY GOES TO DEARBORN STREET

So I took this young man, who, if not permanently, at least for the present, had an absolutely one track mind, to see what might come of his encountering the most complex specimen of the human intelligence I have known.

Bobby was free from tremors or uncertainties. He knew the only interpretation of life, the sole creed to save mankind. He was positive beyond doubt. Sybyl was the reverse. Her every thought was assailed by doubts, promises, and reservations. Her mental intricacy made her seem indirect when she was really extremely frank.

Bobby was sure some dude, to use the vernacular, and in the way women like. He was sizeable, with plenty of bone and muscle and a proud easy carriage. His virile substantial spick-and-spanness was far more pleasing than dapperness. Sybyl tabulated each detail with swift intuitive glances. I catechised her afterwards and she could describe the color of his eyes, the length of his eyelashes, the shape of his teeth, finger nails and feet, and she approved of each detail. The anticipation of her investigation of his clock to see how its wheels were propelled was most fascinating to me. I said something to make Bobby begin on his topic which was highly unnecessary as at that date he was a barrel-organ with but a single tune.

"My friend is interested in the spiritual needs of the age. He is thinking of taking up a career as a lecturer or healer in Christian Science."

"How very interesting. People are starving spiritually," said Sybyl, her eyes softening and darkening with quick responsiveness.

Bobby gazed at her spell bound, "Are you one of us?"

"No. I fear I am merely sympathetic with anything that ministers to our fettered souls."

"But you should become a serious student."

Sybyl sighed a little, flashed a smile upon him and began in a glowing mood that was most beguiling.

"I am more interested to hear this than if you had come back from the North Pole, and tell me, Mr. Hoyne what has it done for you? Were you ill or crippled!"

Bobby waded in. He had been a dashing full back at Yale. He was a prime exhibition of brown-checked, white-toothed, red-lipped health, like one of those male cardboard beauties that advertise summer drinks in the druggists' windows.

"It has done wonders. I never used to be able to eat around at restaurants. My man used to cook for me, but now I can eat anywhere and feel no discomfort."

His idea of anywhere was the Cecil, the Blackstone or the Touraine where an ordinary dinner could not cost him less than five dollars a throw. There had been days in Sybyl's career or self-support when she had gone on two meals and carried a cold cracker in her pocket for one of the two. Now she patronised cafeterias.

Bobby was illuminated by a sort of clogged earnestness and there was not a flicker of anything but perfect sympathy on Sybyl's mobile features.

"And in what other way has it helped you?"

"Well, when I used to take a sleep in the afternoon I got up feeling like a boiled owl. Now I take a sleep nearly every afternoon when there aren't any sports and get up feeling fresh after it."

46

Bobby was a prize specimen. Sybyl's long brown lashes shaded the green blue of her eyes, but she was most demure. I wondered if she were thinking of all the over-weary mothers, the tired little store and factory slaves who could have slept like logs every afternoon and not worried about the boiled owl effects — of her own long hours in the noisy Loop rewarded by short nights of respite, and dinners, not at the Waldorf Astoria or Ritz Carlton.

"I am very interested," she said, and what she thought — but if thought had the power which Bobby's creed claimed for it, women's thought through the ages would have burned a red trail after it.

"Well, now Bobby my chee-ild, you can run along," I said after a little more talk, "I have some business with Miss Penelo."

A quick flush dyed Bobby's tinted cheeks deeper, but he stood up with attempted haughtiness. His eyes lingered on Sybyl's face which to me is the softest, most pleading, alluringly feminine and calculatedly provocative I know. Bobby seemed to find it so also. I was pleased with his discernment as he usually fluttered after the material or empty-headed type.

Sybyl gave him her hand with her characteristic friendliness. "We'll have another seance all to ourselves after business hours. I am one of the heathen aching to see the light."

"I'm devoting myself to people who want to see the light," he said with staggering self-confidence. "Would you like to make an appointment with me?"

"Some day if you have the time."

"Why not tomorrow? It will do you good. You can learn a lot."

"You charming creature," she exclaimed, and I could see it go to Bobby's head. "The only way is to pin me down. You must be a great reader of human nature."

"Tomorrow then for dinner," persisted the man with one idea, and as one idea can dish many every time, Sybyl, caught on the hop, acquiesced gracefully.

Bobby strode out very straight and self-conscious and good to look upon. With the feeling of ownership I had in him since a youngster, I was proud of him. The fruits of his mind were grotesquely simple, but he was a thorough-bred animal and looked it. I feigned disintegration with amusement. It fell flat on Sybyl. She said dreamily, "Marvellous isn't it? Full to the back teeth on materialism all his life and this is the first breath of the wonder of spiritual flight and he is just drunk."

Had she made fun of him I should have offered explanation, but now I grumbled, "Bally ass, some one will have to stick a pin in his balloon before it crowds every one but Bobby Hoyne off the planet."

"Such people are beloved of God," she contended. 'Unto him that hath'. He only wanted to sleep refreshingly in the afternoons and now the Lord has given him that."

"Bally ass," I repeated, "he needs a gag."

"His very assurance is attractive. He is like a dear, rambunctious toddler with his first drum, sure that we must all love the noise as much as he does."

"If he whangs his drum much more in my ears I'll have to put a hole in it or be permanently deafened. You've got me all spread out in the mud like Raleigh's coat waiting to be stepped on, because I'm a mushy proposition, but Bobby is as hard and selfish as nails. I dare you to give *him* a run for his money."

"Is he a bachelor?"

I gave the history of the breach of promise suit and the widow La Pointe and how it had been the means of driving him to religion.

"His unwavering confidence makes me want to whoop for glee. Sure of God, of right, of life, best of all, sure of himself. And his one clear straight idea may give him the full kingdom of heaven, while smart alecs like you and me, so broad-minded that we are bewildered, will be left without a rudder at all."

"That may very easily be true," I conceded.

Bobby commanded me to come to his room that night when I went home. "I want to talk to you about Miss Penelo," said he.

"Fire away," said I.

"She'll make a great Scientist," said he.

"Will she! I had not thought about it," said I.

"There are lots of things you have never thought," said Robert Esq., the old time adoration for my wit and wisdom sunk in contempt for my present day lesserness.

"Don't you do any butting in on this case," he commanded. "I'll make Miss Penelo my special concern. I have already done some telegraphing." He produced a sheaf of yellow slips.

"Bobby, are you sure this is religion?" I ventured to ask. Bobby assumed the look of a stage martyr attacked by an unbeliever. There was nothing for me to do but subside.

I felt like telling him to go further but the words died on my lips. There was nothing to do but be flabbergasted. When a small boy is thumping his first drum there is no sense in trying to depict the superiority of a full orchestra.

"I shall not interfere," I said humbly.

"She hasn't had this presented to her right," said he. "I am writing some articles on it myself that will satisfy her."

"Indeed!"

"You need not indeed, in that tone of voice."

"Kindly consider any superfluous remarks of mine expunged from the record," said I.

"Good night!" said he.

"Good Lord," said I, safe in my own lair.

CHAPTER 15
THE RIGHT OF WAY

Curious to know how Bobby had gotten on at dinner, I left my door open so that I might pass the time of day with him as he went to his apartments. He came about

49

ten o'clock so I knew that it had been dinner and no theatre. Bobby at that era had cut out theatres, tobacco, wine, and even dancing. From a man of robust and every-day lusts he had become an ascetic over night and the novelty of a powerful spiritual jag was repaying him a hundred fold.

He must have been sitting somewhere with Sybyl for about three hours talking religion. Great scheme!

"Hullo, Bobby-Boy!" I called, using an old time term, "How goes it?"

"Great!" said he, needing no second invitation to fling himself into one of my chairs.

"In what humor was the divinity of Dearborn Street?"

"Great! Gee, she's a lively little cricket!" Bobby adopted mundane and secular strain. "Did you ever see any one whip around like she does? I'd give a farm for the privilege of dressing her properly."

"Too small to carry much sail," I remarked.

"Yes, but she'd look too cute for anything in the right kind of sail. She'd be scrumptious in a little belted tailor made with the skirt short to show her pretty feet and ankles, and with a saucy little hat with one of those white wings on it that are always poked in a fellow's eyes. She's as supple as a little walking cane. In the right kind of evening dress she could be made look like a sassy little doll, or in big automobile furs she'd be like a bird peeping out of a nest."

A whole wardrobe thought out after one evening's acquaintance! The toy idea of WOMAN!

"With the blue tailor made," he continued, "I'd give her a string of sapphires for her neck. I'd do away with that cheap dope she has now. Gee, she's a little cutey all right!"

"Bobby, are you sure this is —" I began to remark but I abandoned the sentence and pretended that it was something about the radiator leaking.

Bobby's return from his first evening with Sybyl had given me a considerable jar. I had been sailing along comfortably feeling that Sybyl would ultimately be mine, but here without warning was that mere Bobby talking about a wardrobe — for her, for my precious Sybyl! Such familiarity offended, though common sense told me I was in a world of worldly people and there was nothing more than a tribute to her innocent attractiveness in Bobby's desire.

As he sat there, his rare burst of loquacity spent, other pictures disturbed me. How would it be to see her in the dolly evening dress, standing beside — yes beside that cub of a Bobby, receiving guests — in Bobby's house, fliriting audaciously with them, and with Bobby, for she would flirt with her husband most expertly of all, and her grandfather, and her grandson too I ween when that day comes, the little minx! Yes, Sybyl's wit and adorable audacities in play for Bobby's guests! *Bobby's!* I might be one of them! I could imagine Bobby's ringing laugh when she came off victor in a joust of persiflage.

Bobby after all was a business man. He recognised at a glance a gem hidden in the soot of a Loop office which would have sparkled in a Shore drawing-room, and he spoke of the proper setting quite naturally. It was a case of the smart alec side-tracked in the first try-out by one whom he had regarded as a boyish chump.

I was disconcerted to the marrow. When I got rid of Bobby I telephoned my lady, bestirred to act while yet there was time.

CHAPTER 16
AND THERE IT WAS AGAIN!

Bobby started right in to rush his fences like a headstrong Irish hunter. Even Sybyl, who had had quite some experience, in quaint frontier *argot* remarked that he "made the pace a cracker". I could never go to the office on Dearborn Street but I found Bobby there, or going to be there, or just left. He was as prevalent as the plagues of Egypt, and like me, he did not seem to have to wait till after hours to gain admission. Miss Maguire had too much sense to let him waste office time like that so I had my suspicions that he must be paying for the insertion of pep into a brochure on C.S.

I apologised to Sybyl for the visitation I had brought upon her, but Lord, I dared not say a word derogatory about Bobby! It was Bobby this, and Bobby that!

I battled against sinking to a state of jealousy where I should be prowling around disgruntled and undignified. If he suited her, I was game to pull out. He was nearer her age while I was an old mug-wump nearing forty, and it is useless for an outsider to try to understand why any two people will prefer themselves to any other partners who might seemingly be more congenial.

"Why *is* Bobby so absorbing? There's his health and beauty," I began.

"Other people have health and beauty," said she, flirting outrageously with me and making me feel as much in the running as anyone, "but if I put a ribbon around my neck or a new twist in my hair I feel that Bobby sees and enjoys it, but if I were dressed in a mother hubbard, it would be all the same to you."

There was not a line in her face nor a thread of her dress that was not precious to me, but Bobby had been gifted with the ability to look so that others could see that he saw.

"That's where you're off your trolley, young woman. I may seem as if I did not notice, but —"

"Well this is an age of advertisement — things have to be discernible."

"Yes, as Miss Maguire says, if we continually blow our horn, it at least draws attention to the fact that we have a horn. I know what is in your soul," I said in line with blowing my horn, "and that's what Bobby wouldn't know in a million years."

"I'm not so sure, if I set out to teach him," she retorted; and then with a quick shadow in her eyes, "we women are so used to perverting or hiding what is in our souls that we feel it almost an uncomfortable intrusion when some man comes along with the power to probe us truthfully."

And there it was again!

It was not all angel's cake with Bobby however. He seemed to let loose something wild in Sybyl which I had never seen. She appeared to be overcome with a spirit of perversity and dissembled her spiritual qualities while she set herself to provoking him in the most unseemly way; and what came to light in Bobby was not as his brother Jim had said a "hell of a lot" but a lot of hell in the form of an outrageously uncontrolled temper.

"He certainly is a bad tempered, unlicked cuss," I remarked one day. But Sybyl came back with, "he gets in the silliest rages over nothing, but he hasn't that nasty clever kind of temper with the underground sting in it that I'd remember all my life. In the midst of his worst accusations he generally blurts out something that is a real compliment and which entirely disinfects his fury. He thinks he's going to spiritualise and tame me," she giggled gleefully.

"And you think you are going to tame him!"

"That makes it a great game. We clash — oh, you should hear us clash! It's bang!"

It was the untamed and free which her frontier upbringing had left in her that found something homelike in Bobby's lack of development. I could see that if she would humor Bobby, or if he suddenly became cunning enough to be very gentle with her, he would sweep her off her feet in one of her impulsive moods, and before I could come lumbering along. But I considered that I had the drop on him in how to approach her and meant to keep it if possible.

"He is such a spoiled baby that he flies in a rage if I don't fall for him at once, but he doesn't sulk," she continued.

"You are a pair of spoiled babies. That's why you clash. You both should be spanked. I hope you spank each other."

"*Me* spoiled!" She was earnestly surprised. "Why, I

work like a dog all day and haven't any one belonging to me, and I've had nothing in life but drudgery and hard discipline and there's never a soul to care —"

"Ishkabibble! Also tush, poppycock, and piffle! When it comes to being spoiled, you are worshipped with a more intoxicating essence than poor old Bobby. When a rich man pulls up to think he generally feels that he has no one to love him for himself."

"Bobby has me to love him," she retorted intriguingly.

"I don't think he realises his good fortune!" I was attempting to be sarcastic — a foolishness on my part.

"Then he must be informed by a special delivery letter."

"And what if he comes roaring in on receipt of the transcendental information?"

"I shall tell him that you bet me a five pound box of candy that I wasn't game to do it," said she, tilting her chin.

CHAPTER 17
A SUDDEN SQUALL

"What have you done to Bobby today?" I enquired about two weeks later when I dropped in with the intention of inviting her to a taxi ride as soon as the day's work was done.

"We had one of our frequent final partings yesterday. He is distressed that I am so materially minded and ignorant and wicked that my heart will not absorb the divine principle like his does. I had the audacity to complain that I was tired and he was enraged because I obstructed the triumph of mind over matter by failing on the instant to be as strong and idle and rich and handsome as he is."

"Aw, well," I said patronisingly, "perhaps the rich

Christian Scientist will have as much trouble squeezing into heaven as the rich Presbyterian or Roman Catholic."

"Religion is dangerous in men's hands," she proceeded, "they generally use it to buttress themselves in self-indulgence and compel the real practice from women and children. Bobby has suffered no change of heart. He has found out by reading a book that everyone who isn't as fortunate as himself is an obnoxious error. In ordinary religions people try to sickly over commerciality with spirituality: in C.S. they frankly commercialise spirituality, that's why it is so popular. The only thing men are to be trusted with is the invention of machinery, and they haven't the ethics to use their inventions in this field decently after they have accomplished them."

"Aw, well," I repeated, "I guess it's the first spiritual cocktail the poor kid has swallowed and it has gone to his head. His mentality is like a bit of canvas stretched across two palings. A pin stuck in it would go right thru. It is interesting to see his mind work under its first spiritual yeast."

"Yes, but do you know what he says," she laughed.

"Some hot air dope, I guess."

"He says that I show such a lack of appreciation of the attention and admiration that he has lavished on me that he thinks he had better not see me any more because I interfere with his pursuit of harmony." She was overcome with irrepressible merriment.

"Well!"

"Is that all you have to say?"

"What could, what should I say?"

"Don't you notice the confisticated, pestiferosity of the quintessent one-sidedness of such an attitude! *I* am a source of irritation, therefore he thinks he had better expunge me from his acquaintance. He doesn't think of me, that I may find him —"

"He is very unaccomodating that he doesn't hang around and furnish you with a further study as a booby. I think he has been pretty thorough in that respect. I

55

think it's rather poor sport of you to bait Bobby. The kid's only picked up a few things by ear. He is as raw as a potato while you are a complex little minx, just playing 'possum for the fun of having him teach you to control yourself, when you have nothing to control. He can't control his taste for drink and tobacco — two things inherently nasty to you from the jump. You have no carnal lusts to chasten. No temptations assail you excepting those like teasing Bobby. You should control yourself in those or St. Peter will never pass you. You are a little snare and fake. You are not a woman at all. You are only a wraith which isn't there when it is struck at. You should be indicted by the Grand Jury for deceiving simple males. Poor Bobby-Boy is as badly bitten as a nigger at a camp meeting, but it will soon pall like everything else he gets hold of just to pass the time."

I sometimes felt irritated enough to protect Bobby, but he was so hipped on himself, that at others I rejoiced to see him running his head into an intangible stone wall. I wanted her myself, there was the rub. I was bored beyond endurance with her interest in the cub. Men have never been taught to enjoy a fascinating woman's interest in any man but themselves, and in any case it was sad to see such a mentality wasted in such a way.

"It's wonderful to find a fellow so —"

"Shucks!" I said impatiently, "There's nothing the matter with Bobby but the affliction of being a rich man's son. Rich men themselves sometimes have ability of a high order, but if their sons have any special intelligence it is often undeveloped. You could never have met the rich. The rest of us see them coming. We don't have to waste time in speculation or study. You show a lack of *savoir faire* to waste your brain on a thing like Bobby."

"What would I be showing to waste time on you?" she asked, inimitably contumacious.

"I never expect you to show sufficient sense to waste any time on me."

56

"You are a dear thing."

"I'm not going to be conjoled into being a fool about you any more. I'm not a dear thing and —"

She looked at me speculatively, "you are a dear thing, for my purpose. A mad dog may not be very lovely from the lay point of view, but if a professor is studying mad dogs, the madder the dog, the more charmed the professor."

"Do I infer —"

"I might be talking about Bobby, and then again I mightn't. Bobby's one of the loveliest things —"

"In the mad dog line?"

"His disregard of manners if his inclinations are crossed is —"

"That doesn't take any new words to describe. It's all been done long ago. Any little chorus girl can manage that. 'Too much rich man's son.' He's just a sun flower example. If he had no money he might be holding a small job as a bank clerk or floor walker."

"I have never studied the type in detail."

"Your interest may be excusable under those circumstances, but let this one study suffice. It is inefficient to waste time on an unimportant fact."

"It is never safe to show interest in another man or whew! the fat's in the fire at once. This is my afternoon off. Are you working?"

"Not so you could notice it any."

"Very well then, we will go gallivanting."

She was captivating in a new gown, and pasted above one ear was a white pill box with a pair of wings, such as are never seen on any real bird, attached like the arms of a windmill to the rear where they would first dazzle the gullible bumble bee man and then physically endanger his eye, ear, nose, and throat. She was putting on her gloves when in burst Bobby booted and spurred so to speak, and in important haste as becoming a man who never would be forced by fortune to be of any importance except to pay bills.

"Are you ready?" he asked quite roughly.

"Yes, we are going to see the new exhibit at the Art

Museum. Do you want to come along?" she asked as cool as ice.

Bobby gazed an instant with his mouth open. "I've come to keep my engagement," said he.

"And just in time for a private view of my new dress. I expect you both to be so dazzled that it will obscure the pictures." She pirouetted and spread out her skirt.

When she indulged in such nonsense — a dainty, ironical burlesque of the charming-for-her-dinner business incumbent upon women, I was infatuatedly entertained. Bobby, on the contrary, owing to his unfortunate experience with women, regarded such whimsicalities with grave suspicion. This quaint recklessness of utterance made him uneasy. He had learned to be alert against vampires and his vision was habitually obscured by unnecessary suspicions. He was not sufficiently sophisticated to realise that entirely innocent women with a nimble wit are generally more irresponsible in their utterances than seasoned lotharios. They have nothing to conceal by discretion, and in the exuberance of their clean-mindedness delight to be shocking in speech.

Sybyl puzzled him and to be sure that he was not being duped, he took no chances. His expression became angrily disapproving as she demonstrated her new gown.

"Well, what about our engagement?"

"What engagement?" said she, perversely I knew, for I had never known her to be unpunctual, nor to break her word in the slightest degree.

"Driving in the machine, with something to eat at the Pet Poodle," he reminded her, showing blank bewilderment that she should have forgotten.

Neither took any notice of my presence. I stepped into the other room, but they did not lower their voices.

"I prefer the pictures."

"What do you mean?" Bobby's voice loudened with anger which he made no effort to curb.

"You remember once that I wanted to go to a horse show and you calmly objected because you said *you* were not interested, that *you* preferred a matinee."

58

"I'm not interested in that now. It has nothing to do with the present proposition. You said you were going with me today."

"Yes, and I always keep my word, barring accident, but you promised me a book last week. It is not here yet, and you have nothing to do. I wanted that book in my work. Now I prefer the pictures and I'm not going with you, so that you can see how irritating it is for people to act that way; and it does not matter to you so much as to me. I can't flounce off and fill my time with something else if some one fails me."

"Your actions look very suspicious to me," yelled Bobby. "You just act for effect. You will go anywhere with anyone excepting me, and knowing what are the ordinary pursuits of some of your acquaintances, it doesn't look very good to me. I suppose you mean all right, but your reckless innuendoes are too much for me. I don't want to be unkind. I am only making a frank statement."

"I thank you for the rich study you are affording me," said she.

"I suppose you are enjoying some fancied merriment at my expense but I haven't time to be bothered with you. You think because you are clever and attractive that a fellow should be a carpet for you. I'm going to the movies."

"I wouldn't for the world interrupt business of such national importance," she gurgled delightedly.

"I know this is not your real self talking. I hope you'll soon see the light. I must refuse to speak to you again until you do."

"Perhaps that is the end I sought," she said.

Bobby stopped berating her at this and looked as if he were going to say something smashing. His lips moved once or twice, but he said nothing. His mental trigger action could not keep shot with hers. So he strode out slamming the door.

Sybyl stepped after him, inserted her head in the corridor and bending her little middle cockadoodled with exasperating glee. She ran up and down a whole

scale inimitably mimicking every chanticleer in the barn-
yard from a bantam to a shanghai.

"Oh, la, la!" she said coming in again. "Dear child!
He was too adorable for anything as he stalked off
trying to look profound. He was holding up his head so
grandly and his little moustache was sitting up on end so
precociously! Why *do* people try to ape the Czar! The
greatest of us go to dust in our turn. Why put on airs?
He looked so outraged that I should have loved to hug
him, only he has no sense of humor."

"Too much rich man's son!" I reiterated.

CHAPTER 18
BOBBY'S BILLET DOUX

After our cuting we returned to the office to see if there
was any evening work. A special delivery in Bobby's
unique hand was awaiting Sybyl. She opened it. Her
face went white as she read and she sat very still for a
minute. Then she handed the letter to me.

It was such as a cad might write to a gill-flirt of whom
he was afraid, and at that, it gave evidence of the writer
being drunk. I ran through it and laughed.

"You surely have got the noble Christian Scientist's
goat," I remarked. For her sake I was treating it as a
joke. I was in reality disgusted and if opportunity
offered determined to speak my mind to Bobby. At the
same time the green-eyed monster made me rejoice to
see him make such an exhibition of himself.

Judging by the way Sybyl played around naked and
unashamed with full grown subjects, as compared with
the flummery and spurious travesty of purity with
which many of her sex regarded similar matters, I
always felt her to be one of the most conspicuously
clean-minded and moral people I knew. She had worked
for her living for years and her business integrity was un-

impaired. Her code of relations with men was perfect chastity of the old-fashioned sort. And Bobby, until his religious jag, had never felt the necessity of ideals and his conduct had been regulated by the fashion of his set and the laxity of the police regulations. He was one who accepted the superstition of WOMAN as a vice to be bracketed with wine.

That he should presume to discover Sybyl meriting reproach was ludicrous. When he suggested me as the partner of her alleged indiscretions it became hilarious, for I knew from experience and intuition that I had about as much chance of leading her astray as I had of conducting a *liaison* with one of the Greek statues in the Art Museum. His effusion abounded in such phrases as, "The true significance of your reackless statements recurs to me now", and "I am compelled to infer", and "I hope you understand that I am compelled to have no further association with you".

Her indulgence in persiflage, audacious, but uttered, as she thought, only to people as clean-minded and full of innocent mischief as herself, he had described coarsely as "innuendoes". He was judging her thru' the lens of his own doubtful association with women and in the manner of a divine he had taken it upon himself to condemn her. Loftily patronising as only a fellow gauche for lack of discipline by smart social contact would have dared to be out of fear of making himself ridiculous, if nothing more, he wound up: "I do not mean to be unkind. I am only frank and it is for your good. I must decline to have anything further to do with you. You called me up the other day and interrupted my meditations to tell me that you were tired and lonely when no such state exists except as a phantasy of mortal mind. You make me feel inferior and disturb my harmony. Therefore I think it best for myself not to see any more of you. I hope you will soon see the light. I shall be interested to hear of you and shall take the trouble to inquire of you occasionally from your friends."

It was a deliciously silly production. I was on the

verge of enjoying a good guffaw, but Sybyl was not going to take it that way. Two big tears fell on her cheeks. She was pale and trembling as if she had been struck. She was as completely knocked out as a petted child might be upon receiving its first knowledge of harshness.

"He actually seems to think I'm not — I'm not *nice,*" she stammered as if striving to say something frightful.

"I fear you'll have to excuse him. I'm sure he wasn't quite himself when he produced that. C.S. cannot be entirely blamed. I told you he had acquired a taste for drink and this looks like a relapse. Let me apologise for him."

"He wouldn't have had time to get drunk," she said, referring to the hour of delivery marked on the envelope. "He just went over to the Sherman House and wrote this right away. He couldn't have wasted a minute. If the men I grew up amongst saw that letter, they would give him such a thumping that he would never forget it. They understand morals on the frontier. They haven't evil minds like these town dudes."

"I disturb him!" she exclaimed the tears falling, "I must not interrupt his meditations — bosh! He has about as much ability to meditate as a pumpkin. He doesn't think of my side of it, and how he has nearly bored me to extermination. Out of sympathy for him I have read his effusions — they are like the meanderings of a defective, but I've been humble, hoping he might have found some great spiritual truth, and then this is what he writes! My time means money to me too and I get tired if I have to sit around too long, yet I never let him see I was bored and astonished and not quite sure if he were right in his head, and now he says —"

"Well, well, little one," I murmured soothingly, "we've all had a dose of his brilliant theses. You can get one cut of him any old time on the one subject. He's a patent stem winder on C.S. He has gotten hold of a few damn old platitudes wrong end up, and religion gone wrong can have a much sillier effect than alcohol."

"But he actually writes that I'm — I'm not —"

"You've got to remember that he is about the rarest unlicked cub at large. He is a perfectly effulgent example of what a blithering booby the complete want of any fixtures in the way of self control or discipline can make of what ought to be a man."

"But I know lots of self-indulgent men of his class and they have never dared to mistake me."

"But they had some sort of seasoning, which Bobby lacks. He has never chosen people of any culture in his set. If any one showed signs of being fitted with a brain in conversation, he would get up and leave the room. He has never done anything but leather around in an automobile, or dance or swim among the wasters and easy street crowd and he's been stung twice already, so that is why he is suspicious. He is no judge of women."

"Then why on earth did he come bothering me?"

"I have been trying to point out the inconsistency of it, my little pumpernickel. I'm the one who has really been irritated, and about that. Any millionaire's daughter or chorus girl would do him more than well, and here he comes butting in and monopolising the onliest girl extant who would suit me. He has stuck around so long that sometimes I feared he was developing discrimination, but this shows his interest in you is accidental. It's sad to see you waste time on him."

The tears continued to flow. I could not bear to witness her distress even though it might be ousting an obstruction from my path.

"Don't spoil your eyes. Poor old Bobby-Boy isn't worth it. He doesn't know any better. You have touched his vanity in some way and you must understand that there are a lot of rubbishing women about who pursue any fellow with the price of a meal ticket."

"You don't think I'm queer because I have felt real human affection for you and did not keep you at a distance like something contagious," she pled with quivering lips.

Ah, but I was grateful in my heart to Bobby for this opportunity to administer comfort.

CHAPTER 19
DIVERTING SYBYL

I telephoned next morning on some excuse to find out how she was and learned from the discreet Miss Maguire that something seemed to be worrying her partner. She urged me to come and divert her.

With some invented work as my excuse I repaired thither and found Sybyl as described. She began on the affair as soon as we were alone.

"I did not know who they were from or I wouldn't have signed for them," she said in reference to a great box of flowers which lay open on her desk. "It's like his infernal impudence."

She handed me a piece of paste board engraved:

Mr. Robert Van Dorn Hoyne,

on which had been written by the said Mr. Hoyne: "As we are about to sail for Honolulu we advise peace. A little sea air will do us good."

"Who's we?" I enquired.

"Oh, he always refers to himself as WE — like royalty."

"I guess since he has been bitten with religion, it is himself and God. A little religion without a sense of proportion is certainly a funny thing."

"*We* advise peace! And who started the row! And he goes off after acting like that to enjoy himself and I have to grub here! I am the one who needs the sea air."

"Sybyl Penelo," said I, "I am disappointed in you. We can't expect much of Bobby. He is a joke and this is the proof, but for you to be thrown out of kilter by him, is tomfoolery! Forget it! Let him go to Honolulu or Timbuctoo. The ladies there no doubt will appreciate him and he won't be monopolising some one clean out of his depth. He evidently meant well by the flowers. You must admit it was quite an attention from a fellow so grand that he refers to himself as WE."

"His old flowers! He did not even earn the money to pay for them, and he has the damned impertinence to send them to me after acting like a cad. I am going —"

"What are you going to do now?"

"To give bunches of them to every man I know."

"Happy thought! I'm going to have the pick of the box," said I, taking out a couple of dozen lovely Killarney rose buds. "I'll take them home and exhibit them as a trophy from my best girl — eh? And now madam," I continued, "I can't endure a woman to use bad language. You can smoke or chew gum or even deviate from Mrs. Caesar's code, if you like, but not bad language!"

"You're only saying that to divert me," she said incredulously. I shook my head. I was in earnest. I admit it is a silly piece of puritanism that sticks while others have gone, but it gives me the shivers to hear a woman using the mildest oath. Sybyl looked into my eyes questioningly.

"I can't believe it when you are so radical. I just love *hell* and *damn*. They are two succinct little words of clear cut emphasis and it's only evil-mindedness and luny sentimentality that have put them out of court. "Damned impertinence" and "You be damned" are two delightful expressions and "Oh Hell!" is simply great if some noodle is flapdooling."

"It makes me shudder to hear those words on your lips even in fun."

"Then you must be cured of such tomfoolery right now. Here goes for a whole page of *hell,* and then I start on *damn*."

I arose and put my hand over her mouth. She drew away from me with shrinking and incredulity as if she had discovered another case of madness.

"Perhaps Bobby is not the only lunatic. Take those *damn* flowers out of my sight."

She laughed mirthlessly. "Oh, I say, I've just thought of something. Decorate the vases in your establishment and say they were sent by a strong minded spinster who is paying her addresses to the weak minded manager."

65

"Done!" said I, taking the box under my arm and walking off with it.

The posies made a pretty display in the dining room that night and Bobby had not yet packed his grip for Honolulu.

"Fellow inmates," I announced, "these flowers which you see on the tables are the gift of a lady friend of mine, sent to the house with her compliments because she is paying her addresses to me."

I watched Bobby as I was speaking and had the satisfaction of seeing the scarlet mount under his healthy skin. The others of course, thought Aunt Pattie was the donor. Harold Brubaker called out from his far corner, "When is Aunt Pattie coming to dinner again? I move that we invite her to come over here and live with us altogether."

"Second the motion!" called a rousing chorus.

I gave Bobby every opportunity of conversing with me but he ate his dinner quickly and left the dining room. I crossed his path later as he made for the elevator, the fumes of his cigarette — a particularly offensive expensive brand — fouling the corridor, and he gave all the signs of a flourishing grouch. I was sure he had no doubt of the fate of his flowers.

CHAPTER 20
HERSELF AGAIN

I did not see Sybyl for two afternoons and then I found her in high spirits. She was humming a tune, the personification of mischievous glee as if nothing had ever disturbed her equanimity.

"Well, how's our friend."

"Wasn't I silly to be upset! The other night, after you left, all at once I saw the funny side of it. Just think of the joy and delusion of Bobby being afraid I was going to lead him astray, when I don't suppose he'll find any living creature except his mother who would be so anxious to see him grow into the most beautiful being possible. I've got him a little packet."

She produced first a post card decorated with the face of a cherubic infant with wings in the background. Under this was written: "Pretty little Bobby. The growing pains in his wings make the little lambkin cross."

"I can't imagine why he hurt me so," she remarked. "I must have been very tired. It is a howling lark the more I think of it."

On the other side of the card I read:

Darling little Bobbykin, Dollykin, Dimplekin, Duck! was 'um lil' precious afraid the great wicked giantess would tuck him under her arm and spoil his pretty curls and run away with him and eat him. Too bad! He should be careful not to stray away from the other little girls into danger. Dear little Precious!

Next exhibit was a box full of pink cotton and reposing therein what she called a "pacifier", one of those dummy nipples such as inefficient mothers give their offspring to suck wind into their tummies, it seems I have heard it said or saw it printed somewhere.

I was aghast. "You're never going to send that to Bobby Hoyne!"

"Certainly, by special delivery."

A note under the wadding ran: "For little Precious when he goes on the big ship. If he will hide his head under the blankets it will scare the bogey man and keep him safe and sound. Dear little thing!"

"And what do you think will be the offset of sending this to his lordship? Men are used to being babied you know. Ridicule raises Cain in them." I tried to be calm as she was so sure that she was sending a flower of good will that would entertain Bobby as much as herself.

"As soon as he gets this, he will see how silly he was, just like I did. He is only an undeveloped kid."

"Yes, but so are ninety per cent in everything but their vanity and selfishness." It was on the tip of my tongue to ask her to desist in sending this rubbish to Bobby. I expected it to raise all that was evil and spiteful in him. Perhaps it was a touch of malice that kept me silent. I chuckled a little to myself.

"You don't mean that lay-out to be insulting then?"

"Insulting!" she exclaimed in utter surprise. "How could it be? To tell a great breezy pirate like that to put his head under the blankets and use a pacifier cannot be anything but ridiculously funny. Why, the silly booby, suppose I took a notion to pursue him, he could vanquish me with one hand!"

I went home. I determined to have a great deal of business around Dearborn Street both in and after hours until Bobby was safely on the way to Honolulu. I meant to be on hand if help were needed. I was not game to tell her not to send the pacifier. I took the path of procrastination which breaks and makes lots of problems. I limbered up my muscles with the punch ball that evening and stood ready to administer a licking to Bobby should he try to act the cad with her again; and the case so far as I was concerned was already tried and did not admit of arbitration. I could not be sure how Bobby would act, but from my experience of men in the Loop I knew that there was nothing too saintly, too devilish, or too unexpected to happen.

I hoped devoutly that I should not have to try my hand on Bobby. The chances of being licked might be about even, but I always remembered him as a little chap. He had had a hard time keeping up with us older fellows, but with the fortitude of a pugulist he never whimpered and had always been in at the finish. When his elder brother Jim had thought it necessary, as big boys will with little ones, and big nations will with small ones, to administer an unmerciful thrashing now and again, he would scream with rage and strike back for all he was worth but he had been a dead game sport and took it whether just or unjust, like a gentleman and a hero. After the engagement he never seemed to think of it again but insisted upon still being in the marching squad. He took such punishments as acts of nature rather than as any sign of humiliation. Great little Bobby-Boy! I never thought he would come to cross me in the one desire of my life.

I had always despised men who let a woman come between old friendship, but this case was, of course, entirely different. It was not because I wanted the woman myself but just pure chivalry, and outside and above any tender interest in her I decided she was not to be bothered by a fellow for whose introduction I had been responsible.

Bobby was not home for dinner that evening nor did he put in an appearance for breakfast, but that was not surprising as he had the feather bed form of indulgence, among others, and often did not arise till near noon.

The late afternoon found me on Dearborn Street, where I saw him leave the Concord Building as I entered it. I was standing at the revolving doors as he passed and he did not notice me. He appeared to be occupied with something far from rancour or violence.

I found Sybyl in great spirits.

"What's the news from the front?" I enquired.

"Bobby has just this moment left."

"How did he take your *billet doux*?"

"Just as I thought. He walked right in with the loveliest grin and said he was going to choke me and that I was a "sassy" little thing and had no right to be alive. He threatened to kiss me as a punishment."

"And did he?" I enquired, much interested.

"Oh, no, he didn't because I didn't want him to."

"What had that to do with it?"

"No decent man ever takes a liberty like that unless a woman wants him to. He may threaten and even think he's going to, but not *really* unless he's an irresponsible. The Anglo-Saxon doesn't play the game that way."

"And you mean to tell me that he took it all right! That he stood the gaff fair and square and good humouredly."

"*Of course*! He says he doesn't know when he laughed so much as when he saw that pacifier. He had it with him and threatened to make me use it while he was looking on, but of course he only threatened. He would be afraid to hurt me."

Such assured knowledge of the male of the species left me nothing adequate to say. I was well acquainted with my own mental and physical paralysis in her presence, but had thought it individual rather than typical.

"So Bobby took it all right," I repeated. "Did he apologise for his letter?"

"Oh, I forgot all about that, and I bet he did too."

"Forgot *that*!"

"Yes," she mused irrelevantly, "the bigger one's forgettery, the less call upon her forgivery."

I reached for my hat. I felt as if I could get my bearings better if I stuck my head into it. A man never feels sure of his "virility" unless in his war-bonnet; and yet we have inverted nature by permitting women to live in their hats and wigs while we are exposed to a vulgar and unsympathetic public, not infrequently with a shining skull.

CHAPTER 21
MAN PROPOSES — WHEN WOMAN WISHES

Bobby did not go to Honolulu. He settled right down at The Caboodle apparently for a life term and the epidemic of Bobby this and Bobby that intensified on Dearborn Street.

It made me very cross and as I found that Sybyl was dining quite frequently with Bobby at the Blackstone or Congress and that she did not impose the self-respecting rule of paying for herself when with him I made it a peg on which to hang a lover's quarrel.

"You'll let that fellow pay for you and you wont let me, and all that a woman is to him is a toy to be petted while attractive or a creature to be bought —"

"You have expressed it exactly. I should be worn to a frazzle trying to explain my attitude to him and would succeed in nothing but making him think I was "queer". I'm not strong enough to wrestle with Niagara. I keep the self-payment rule with you because you are sufficiently evolved to understand."

Not entirely mollified by this I contended, "In that case you needn't work it on me because I would not misunderstand."

"He is entertaining and I love dining in a beautiful place with the orchestra playing. I couldn't go by myself: I'd be afraid of the waiters."

"I take off my hat to the waiters. They must be great men to fill you with fear."

"They are. I just love to watch Bobby strutting around ordering things. He does it with such a grand air. All I have to do is to follow after and look at people."

"Gee! If any one could look more insolent and sure than youself I'd —"

"Of course I walk upright and am not in fear of the police, but I am conscious of every living being all the time, whereas with Bobby such worms as menials never appear above the horizon of his consciousness unless they make a mistake."

"I could hire one or two waiters to let me treat them like worms while I swagger into the Blackstone if you will change your patronage to me. It's your inconsistency that upsets me. You pretend to be advanced, but like all the rest you'll fall for a cave man cub who tramples womanhood in the mire, and a really evolved man who understands things, you'll treat like a dog, and compel him to go to some horrible grab-lunch, hand-me-out joint —"

It was delirium to make such a statement. I had called to try my luck with another proposal, and this is how the thing had gone. I was startled by the cut look which swept across her face.

"The Fireside is the best that I can afford and it is run by lovely people. I trust you will select more congenial eating companions after this."

She opened the door indicating that I was to go. I took my hat. I was too savage to apologise at once. My remarks had been utterly uncalled for. It was none of my darn business if she let one man pay for her dinner and denied another. I held out my hand but she wouldn't take it, and she hadn't a sulky thread in her so that I knew she was wounded to the core. The Fireside was the apple of her eye, her retreat and her refuge when the day was done, and I had belittled it.

I wanted to go and punch Bobby, but there lacked excuse other than that the lady appeared to prefer him. Then I was hit by a brilliant idea. I went to the Fireside and sat in the rest room and read a paper — upside down — I was so busy thinking of her!

Mrs. Laddy came up and greeted me with a charm that the chatelaine of a Shore drawingroom could have envied, and yet I had called it a grab-lunch joint! I was not in the habit of losing my temper, but there was a nerve-racking element to this being in love which I had not sufficiently discounted. The sensibilities seemed to be exaggerated so that more ballast was necessary than in ordinary emotional experiences. Perhaps poor little Syb was feeling the same, and yet there were Bobby and I, as well as others all plaguing her, and in addition she was a highly strung piece of sensitiveness and had to work all day in the clamour of the Loop.

In due time she came in. I followed her sedately and so anxious to keep out of sight that I selected about seven kinds of bread and a few potatoes. The checker smilingly remarked that I seemed to be bread hungry. Sybyl went to her usual seat and when she had things comfortably set out, I rushed in as the creatures who fear not and dumped my stuff near her.

"Have a piece of bread old pard," I said. Her sense of humour was not proof against that but she was white as a little ghost and was very quiet. I did not know what to do about it. But she opened the ball. There was no sulking or glowering over injuries with Sybyl. She always fussed about them until they were entirely cleared up.

"What are you doing in such a questionable place?"

"Best food and best company in Chicago here. There is not a hostess anywhere to eclipse Mrs. Laddy."

"Then why did you say those terrible things? When Bobby carries on like that, it is because he doesn't know any better, but you do, and that's what makes it hurt."

"But that's just it, you'll go out with that rip of a Bobby and he doesn't —"

"Yes, but I have to take him as he is because he doesn't know any better."

"There it goes! Men always say that a woman prefers a belswagger who ill-treats her. It doesn't matter whether she does it because she prefers him or because he doesn't know any better, the result is the same to the decent man who is left out in the cold."

"There is nothing else to take and one gets tired of being alone," she said plaintively. "I wasn't designed for a nun."

"But you have a choice between Bobby and me," said I "and you tolerate Bobby."

Then she was herself again. Her eyes opened wide with amazement and danced with merriment. "The brazen conceit of men is a colossal *phenomenon*," said she with humorous emphasis on a word I overworked. "They neglect no opportunity of drawing attention to the possession of a horn by continuous tooting."

"We have to if we mean to survive in the business of being a man," I maintained, and the breach was healed. I began to think I might get the proposal in after all but she diverted me by becoming analytical and inquiring, "Now what are the things you like in me so that you are always here?"

"I like you for being the most pestiferous little squirrel with no more idea of logic than a caterpillar, and because you talk more rot in one hour than a real womanly woman would be able to think up in a year, and because you seem more like a toy than a real person."

"That's just it, and I love you —"

"*Love* me!" I gasped.

"That was just a figure of speech," she said making an irreverent grimace. "I *enjoy* you because your hair is made of straw, and your eyes are like a china doll's, and because you always get your clothes rumpled up, and because you're such a nice great blunderbuss that's neither useful nor ornamental, and because you are always cluttered under my feet until I have become inured to you, and just *because*!"

I'd have risked ten years in jail to call the bluff in her stimulating coquetry, but I behaved like a shorn Samson.

That night I had an interview with my mirror. I rejoiced that my teeth were every bit as big and white as Bobby's, but my eyes were like a China doll's — a weak minded doll's at that, and no good at all without specs. My hair might have been becoming on a little girl under one year old but it did not add to "virility" of appearance. There was my nose, a little bigger and more bent than Bobby's. It had more the curve of a Sioux Chief's, while Bobby's had the insolent height combined with shortness found on many of the governors of England.

"One prominent probosis, one pair of broad lips a trifle thick that shut up like a steel trap and ornamented with a pale yellow tooth brush — a face which might be described as open, no hidden corners or mysteries," I inventoried. However I decided to send the crumpled clothes to the presser — several sets of them.

CHAPTER 22
THE MEANING OF FLOWERS

It became a sort of race between Bobby and me to see who got most of her time and I did not know when she did her work.

"You are cluttered under my feet again," she complained one day that I had paid her both a morning

74

and afternoon call to see how a circular that I had ordered was progressing, and each time the door opened we did not know whether it was to be a special delivery, a telegram, or a registered letter from Bobby. He sat up nights writing her reams of the tamest bromides in circulation since before Noah designed the ark, but Bobby considered them flash lights of new wisdom. Things already in print were not good enough. He had to compile something super-excellent out of his own skull contents to save her.

"It *is* silly of me to waste so much time," said I. "Nothing in the game for me. I'm going away and I shan't come back." I was watching her face with a hungry feeling but I watched in vain.

"Then I'll be able to get something done besides gossip."

I leant forward and caught her hands in mine. "See here, would you be glad if you never saw me again?"

"*Dee*lighted!" said she baring her teeth in mimicry of T.R.

"This is no joking matter," I persisted. "I want the truth."

"*Dee*lighted!" she repeated, but her lashes were down and her lips straightened in a giggle.

"Now young woman," and my grasp became desperate, "I want the truth. Look me straight in the eyes and tell me you wouldn't care if I went away and never came back."

Her face was provokingly cool and her lashes still down. A coldness passed from her to me.

"I know you wouldn't care," I said, and life dropped fifty degrees, but as I was loosening my fingers she caught them tight and raising her eyes as deep and dark and clear as a pool where the shades fall, whispered softly, "if I tell you the absolute truth will you promise to take your hat and go without arguing?"

I promised, and life went up seventy-five degrees.

"Well, there's your hat, and now you have promised." She looked at me steadily. "If I thought I should never see you again, I should *die!*" Intensity of emotion conveyed the sense of her anguish in contemplation of my loss.

I took my hat, I halted irresolute, but she motioned me to the door. I was Lot's wife many times over and being turned out of paradise, but her back was resolutely towards me and I had given my word. I went home. Every thread of my being sang, an enchanted organism, the medium of spiritual magic.

I sent her a great bunch of violets next morning. I followed them by a call after hours, but she was as if the episode of yesterday had never been.

"Miss Maguire says that to send a young lady violets means that she is yours practically. Is that true?"

"Miss Maguire is a highly informed young lady."

"Then there has been a mistake. I got some violets with your card in them. Now you must tell me what young lady they were meant for," she demanded.

The darned little squirrel! I gazed at her flabbered. I felt my mouth fall open like people's whose minds are not quick on the trigger. Whether the ventilation seems to help as when one is short of wind, or whether it is laborious to attend to everything at once, I am not scientifically equipped to state.

"Well, after yesterday," I was blundering enough to say.

"After yesterday?" she repeated.

"You said you'd speak the truth."

"Did I tell any extra lies yesterday?"

"You said you couldn't bear if it —"

"You dear darling duck, of course I couldn't bear not to see you again. You are the joy of my heart. I couldn't bear to lose Miss Maguire or Dr. Margaret either. *You* are a love to send me violets for *that!*"

"May I keep on sending them?"

"At your own risk, but if you send them with the meaning that Miss Maguire says, I'll, I'll —"

"Yes?"

"I shall give them to Bobby and say they express my sentiments towards him."

The game was up. The only thing to do was to meet her on her own tack.

"Well, what may I send as being appropriate — thistles and brambles?"

"As an expression of yourself I should suggest something modest and retiring like a sunflower — with a horn attachment."

"I'd rather express *you*. I'll send a cabbage."

I did next morning.

CHAPTER 23
THE KING OF INDOOR SPORTS

Many times I anathematised my younger friend as "That beast of a Bobby!" For Sybyl to permit his attentions was in my point of view a casting of precious things before the uninitiated, and, I began to think, the uninitiatable, but that may have been the green bias. I wondered how she played the game with him and how he returned her play. One afternoon I inadvertently found out.

It was a long time after hours. The office was very quiet. I stepped in softly hoping to find Sybyl alone, but getting as far as her door I was arrested by the fact of her having company. It seemed more embarrassing to declare my presence by going than staying and what I saw in a big tell-tale mirror which chronicled in a second room what took place in the first, was an old, old story.

There being enacted was the sex duel as it is fought with slight variations by the English speaking peoples the world around. And what I wanted was to play with her a spiritual duet. Perhaps she preferred the duel for she was well-equipped for it, in its finer aspects, and in a multitidinous majority of cases it is all that women are called upon to play. She may have been as a musician capable of Beethoven but who finds it easier sometimes to turn to Nevin.

In the king of indoor games as played by those designated Anglo-Saxons, the participants race to the precipice and stop with easy precision before going over the edge. They toss fire balls without being scorched — if the contestants are skilled, and Bobby and Sybyl were skilled.

Bobby lunged gaily threatening the familiarity of a kiss. Sybyl returned a caressful thwack on his healthy cheek leaving a deeper tinge under her fingers. He grasped both her hands in his large one, pinning her easily with one arm leaving the other free for action.

"I really will kiss you for that!" he exclaimed, a thrilled delight in his tones.

"You will not!" said she, the arch face of hers daringly tilted and flushed in the joyous excitement of the game. Well she knew that a man of his upbringing would not dare, that it was her royal privilege to coquet to the last line and then coolly turn and say good day.

As they confronted each other flinging the immemorial challenge Bobby's blazing eyes softened. "I think you are a witch," he laughed with ringing gladness. "You little — little — little sassy thing! You know what you deserve!"

"I deserve —" she left the sentence unfinished. What need for words?

"Well, you know what you are going to get right now," he bragged, but suddenly relaxing put a hand as tender as a dove under her chin.

"You little fake! You little snare and delusion! You drive a fellow just crazy with your airs and then you give him — nothing. What shouldn't I like to do to you!" His voice breathed an ecstasy of tenderness — a Samson biologically right and luckily safe.

I slipped out like a thief. In this game as it is played by the Anglo-Saxons there is a part for the other man, as skilled as the roles of the principals. I took myself home for the contemplation of it. It demanded first of all the ability to keep my head shut and to expurgate the antics of a fool from my ordinary conduct. If Sybyl and Bobby were fairly matched in that duel, which might very well soften and spiritualise to a duet, my part had still to be put through.

To love and be loved is perfection, surely, but if one can have but half of this perfection, to love is a greater gift than to be loved. Poets have admitted this, so mere business men need not be ashamed to prove it true.

And I had had my love. Nothing could ever take that from me. I had been blessed to feel in my inmost being that it is the loving so much more than the being loved which gives the spirit wings. To realise that we can love greatly is to some of us the power and glory for ever. This sanctuary I had entered, thanks to little Sybyl.

I sat down to smoke a rare pipe upon it and pull myself together. A man may be the private owner of a heaven and hell and have the beauty of Apollo, yet if his spiritual processes lack oil it will avail him nothing. It is a platitude, that by the spirit we live. So I had to get this thing straight. If it was Bobby, then Bobby it was. Even as my rival, the old love kept me from really hating him. The vanity of man is ineradicable and it was ME he had chosen as a god when a little fellow. That had shown he had some perception. Now it was Sybyl, a further evidence of discernment on his part. I could not blame him for that. He was coming on apace. His was a case of delayed development but he would be none the worse for ripening late.

I could see all this in the refreshing blue wreaths circling above my head.

And after all, the last card had not yet been played. Hope springs infernal in the lover's breast.

Bobby came in to dinner a little after I entered the dining room and he was madder than a wet hen. When I was half through the meal I was called on the telephone by Sybyl who wanted to know why I had not been at The Fireside. She upbraided me for being eternally under her feet when she wanted to work and systematically deserting her when she was a victim of loneliness. Weak and spineless worm that I am, I suggested the theatre and gobbled up my ice cream and cake and tore down town.

In the darkened auditorium she slipped her hand into mine, leaning thrillingly near to whisper, "I am so grumpy and out of sorts and you always smooth out my feathers. I'd like to chew off some one's head."

"That's just what mine was made for."

I was so transported that I suggested the seeing her home process should be prolonged a little and we drove nearly out to Evanston and back. The taxi man was discreet and went slowly and I had to hold her close inside the rug and the wing of my coat for it was a cold night and she had not been dressed for driving.

She did not mention Bobby. I wondered what snag had quenched the light which had been on their faces a few hours earlier. What mattered it! All I cared was that she had come to me for comfort and snuggled against my heart as unselfconsciously as a tired child. To ME she had come for refuge! I was not going to spoil it by nagging curiosity. What she had to tell me I should know in her own good time. She was worthy of fullest trust, innocent coquetry, whims, and illogicality notwithstanding.

CHAPTER 24
NOW UP! NOW DOWN!

Though not making any perceptible headway, I began to think I was at least holding my own till the young cub brought a big green car on from New York. He drove like a gay-hearted fiend and a mechanician combined, by all accounts. Certainly he could handle the wheel like a gladiator with the nerve of old Nick, or so it seemed to me, who could not drive at all because of my bad sight. Not that I was afraid for myself, but I had an unholy terror of running down, say a gentle old

80

lady or a little child. So I employed a chauffeur and generally sat like a hatching hen while he toted me around. I told Sybyl it was the hotel 'bus.

She preferred to sit beside Bobby, wrapped in one of his heavy fur coats, and looking indeed like a little bird in the nest, as he had once described her in fancy. He had surrounded her with every comfort. He had a bear skin bag to put her in when they sat in the tonneau and hot air when they sat in front, and she took such care as her natural element. I had to admit that Bobby was not too slow after all. He had left me a hundred miles out of sight.

Coming from the frontier, Sybyl despised with all the fervour of a cave woman the man who had to have other men to wait upon him, even chauffeurs. As for the fellow dependent upon a valet, she would cheerfully have exterminated him with rat powder. She was a curious mixture of the cave woman and the over-feminised girl so prevalent in American society. She admired many of the old swashbuckler, frontier accomplishments in men. A spiritual man who could not also on demand be a pugulist or perform doughty physical deeds had little hope of attracting her.

So Bobby took to driving entirely himself and his prowess with the wheel was one reason of his success with her. He taught her to drive the beast herself and her delight was boundless. The only thing that Bobby had ever done after leaving the football team was to drive a machine in a few automobile races and he talked of taking to the race track in earnest now. He seemed to be growing more seasoned and purposeful while it was I that was reverting to his former characteristics.

"You little cat fish, what did you really ask me to come in for?" I demanded as belligerently as I knew how one afternoon that she had telephoned that she would be glad to see me. "Wasting my time! What do you suppose I am?"

"I don't know." Her voice was soft and sweet, and her airs, (that's all I can call them), enticing and disarming. "*You* know," she added, dropping her glances her manner full of tremulous invitation. I stepped forward to take it but when I was deliriously on the brink of the precipice she looked up with boyish mischief and chirped, "This is so sudden. It is also premature, as I limited you to proposing once a week and the week is not up yet."

"I'm going to forget you. I'll never propose to you again at all any more for ever and you'll be sorry when I'm dead."

"That is also very sudden. I'll be a sister to you lovey-dovey-deary-me," she prattled with bubbling mirth, bewitchingly provoking. I hungered to smother her in love's embrace.

"It's true. I'm not going to think any more about you. I shan't even be interested to know how you and Bobby come out. You're nothing but a waste of time. I hereby forget you," I said with a brave show of indifference, but as I went about my business, more than ever in front of my vision all day was a little face with a tang to it which wiped out all the beauties, old and young, that I had ever met.

When I got home that afternoon I found there a box from a florist's. It contained a tiny *boutonnière* of forget-me-nots and a card inscribed "Bet you can't".

What a joy to have spanked her! Drat it all, and there was that fatuous Bobby taking his place in her affections by sheer force of energy, and taking it for granted. Did he think it such a simple matter to entrap that little squirrel? "Where angels fear, fools dare to tread." I muttered, but it did not help any.

In return for the forget-me-nots I sent a special delivery, the mails being slow as molasses or a prairie waggon, and in it I said, "I don't want to forget you. I am going to remember you always no matter how Herculean the effort, because that is what you were made for — a souvenir. I couldn't be hired to forget you, you little grass-hopper!" Then I should tantalise her by absence. But back by special came another note. In it was my special delivery unopened and written across the back, "It seems so inhospitable to send back a dear little note but I am engaged upon very special work these days and have to concentrate my feeble feminine intellect to keep it from frittering. You will forgive me."

Jehosophat! I had met the chief boss tantaliser and saw that I had better take off my hat before it was knocked off by the police. I had no redress except to be nasty and that would have been to prove myself a gross inferior — a tapir trying the dance of the gazelle. Ah, Ha! The next time a letter came in her writing I should send it back unopened with a parody of her message on the back: but the next note from her was type-written and post marked New York so that I opened it unsuspectingly. It contained a crushed red rose bud and the words, "I've taken the thorns off!" Bless the saucy baggage, the thorns on her rose pricked ecstasy!

I sat down to face a few facts head on. Resolving to forget her was useless. The only cure for my state was marriage, the right to hold her in my arms conquered! Mine! That would be a full and glorious revenge. Ah, to get her completely in my power, though I should have to build a yawl and turn pirate to do it!

But I seemed to be entirely out of the running. That accursed Bobby was the leading man by every test I could apply. What made it more exasperating was that I had taken him to Sybyl's office and introduced him. He could never have guessed she existed but for me. What she could see in him besides his teeth and hair and his ready money almost shook my faith in women's selective instinct. I had been waiting for her to tire of him and return with relief to a creature of ideas like myself, and failing that I had counted on the call of the chorus girl, the pet, or the parasite to have been too strong for him long since.

I was still sufficiently neutral to admit that he was a strapping good-looking lump with his clear hide and black moustache clipped in the latest tooth brush effect from England. Sybyl pointed out that it was cut on exactly the same pattern as mine. It was, but I had worn mine from boyhood. There had been a superstition that to leave the male upper lip intact strengthened the sight.

Such a facial garnish was old-fashionedness on my part, whereas for Bobby to leave hair on his face was a dandified following of a fad that had just come in. Bobby seemed as settled as if it were all over but the wedding march. Only Miss Maguire cheered me still. She maintained that it was a long way from time to throw up the sponge. She held that I had a show if I would only think up something to eclipse the automobile. She was a good business woman even in advice about love.

"Just think of all the people you know," said she in her soft-voiced wisdom. "Nearly everyone you thought was going to marry some one, married some one else, even after the engagement was announced, and those two are not engaged, I'm sure. Can't you do something striking to please her like Mr. Hoyne does. He captures her imagination. Girls like to have things done for them. And *she's* worth doing something for. You'll never see another like her as long as you live. She's the only one in the world. If I only had the mind and the personality of that girl!" said Miss Maguire, who was the best and truest press agent woman ever had. She told me that her partner had a perfect craze for aviation and had tried to persuade Bobby to take it up, but tough as was his nerve for automobiling, by some quirk he balked at flying.

"Try flying," faintly murmured Edna Maguire.

"Miss Maguire," I said, and I meant it, "if the fellow who gets you doesn't stand on his head or anything else to prove that he's worth you, just let me know about it."

Oh, to see her blushes!

CHAPTER 25
AVIATION FOR SYBYL'S SAKE

Had women been free to put their imprint upon civilization, men by now would have been super-men, demi-

gods, and what would have happened next is speculation. For, a woman is always attracted by the daring and
different. If she has free choice, she never singles out as
an ideal a man with all the miserable traits and the
prettified delicate physique, so that owing to a handicap
of subnormality she can strut about and crow, indulging
in an illusion of superiority.

Acting on this thesis and further instigated by Miss
Maguire, it happened that I, a sane, slow, sure and safety
first citizen in my late thirties, with little penchant for
machinery and defective sight as a further drawback,
relinquished a policy of watchful waiting and took all
suddenly to being a show aviator.

One evening after seeing her and Bobby pass in the
snorting green monster I strolled round to see Otto
Brent of the Aero Club and surprised him by announcing my intention of learning to fly and probably
investing in a machine of my own.

I went at the venture methodically and though not
brilliant became a creditable bird in a short time. I had
a powerful incentive. Strange to say I made a good
aviator though I had no intention of making more than
one or two public flights. I could wear my glasses and
the apprehension of running into some one, which had
circumscribed me all my life, did not apply in the air. It
was inspiring to plunge along feeling free at last from
the danger of hitting an innocent bystander.

In a few weeks I acceded to Otto Brent's request to
give a public exhibition on the Lake Front in a new bi-
plane of the Curtiss type.

It was to be a great day for me. I called at Sybyl's
office the evening before and invited her to come and
see me loop around in the clouds. I tried to be casual
but I could not keep all the triumph out of my tones.
"If you are game, I'll put a crest on the occasion by
taking you for a baby flight afterwards!"

Oh, to see her eyes! Where was that mere Bobby with
his mere automobile then!

"You don't mean it! I didn't know that you could

85

fly!" She clapped her hands and shook mine in congratulations.

"I can, a little," I said modestly, hauling out a paper to exhibit the sporting page where it was announced that Cavarley, an entirely new recruit to the noble order of Condors was to give an exhibition on the Lake Front, landing in Grant Park at noon.

The day was first class, warm for the season and with very little wind. There was quite a deal of interest in the event. Otto Brent understood the art of advertising. The machine was a daisy and in perfect order. Machines to fly with need to be or the flyer doesn't live to tell the tale. Up and up I sailed, thousands of feet, then looped a bit and did a few spirals, though I was not very spectacular in this. The interest lay in that it was the first big public trial of a new type of machine and by an elderly aviator who had learned to fly as speedily as a man may become a licensed chauffeur.

I was in fine form and much elated but when it came time for landing a strange nervousness overtook me. I found I could have done with a little more seasoning in the landing stunt before taking it on in front of that blistering crowd. All those people paralysed me. There did not seem to be a spot where people were not running around like ants and I shuddered at the possibility of squashing some of them.

Once or twice I came down to within a hundred feet of the earth, but not sure of my distances went up again to get out of the way of that accursed, drivelling idiotic mob. I thought of clearing out to the suburbs and coming down there but that would be defeat before Sybyl and Bobby and an occasion not only crestless but robbed of its very scalp. So I came back to the ordeal.

No doubt it was this fussiness which made me throw the joy stick out of gear. In adjusting it I lurched forward and lost my glasses. They fell broken. Now I was in a mess. The lever would not work very well but I fumbled for the emergencies and came down all right excepting that I could not correctly gauge how near I was to the earth. It was nearer than I calculated and it hit me before I hit it.

CHAPTER 26
RECONSTRUCTION FOR MY OWN SAKE

When I came to I was in St. Luke's and what with the smell of iodiform and bandages and things I seemed to be in a patternless mess. My head was large but I could think with it, but my trunk, oh where was it!

I discovered from the nurse that it was tomorrow and that I had enjoyed a fine sleep. My good friend Dr. Duff Devereux had been watching the exhibition and with the assistance of Bobby took charge of the remains as soon as they eventuated and conveyed them to the hospital. A great surgeon had fixed them together again and now Dr. Devereux, who was in charge generally, had dropped in to assure me that there was no cause for worry. A broken collar bone, a cracked thigh, a sprained wrist, perhaps a rib and some severe abrasions all on the left side, slightly cut about the head and stunned, but mere scalp wounds. That was all. From the surgical point of view, a mere bagatelle. The work of restoration had not been sufficiently arduous to be interesting. Considering my virtility had not been of the order which is visited upon the children even to the third and fourth generation, Dr. Devereux said there was no danger of complications. I should be about again as good as ever in a short time.

"As I was coming in I met a little friend of mine who will not eat or sleep till she hears you are all right. The accident threatens to have a more disastrous effect on her than on you."

"I want to see her now," I said promptly. I did not feel so bad considering, if I only kept perfectly still and did not attempt flights of logic.

Sybyl came right in as the doctor withdrew. She looked at me quietly and caressed my right hand.

"Good morning! The water's fine!" said I, in high spirits — that is comparatively.

"Are you all broken up? Are you paining all over?" she whispered stooping down to me. I put my uninjured arm around her weakly, and in a voice which I tried to make clear and steady, assured her that I was all right. Whereupon she let the tears splash down on what was uncovered of my face.

"I was afraid that your beautiful body would be all broken up and you would be lame for life, and we're all too ugly as it is without messing up our framework."

"If I don't regain my ordinary perfection Dr. O'Donnell shall have to reckon with me." I drew her near as I was able. Her distress filled me with ecstasy. Accident was surely its own reward.

"Little heart of mine, would you have cared if I had gone out this afternoon?"

"Do you think I am made of wood — one of those cigar store effigies?"

"No, composed of electricity throughout."

"It was terrible to see you come down there! I thought my heart had flown away but I never made a sound though people all around me cried out! You fell such a little way but it was the weight of the machine. I can't stand it. Supposing you were killed! I'm so lonely! Don't you ever dare go flying again! Promise me you won't! You don't care whether you get killed or not! You didn't think of me, you thought only of yourself."

It was like being bullied by a butterfly or henpecked by a canary. I must have felt like the young mother with a new born babe who is represented as saying the rapture of maternity repays a thousand fold for all the pain and danger. I caressed the silky head as it lay against me and she sobbed on unrestrained. I let her alone.

"I'm sorry I've made such a fool of myself. You are sure it is you?" she said presently.

I dried her eyes on the sheet. "Did you think it was a

88

dummy they had done up here? I'm quite alive and I can wiggle my toes on one leg, so my back is not broken".

"Why, now I can see the dimple. *It* isn't spoilt at all events." She placed a finger tenderly on my chin. "That doesn't hurt you does it?"

"Hurt! Little Heart of Mine!"

"And your eyes looking so sleepy and strained because they haven't got any glasses."

"I've sent word for Harold Brubaker to bring me a pair."

She stopped sobbing and moved away from me a little but retained my uninjured hand and stroked it with a disturbing tenderness. After a silence I said, "Sybyl, I went up flying for your sake and now I suppose I've made a bigger fool of myself than ever."

"No, you flew very well. Those who know about flying said you were fine and not the fool-hardy kind. Your fall wasn't sensational enough to make a stir. Accidents happen all the time every day. But you mustn't fly again."

"Would you have me sit down like a muff and acknowledge myself defeated by a few scratches like this. I must have some special goggle spectacles made."

"I'm going flying with you in future and then if you are killed I'll be killed too instead of being left lonely," she announced. She broke down all over again so that I had to comfort her all over again, and assure her that my strength and beauty were unimpaired, my courage reinforced. Then I had the impulse to strike while the iron was hot. "If you will marry me I'll not fly any more."

This crudity was doomed to instant defeat.

"If I married you I might want you to go flying," said she drying her eyes and beginning to flirt again right away.

"I believe you'd flirt with me if I were dead."

"It was you who began to flirt with me again," she contended.

"Well," I continued grimly, "if you won't have me I'll

go and fly as my profession. Any stunt that has been done in all the world — Pegoud, Vedrines, or Beachy — I'll outdo them and keep on at it. You know what that means."

"You shan't do any such fool thing."

Dr. Devereux returned at that moment and saved me from any further indiscretions I was on the verge of uttering. When he saw that Sybyl had been weeping and was still nestled against my pillow he began badgering her.

"Why Cavarley, how have you kept it a secret? And this little puss, I've always been telling her that love was —"

"Oh yes, Dr. Devereux always recommends love and grubbing in a garden among chickens as a cure-all for dissatisfaction, and loneliness, and psychic enervation, and corns, and indigestion, and near sight, and tooth-ache!"

"Well Madam, have you not seen it prove effective?"

"In a way, but the cure was worse than the disease. Among parasitic wives I think fatty degeneration of the soul is worse for the race than dissatisfaction and rebellion among mother-hearted spinsters."

"Falling in love — darned good advice — will cure nearly anything," reiterated the doctor.

"It might if it could be followed. But you ask people to make bricks without straw. What could they fall in love with?"

"With you, you little sinner! Why do you make such a noise about Cavarley here, if you are not in love? How dare you lead an honest man astray! Is this your idea of platonics? If it is so hard to love a mere man, how do you account for all the lovely ladies who have been here weeping over Cavarley's few little scratches?" demanded Doc Devereux with mischief in his eye.

"That all men are liars, as one who knew them even better than I testified," she retorted with a diverting promptitude which left her some points ahead.

"Grubbing among chickens and falling in love, those are the only two remedies you have in your bag of tricks," she repeated with the relish of the vanquisher, "I hope that in heaven you will have your reward and be a super-woman or super-mother and have triplets first go off. How many lovely society ladies have fallen in love with you since last we met?" she inquired with breath-taking audacity, for he was the adored of more than one woman who had the widest choice that is open to her sex today.

"How many people have *you* pulled to pieces just to see the wheels go round, young woman since last we met?" he parried, taking her face between his palms and looking near and deep into her eyes. "It is a pity your own wheels go so swiftly. You should be out in the garden grubbing among the chickens — more fresh air —"

I knew it was useless my entering the game of pitch and toss.

"Now you run down stairs you little Tom Tit, till I say a few words to the world's greatest aviator," said Doc. "and then I'll take you home in my machine and let you see how my wheels go round," he concluded with remarkable indulgence on his saturnine face. She went out blowing us kisses.

"I'll be switched," said Doc. "Cavarley, why do you hesitate?"

"I'm more than willing, God knows. It's she that's hesitating."

"Form of coquetry, and yet she thinks herself of the emancipated type. What she needs is a level-headed fellow to impose his will upon hers and take the whims out of her. Chickens, a garden, and fresh air are a good remedy for most of the ills that try pills after all, you take my word for it," said Doc, and he ought to know. He put his head in at the door after he had said good night to repeat, "You've got such a hand that you can't lose now, no matter how you play, but how have you been so sly about it?"

In truth I felt myself that I was several laps ahead of that mere Bobby-Boy, in spite of his big green car and his black hair.

CHAPTER 27
THE GAME AND THE CANDLE

Whether the game of aviation for Sybyl's sake was worth the candle I am not sure. Some days I thought not when I lay there helpless and darned uncomfortable and, ouch! those knitting bones! But there were other times when I felt I had scored. These were the days when Sybyl tripped in and all in one breath called me a blunderbuss, and a sweet lil'boy with yellow eyes and blue hair, and a dear adorable thing, and a lunatic, and a Silly-Billy, a slap-up trump, a real duck, and a gosling, and a goose, and a dilliwig, and a crocodile and a polly-wog, and a Hottentot, a dear lamb, a mad bull, the son of a sampan and a sea cook — each individual epithet a delirious term of endearment from her lips.

Making a fool of me! Why should a man feel fooled by sweet moments which take him near the angels! Deluded! Not so. Let us grasp confidently that paradise irradiating the soul with lofty purpose, tender, glowing, selfless.

The things she could think up to entertain a man were inimitable. There was a delight in tantalising in her which never permitted her to cloy with too much attention.

She sent me a dull advertising circular in a beautiful envelope by special delivery. Next came a tiny gold thimble with instructions to stick it on the ends of my huge digits and try to make them taper so the girls would like me better. The following day I received peremptory instructions to return the thimble at once because it was Miss Maguire's, the gift of a lover, and Miss Maguire had missed it. She sent instead that which she said was her own thimble, a one cent tin affair large enough — yes, really large enough for myself. She sent little bouquets, and ribbons for my hair, and a lively book of poems entitled *In Vivid Gardens,* with a sweet wild woodnote of purity running through them, especially refreshing.

On April first I received a large fat envelope sealed almost to invulnerability. When opened another envelope came to light on which was:

Dammmmmmmmmmmmmmmmmmmnnnnnnnnnnn!

The next was inscribed:

HELLLLLLLLLLLLLLL!

Another:

GOLDARRRRRRRRRRRNNNNNNNNNNNN!

Then one envelope after another:

DEAREST!
DARLING!
BABY!
BOOBY!
BLUNDERBUSS!
XXXXXXXXXXXXXX!!!

Surely these were intended for kisses!
Next:

REMEMBER THAT AS SOON AS YOU ARE
WELL WE SHALL

There the story ended. The ensuing envelopes were plain and I opened them with delighted expectancy till I came to the last. It was inscribed:

REMINDER OF WHAT WE WERE TO DO WHEN
YOU LEAVE THE HOSPITAL.
POSITIVELY NOT TO BE OPENED UNTIL YOU
ARE REAL WELL!

Of course curiosity kept me from obedience. I hoped for some message with a sunbeam of promise for me. I hurriedly opened the envelope in spite of instructions and read:

CURIOSITY KILLED A MONKEY!

The saucy Tom Tit!
My nurse was as interested as I to see what she would

do next, but two days passed and no message. I missed her mischief. The nurse said I grew unendurably cross but then relief came:

> IT IS UNWISE TO BE AMIABLE TO THE MERE MALE OF THE SPECIES AS THE HUMBLEST OF HIM THINKS ANY WOMAN WHO LOOKS AT HIM MORE THAN ONCE WOULD RISK HER LIFE AND HONOR FOR A SMILE FROM HIM!!!

I wondered from this if Bobby had broken loose again. He appeared to be in working order and dutifully came to see me and supplied me with everything under the sun excepting much of his company or conversation.

There was a red letter day when Miss Maguire dropped in dressed in a spring suit as blue as her eyes and bringing me handy little things as well as jellies brewed by her own dainty taper fingers. She sat and blushed and I think did not know what the Dickens to say till I started about Bobby. To my relief, she reported that he and Sybyl were seeing very little of each other. Miss Penelo had no time for company these days as she was very busy with an intricate contract — a volume on the reconstruction of the universe by a millionaire who hoped to win a fat nimbus through philanthropy. She assured me that her partner had acted like a lost soul till it was certain that I was out of danger. Miss Maguire gave me to understand that she had her money on me and she believed that Bobby was a passing show. She had seen other young gentlemen like him pass through her remarkable partner's laboratory.

In the middle of these inspiring confidences who should call to see me but Harold Brubaker, Esq., lawyer, wag, and young man about town, a fellow as full of temperament and vivacity as Sybyl herself. I laughed in my sleeve to see that Miss Maguire's blushes and timid utterances deeply impressed him from the first. I suggested that he should see her home as she was my most precious friend. Miss Maguire of course demurred and looked as if she would surely cry if any big boy pressed his attentions upon her, where-upon Brubaker became mightily insistent, and to my joy, I discovered later by accident that not only did he take her home but that they went out and made an evening of it first.

Harold accused me of selfishness in keeping her all to myself. He said he had lots of law work and he had discovered that Miss Maguire was a full fledged member of the Illinois bar but, in the present stage of prejudice against women lawyers, found it more profitable and comfortable to open business with Sybyl.

CHAPTER 28
REWARD

As soon as I was dismissed from the hospital and able to hobble around on crutches I ordered my chauffeur to take me to Dearborn Street. There was a lot of business I was glad to turn over to the perfect and competent hands of Miss Maguire and both she and Sybyl had cordially invited me to come and see them at any hour of the day as soon as I should be able.

How enchanting to be welcomed by them both and put to rest on the couch in the reception room. Sybyl in particular hovered around like an agitated Tom Tit. I found I was weak after the journey and glad to lie down? The rear of the Loop traffic was soothing in the distance and the busy click of the machines near at hand gave a homey informal sound. Next thing I knew Sybyl told me I had slept for an hour and had snored like a grampus till the police had come up to investigate if the building had started to crumble, and did I feel like tea? It was all ready brewed by Lieutenant Yellow-Hair and then Miss Maguire came in and smiled upon me and presented me with a box of candy. How comforting it is to be petted by a number of the nicest women in creation whose motive is real motherly hospitality.

From time immemorial it has been a fascination for men to watch women work. Perhaps that is one reason why the office on Dearborn Street was more enticing than any drawing room that was open to me on Sheridan Road or Prarie Avenue. It was sweeter even than my cosy precincts at The Caboodle, for I was run down by the accident and lying a-bed and inclined to depression, and though I do not think Sybyl was soothing, there was no doubt of her being the most stimulating little contraption the Lord ever devised. She had the power to take me by the crop of the neck, and yank me from the deepest dungeon of blues and dissatisfaction to a plane where everything was glowing and paradisaical. And Miss Maguire had also distinctive gifts. There never was any rush or disorganization perceptible in the division of her business quarters open to the public. She was never flustered, never in a hurry. She had the secret of imparting to each client the idea that her time and inclination were entirely at his disposal. Such an atmosphere does not happen haphazard. It is the result of untiring energy, capability, and the ability to organize and train a skilled staff — efficiency at its best.

I quickly formed the habit of dropping into the office for a dawdle and a cup of tea. It takes eternal vigilance to escape lax habits and retain any manliness of fibre. I dreamed sweet dreams of the way I should return this hospitality should Sybyl ever come to my abode. I was aching to supply her with an abode. I was not idle in pushing my suit. All roads of conversation apparently led to that enthralling subject, but she always put me off with ridiculous statements and the stipulation that I was not to propose more than once a week. Still I hoped on and on. The thought that she would never be mine would have been insupportable. She showed nothing but pleasure in my company and petted me like a mother bird. Miss Maguire too, feloniously encouraged me.

Bobby had gone to Paris to investigate the merits of new kinds of machines for racing. Thus I had the joy of thinking I was the only toad in the puddle, and Miss

Maguire, I repeat, feloniously encouraged me. According to her the logical thing to happen was that Mr. Hoyne would not come back to Chicago at all for an indefinite period. There would be too many expert charmers more to his congeniality in Paris and other resorts of idleness, luxury and beauty.

So I went on serenely, delightedly in my fool's — no, I am still sane enough to say, angel's paradise.

CHAPTER 29
BOBBY, THE PERSISTENT BOGEY

But Miss Maguire and I were wrong about Bobby. He came back from Paris in a few weeks with a couple of cars behind him, or in front of him rather, as they were these insect looking racing contraptions and carried most of their bulk forward in the hood.

He talked of contesting a race in dead earnest and produced old-time portraits of himself, when as one of the most daring gentlemen drivers, his picture had been wont to appear in sporting pages. There were many poses of him including one with his head thrown back, his goggles raised to his forehead, and his big square white teeth gleaming in a boyish smile.

Sybyl's attitude towards him was beyond fathoming. She was so complex that it is doubtful if she understood it herself. Any mental or emotional reaction with her became complicated to the degree of entanglement in a web of indirection. If a situation were laid before her, whether it involved love or hate, selfishness or sacrifice, and particularly decision, she had to look at it from every side of the prism and juggle with it before she could take action. She would climb up behind the barn and take a peek at it from that angle. She would pass by as though she had discerned nothing. She would walk right out in the open and recklessly invite the problem to her. But she would never embrace it. Oh, no! When it came near she would scamper off like a squirrel. If cornered she would make a desperate retreat and a firm repudiation of the whole thing, but if the situation retreated she would come squirrelling right back again, just to see, well, just to see if it had been as much so as she had imagined, and she would begin in her intricate, penetrating, puzzling, misleading way to find out.

Little puss, free from carnal appetites herself — a sort of disembodied spirit, I don't believe it was in her to understand the terror and urge of carnal appetites in the average poorly controlled male or to realize how sharp were the edges on the swords which she used as playthings. It was impossible for a fellow as elemental as Bobby not to mistake her at times, though to do the youngster credit, as a member of the lobster brigade, he was doing pretty well to persevere with her, when there were so many lady lobsters which should have been more congenial. Now that his anger no longer had the power to wound her she was highly entertained when she drove him to accuse her of dark intentions such as the breach-of-promise ladies and sisters even farther on the road of exploitation were capable of.

I saw that he really wanted her, should his desire last till he could win, but self-indulgence and lack of discipline had so encroached upon the art of patience that I continually expected and devoutly hoped that the call of the magazine-cover beauty would lure him to his rightful sphere. He frankly confessed it was her extreme novelty which titillated his appetite. He had never seen anything resembling her and being of that set which considers itself an explorer greatly rewarded by the discovery of a new dinner dish or smoking room joke, Sybyl was some novelty, to use the vernacular.

However, though it was her uniqueness which attracted him he was not content to leave her as she was. Her independence and complexity irritated him and he was always bullying and nagging her. Why such a little creature of spirit and fire should please him at all I did not know. It almost gave proof of inner depths in him not yet uncovered. There was I, on the other hand, knowing enough to leave her just as she was, and thanking God she was not as others. I was willing for a month of her in preference to a cycle with any other woman, delighting in her complexity and responding to it. I enjoyed nothing better than her squirrelling over me though she tantalized me to distraction. If Bobby had not appeared to endanger my game of watchful waiting, I should have been content to stand pat until like a real squirrel I had adored when a boy, she would come quietly and restfully to me and to no one else.

Bobby was militating against such a finale for me. He was writing her the most extraordinary series of letters. He showed me some of them. They were intended to convey his adoration in such a way that if the public fell upon them they nevertheless could be taken for nothing but the meaningless effusions of a gay flirt. I felt myself superior to Bobby in this. A man, I take it, is only half a man and has never fully entered the magic heaven unless he has acted Samson to some Delilah. Samson is biologically right to surrender; the trouble lies in a civilization which has perverted Delilah making her a vampire to betray her Samson's manhood, whereas Delilah undebauched would make of his surrender a time of growth and inspiration that would but reinforce and spiritualise his strength. Where a man shows himself a raw fool is in picking a perverted Delilah when there are others a-plenty who would not shear him but glory in enhancing the splendour of his locks.

Bobby betrayed himself of shameful experience that he feared a Delilah in every woman. My "old maidism" and belief in women left me ahead of him there.

"You had better be careful," I warned Sybil in regard to her replies to Bobby. "Some day when a chorus beauty or millionaire's daughter traps him and then wants to get rid of him in a little while, they'll bring out your letters among the dozens of others he's likely to have received: and what would you feel like to have them spattered over the front pages of the newspapers?"

She flung back her head and laughed in triumphant merriment. "I never write a letter to a gentleman unless I should be amused to have it appear on the first page of the *Chicago Tribune* or *London Times*."

"Does that mean, you little Tom Tit, that you never care enough for any man to write him a decent letter?"

"Might it not mean that if I write a man a love letter or any other sort of letter, I am game to stand for it even to the extent of its being put on a bill board?" She looked down her midgit nose at me, backed off the boards as usual — the elephant defeated by the squirrel.

"And besides," she added provokingly, "I feel quite safe with Bobby, for it not by practice he is at least by breed a gentleman, and that is a whole lot. I'm sure he wouldn't do anything —"

Here was that accursed family business again. She had discussed of yore with me how superstitions hold us more firmly than chains and confessed to curious streaks of snobbery which transcended reasoning. She had said that she would prefer to marry an aristocrat — a man whose mother had been a lady in the best sense of the word, even though he were only a very ordinary fellow, rather than the greatest and most wonderful being whose parents had been of the gutter gutterly.

"If Bobby were the child of some unknown and disreputable woman picked up by the Hoynes out of an orphanage?" I inquired tentatively, "Would you be so reckless with him?"

"It would certainly put a different complexion on things," she admitted. "But he's a thoroughbred. It's that which puts the dare-devil in him that I enjoy. I always feel that he might kidnap me any minute if he took it into his head."

"But," I argued, thereby illustrating what a mere fool I am, "you are entirely your own mistress, from whom or what would you need to elope?"

"From myself, Silly-Billy. I never can make up my mind, but if some man would just take me by assault and battery I'd be so infatuated with his surety of purpose that I'd live happily ever after."

I entertained dreams of taking her at her word. A house could have been secured somewhere. I could drive up behind her some night when she was walking home, as she frequently did at a late hour, and flinging a cloak about her lift her into an antomobile and decamp. That part of the business could have been accomplished by a civil war veteran with one leg, for she wasn't a decent handful. But then would come the mental gymnastics. Suppose the little creature when released from the 'cloak should confront me with eyes flashing fire and demand what I meant.

"To make you my wife." Then if she flashed back "And who are you sirrah, and what your antecedents that you should take it upon yourself to capture me by force?"

That's where I could discern my retreat, cowering, apologetic. It would not be a retreat but an elimination. I cursed my unknown origin and decided I had better not elope with a mettlesome one who could not be impressed by money to any vulnerable extent.

That blithering Bobby! He did not have to suffer such tremors. If he had taken it into his head to kidnap a duchess his family pride and confidence were such that he would not have thought of the question of lineage at all but would have been free to concentrate on the joy of the adventure.

I went home that night determined to wrest from Aunt Pattie the facts about my mother. I was so sure of my father that it never occurred to ask about him. Aunt Pattie was in California and had not received or sent anything but the most casual post card for weeks. I took a long time asking who and what was my mother. I was glad Aunt Pattie was at a distance. The unbelievable timidity that overcame me on approaching this question had often sent me from her presence without putting it and would have done so again. I found the letter so hard to compose that I wished the services of "Maguire, Penelo and Co., General Letter Makers", could have been at my disposal, but I got it off my chest at last. Then to await the reply!

CHAPTER 30
PUTTING MY FATE TO THE TEST

When I had graduated from two crutches to one and noted that The Caboodle was calling for special attention, I discovered also that its master was at sixes and sevens. I had ever been a prosaic creature who early put life on a practical basis. I very rarely got out of hand even as a youngster, and habit had intensified my leaning towards order and self control and fastidiousness. I was getting the wild bull that is in all healthy young men thoroughly gentled, and was taking each year deeper satisfaction in the mental or spiritual as distinct from the material aspects of existence. Now to my dismay I found myself undone.

Where were my sane and disciplined habits of thought? All dispersed. I was as much enslaved as a tobacco fiend or a drink sop or a man who loves women not purely but too well.

My failure to win my love might have been easier had I been given to lesser amours along the way. Like many others I might have diffused my emotional powers in various passing incidents. But my life had been otherwise and the pent up stream of desire, unleashed for the first time, broke forth like a grandly flowing river which had never been thinned in numerous lesser channels and it had to have its way, or I to right about face and start life all over again. There could be no half measures or panderings without inevitable shipwreck and the waste of the work I had done on myself from boyhood.

Of course I thought I had some chance with Sybyl. It seemed to me that she never let me alone. If I experimented with a policy of unadulterated friendship, she would certainly do or say something that brought it all about my ears. But there I may have been blaming the child wrongfully. I tried to be fair. I know that a man enamoured will see encouragement and a hidden meaning of love in a simple "Good morning!" or "I'm glad to see you!" the same as she might address to a grandfather — and her own grandfather at that — But still.

And then Aunt Pattie's letter came.

> Dear Boy,
> Better leave the subject of your mother alone. As I told you long ago, if it does not matter to me, it has no right to matter to you. I will tell you this however, you are the result of an experiment by a woman who thought that she knew the meaning of love, and who afterwards found out that she was mistaken. If some good woman has come into your life, and you, like your mother before you, fancy that you have discovered love you had better come to me, or I will go to you, for in such a belief of love you might understand, and you will need understanding for possibly you will feel that it is yours to forgive; but take my advice, let sleeping secrets lie.
> Your affectionate Aunt Pattie.
> P.S. Have you found the woman?

No thought I, on reading this, I have lost her.

Nevertheless I meant to go to Sybyl and put all to the test. If she cared for me, I should confess my fears to her, shew her that letter and in her sweet sympathy she might help me to unravel the mystery. Perhaps she had more rumours upon it than I. I knew of at least three members of society families whom report said had other fathers than they themselves suspected, and whose real progenitors were a matter of common or perhaps erroneous knowledge. Might there not be some such rumours about mine? That letter however confirmed my worst fears. My mother was some betrayed weakling — ah, this uncertainty was insupportable.

Once for all I determined to find out my chances with Sybyl, regardless, in spite of my mother.

I waited till late one afternoon and saw her by special appointment. I stumped in, put down my crutch and drew her to me without preliminaries. A sudden trembling took possession of me that I was at pains to dissemble, as one breath of passion sent her scampering to the farthest branches of her tree of retreat.

"I have come to ask you a serious question," I said, and my voice went back on me so that I was silent for a minute, "I want to know once for all if I have any hope with you."

"Now, now," she said playfully, "you were not to propose more than once —"

"You've got to be serious for this once in your life," I said rather roughly. Responsive as a flash she was immediately serious.

"It is not a matter of proposing or playing. That has been entrancingly entertaining, but you are always picking at me. You never leave me alone, and when a woman squirrels around a man like that he wants to know how much she means, and he hopes if he l — if he cares — if he is as fond of her as I am of you, that she may one day mean something serious. You must tell me frankly if there is any hope and if you don't care for me — I don't blame you — but you must let me go and put my life in order again. While I'm like this, eaten up with uncertainty and longing I'm only making a blamed fool of myself and everyone else."

The little form was trembling in my arms and I was becoming a weak helpless muss again. In a moment I should be back at heel apologising and ready to hang around on any terms so long as I might be near her, so I tuned up my will, "You wouldn't want to make a fool of a man who worships the ground you walk on, would you?"

"No," she whispered, "I wouldn't want to hurt anyone. I'd rather that they should hurt me."

"You haven't hurt me," I replied, that divine warmth and softness stealing away my determination like a drug, "you've put me nearer heaven than I ever dreamed of being, and made me feel a better man. I'm proud of loving you, but now I want to know have you given me all that is coming to me — have you given me my full share, because if you have nothing more for me I'll have

104

to get away and pull myself together." I hung on her reply. Ah, the tumultuous hope of that moment!

"I'm never going to marry anyone, so you can please go away and not let me be a plague or worry to you in any way. Please go away, it will be easier."

"But don't you care a little?" There was that softness and warmth reflected on her face too, or did I imagine it?

"Care! I always care ever so much," she cried impassionedly, "but what is the good?"

"If people care for each other, all is good, everything can come out all right."

"It is not so simple as that. There are all sorts of superstitions and mental reactions that bind us more than chains or laws."

"But why can't you take me?"

"I can't take any one."

"Well dearie, I wish you had made that plain at the start — you could have let me go long ago," I said, perhaps unfairly, as the warmth and softness faded like the rosy morning mists leaving only the far reaching desert yellow and dry.

"That is true, perhaps I have been unwomanly."

"No, you couldn't be that if you tried, but perhaps you didn't understand that it would have been easier on me if you had let me go."

"I understood, but it was weakness and selfishness — and loneliness, that made me want you near me. I'll try and explain. It is a game between men and women, but the whole of life is on men's side so that a woman could not get even no matter how she cheated. But you came right out in the open from the first ready to give all without haggling or trying to see what kind of a bargain you could drive. Oh, how I have loved you for that! You walked around there like a splendid caribou with his head high and I could not shoot you for your hide and horns. So I left you there browsing around in the open expecting you would one day go off to another hunting ground — men are fickle — or as long as you

105

liked to play around on my demesne I should never have harmed you. Do say that you understand?"

"I understand and I am not going to blame you. It has been a joy but now if you don't want me to be ever so much more than a friend, I'm going away off out of your hunting ground."

A little gasp escaped her and she held me closely a moment.

"I can't bear to be without you. No, that is not fair," she added recovering herself, "I am picking at you again. Yes, you must go away."

"I don't have to go away unless you send me."

"You see how I am situated, it isn't fair to keep you and I haven't the pluck to send you away," she said with deepest dejection.

"I understand. You have oodles of pluck, but with you, there are so many angles that your decision gets lost. Just try taking one little thing at a time. Must I really go away? Surely that is a simple proposition. Can you never be mine?"

"Oh no, it is of no use. It isn't a simple thing."

"Was there anything in your past life or heredity that makes it impossible or inadvisable that you should marry?" I asked gently. Imperious and wilful she instantly retreated on the far heights of her maidenhood.

"There is nothing in *my* past life that would prevent me marrying into the nobility if I should so desire — it is not on my side that the barrier exists."

I knew the game was up for me. With that dmanable letter of Aunt Pattie's against my heart I felt sure there were rumours of my parentage so shameful that I should not have offered myself without apology. That closed the matter. I rose to go.

"I know I'm a fool," she said; "not a woman in a million balks, so just pass me up as a freak. The hurt of it falls on me far more heavily, and it is no fault of mine."

"Nor of mine."

"I realise that. I am very, very fond of you. There can

surely never be another man just so lovable and suited
to me. Thank you for caring."

I stood awhile on Dearborn Street as I came out of the
old Concord Building. I looked south where, unlike its
fellows, this street is broken by an obstruction and is
marked by the spire of the Polk Street station. I looked
north, where it runs under the elevated and falls into the
Canal when the bridge is open. It was very ugly and
dirty and blatant, lacking in any character excepting the
coarse earmarks of driving Business. How all such details
stand out when a man is either elated by joy or
depressed by despair.

I should go away at once and I cared not tho' I
should never again see Dearborn Street. I hated it. I felt
I could never visualise it without a leaden feeling of
defeat and loss.

I went straight up to my rooms without any dinner.
The world had fallen to grey dust. I was old enough and
philosophic enough to know that men have died and
worms have eaten them, but not for love. I knew there
were millions of other fellows who couldn't get the
particular girls they wanted and afterwards were glad of
it and found others filled the bill just as well. I knew it
would all be the same in a hundred years, or in five, or
in three. I was sufficiently acquainted with life to know
that my despair would probably be better in one year or
in a month, or a week, but no such senile understanding
kept me from being just as miserable, just as down and
out as the young chap with puppy love who really
believes that the world can never be the same again.

I hated Bobby in that hour. It was as clear as day. He
was the average fellow, but his father and mother were
on record. He had a good name, his mother had been a
lady, and mine, God knows, she was doubtless some
unfortunate Irish servant girl, perhaps worse than that.
I almost cursed Aunt Pattie for bringing me up as she
had.

The picture of Bobby with his goggles pushed back
and his mouth wide open in an ingratiating grin faced

me, and did not ingratiate. There was another of him on the opposite wall with a girdle as his only costume and he was a thing of joy. I suspected that he had had this taken expressly to show his beauty to Sybyl and then had allowed the little puss to wheedle a copy from him. I gathered the whole collection and flung it in an empty drawer.

After all, the belswaggers were right! Women deserved all they got. The man a woman cared for was the one who had the hide to treat her like a dog. I cursed my fate that I had not been born to be a swashbuckling, brutal, lascivious, cowardly brute — then perhaps Sybyl would have preferred me.

There was another picture of Bobby when small which I kept in an old-fashioned album of boyhood's friends. I looked it up now and did not throw it with the others. I left it there as it stood, the little boy looking up at me with adoration in his proud young face. Bobby had given me this picture as a great trophy and love offering long ago. He had I think, purloined it from his mother's family album.

I sat down all undone and the young fellow with puppy love and no philosophy could not have felt any worse, for I was as complex as Sybyl and therein I was able to appreciate her as no one else could. But that limb of a Bobby, he would get her, and for him to have her was like taking a Sévres vase to drink from on a camping trip, when a tin pannikin would have been more appropriate. If I had had her I should have put her in a shrine.

But perhaps women do not care to be worshipped or appreciated or understood, they want — God knows what they want! The screw that was loose with me was that the one woman of them all did not want me.

I was diverted from my painful state of mind by the arrival of Aunt Pattie. She whirled in from California having but recently heard of my accident.

"So it is a broken leg!" she said, "not a heart!" Then with a shrewd glance, "Is there a woman in the case?"

"Nary a one!" I replied, thinking of my defeat.

Aunt Pattie was concerned to find me thin and pale. Morose and ill-contained, I turned to her, thankful that some one wanted me.

CHAPTER 31
RABIES

That, as Aunt Pattie expressed it, was the first honeymoon she and I had had together since I was a youngster.

We went first to Bermuda while the weather was still cool, and to the east ports during the latter part of June and July. We floated with the stream and sea-shored and hee-hawed and bazaared and flower-showed, afternoon tea-ed, regatta-ed and gymkhana-ed day by day. For a change in this menu Aunt Pattie took me to the big suffrage meetings which had penetrated even to the mansions of New Port and Bar Harbor.

I dedicated myself to tagging along. Aunt Pattie was anxious regarding my listlessness and poor appetite and she and the doctors devised porch sleeping and tonics, massage and salt rubs and talked gravely of the possibilities of internal injury. They failed to discover that it was of the heart. Had I been a lady of eighteen or twenty-eight in need of a husband, Dr. Devereux's cure-all of love would certainly have been considered the thing for me, but I was protected from such aspersions by the accident of sex. Also my unblemished record of immunity and old maidism stood me in good stead, while Sybyl, bless the little self-supporter, did not scintillate in circles which could have wafted tales of my devotion to Aunt Pattie.

She had decided to take me abroad as soon as my leg should be strong enough to get about on ship board. I was willing to be taken. I meant to get myself in hand presently but life was endlessly long in which to accomplish nothing and for the time being I was willing to drift.

I wondered as I sat by the sea or watched the young bloods galloping after a ball if SHE were calling Bobby a slap-up trump, the son of a sampan and a sea-cook, a Turk, and a lunatic and dearest, darling duck, all in one breath. What irritated me was that Bobby would be thus addressed without appreciating it, and what was worse, Sybyl did not seem to need appreciation. Such vivacities trilled from her lips as naturally as the song of a wild bird on the bough, and when in an unbiased mood I was bound to admit there was less of amoristic taint in them than in the formal "Good day Mr. Cavarley!" of some women.

It had been a full surrender on my part. In one grand all-consuming passion had accumulated all the loves I might had had — first for the little girl at school, then for the pretty debutante, next for the "misunderstood" wife, who would go the limit inside the dead line, and for the discontented wife who did not recognise a danger line, and for the other class of girls which men find necessary to demonstrate their virility.

Many a time I came near telling Aunt Pattie about Sybyl, but the simplicity of the tale kept me silent. There was nothing to tell but that I was absorbed in a girl to such an extent that there was no cure but marriage, and the girl preferred an unseasoned cub to the diversified me because he knew where he came from and I did not. After Aunt Pattie's heroic solution of her problem I could not wound her with mine. I recognised the justice of her demand that sleeping secrets should lie.

So we meandered through the days in that exclusive earthly paradise, alternately bored or amused, and came to the last week of July 1914, when into the regular routine of flirtations, *liaisons,* engagements, intrigues, dances, regattas, automobile jaunts, and other items of the social tournament crashed the appalling news that Europe had gone mad over night and was at war.

One pack of pampered hell hounds, maddened by the

delusion that it was menaced by all the other packs, and freed from leash, had almost annihilated a nation before the other dogs of war could be whipped into readiness. The rabies was spreading like a prairie fire till it seemed that no packs of any magnitude were to be left uninfected.

It could not be true! It was a ghastly accident, a false rumour, a mistake! It would be settled in three weeks at the outside.

Had not the nations been building great navies and armies and other equipment for two generations for the one great purpose of preserving peace! This was but the running amok of a few irresponsible dogs with hydraphobia. It was a terrifying slip but they would be back in kennel in a few weeks.

Yes, it was not really true. Real people, modern, highly sensitised, educated, civilized, just like ourselves, were not going to kill millions of other people just like themselves, in the most excruciating, filthy, barbarous, senseless, disgusting fashion! The brain reeled before such a prospect.

All was confusion, excitement, horror, dismay.

The folk who worked the year around at play stirred to the delight of a new and splendid sensation. Here was something really worth while at last. One society leader in the pavilion where we were having afternoon tea arose and throwing up her arms exclaimed. "War! Glorious War! I hope it comes to America too! We need its quickening influence!"

There was a renewed zest in being among individuals of a certain type but a total collapse among those whose roots had been in the spiritual side of life. To my circle and Aunt Pattie's it meant only stupefying astonishment and despair.

The newspapers whooped up the excitement and panic of the American sight-seers abroad. Nearly everyone had friends or relatives in Europe. Some could not be heard from. There were long lists of nonentities rich and poor, and quidams large and small who could not be heard from, or who did not want to be heard from, or who cabled reams of balderdash about it all.

In those incogitable first days we read every line about the war in every paper as soon as we awoke in the morning, and then read all the contradictions in the evening papers at luncheon. We could not depend on a word of it, we said, but we read and remembered every line of horror with painful avidity.

Hideous nighmare! Vast incredibility!

Had not science worked for decades on deadly inventions to protect us from war by making war so horrible that it should be impossible, that the human being should reel before it! All the great men in high places with letters after their names or millions in the banks had proven by the processes of that masculine logic which my little Sybyl holds in such high derision, that the only way to preserve peace was to prepare for war. So war could not be. But, the nation most logically, most efficiently prepared was already far out of her own boundaries devastating another country and attempting to conquer its people. Surely there had been some ghastly miscalculation in such peace preparations!

All the while our brains milled round on the impossibility, the unreality of such a disaster.

Some rejoiced that they had not gone to Europe that summer, others thought it just their luck to miss such an adventure and the chance of being dinner heroes during the coming fall.

I had been lumbering along getting myself in hand so that I could encounter Sybyl without the abnormal exaggeration of all the sensibilities which endangered poise and was beginning to feel sober when the European holocaust threw me all out of kilter again. Life had been changed overnight. All old proportions had shrunken or enlarged so that complete readjustment became imperative and I knew where I stood with Sybyl Penelo. I wanted to go straight back to her. She was the one being who vitally mattered to me in this earth quake. I must know her attitude. Would she be changed by the hysteria which had smitten Europe?

Aunt Pattie and I were of one mind. We gathered up

our traps and scurried back to base without delay. We were like a pair of startled children who run to their mother's skirts. It seemed as if this enormity might be less lurid if we could view it from the safe ramparts of home.

CHAPTER 32
BOBBY'S ANNOUNCEMENT

I returned to The Caboodle on a Friday night a week or two after the war had started. The next forenoon I called at Dearborn Street but found that Mr. Hoyne had taken Miss Penelo out to Highland Park to spend Saturday and Sunday with his Sister Mrs. Hastings Howe.

I chatted with Miss Maguire for a while about the one topic, finding her quite sane and untouched by militaristic hysteria, though anxious about the dull business season which threatened. There was almost no work in her line just then but she hoped prospects would improve by fall. The war surely could not last very long.

That evening a committee from The Caboodle inmates waited upon me to discuss the possibilities of curtailing the luxuries of the place and generally reducing the scale of living so that in face of the financial panic which threatened, they could manage to keep their comfortable quarters. Some, whose way of living had immediately come to a standstill, had to leave.

Late on Sunday evening Bobby burst into my quarters and expressed his pleasure to see me home. He was radiant and dusty from speeding along delightful summer roads and in high spirits regarding the war. He expressed himself as "just crazy to get into the fun, the greatest thing that ever happened!" He was preparing to contest a road race in a new French car. He considered it would be good practice in the line of what he was going to do on the other side racing away from exploding shells and bombs. He hoped to serve as a demon driver or officer chauffeur in an Ambulance Corps which the American Colony in Paris were sending to the front. Tony Hastings had written him to come over and help. Tony's mother was already fitting up one of her French houses as a hospital and Tony was directing the assembling of the Ambulance Corps. Tony was to jump right into all that was going on and Bobby was to join him as soon as the big race was over. Tony was taking a recess from his operatic ambitions. Doubtless he had abrogated his broken heart and Christian Science.

Inquiries in this direction were blocked by an admission of Bobby's made elaborately casual but from which not all the bombast of conquest had been purged. He said Sybyl was going with him and that he looked forward to an exciting honeymoon.

"Sybyl going with you, to the battlefields, that little thing!" I was startled into exclaiming.

"Why yes! We're not going to fight. We're only going to gather up the remnants of the Frenchies and give them a chance for another go at the Germs. I don't think you could frighten Sybyl with a bomb or a battle axe. I've done the craziest things with the car just to test her and she simply loves it! Jimmeny she's got courage!"

"She's got the courage all right, but a *honeymoon*! When are you to be married," I managed to ask somehow.

"We haven't set a date. Sybyl is very cut up about the war. I don't like to worry her. We can be married any time over there at the Embassy."

"Are you going without being married," I asked, amazed yet relieved by any postponement of the ceremony.

"Yes, you old maid, but it's as right as a church. Nancy is going over to help Tony's mother in her hospital work. Nancy has never settled down the same

114

since that smash up among her kids. She wants to do something like this and Hastings is just going to tag along to take care of her. He's a roaring pro-Ally. Says if we don't help lick the Germs over there we'll have to do it ourselves over here. I guess Nancy isn't going to let him do anything though except to subscribe and take care of the women. Sybyl is going as general secretary to the whole outfit under Nancy."

Bobby got up to leave me. He turned back in the doorway.

"Listen! We are not telling anyone our business. But I thought you would kind of like to know as I've told you most things since the year one."

"Thank you. I'm glad to know." I managed to get out. He did not guess that his words were like a final knell to me. There was still a ray of hope in that Sybyl was not going as Mrs. Bobby but as secretary to Bobby's sister, Nancy Howe. I immediately thought of asking Aunt Pattie to get in on this Ambulance business and go too. I felt sure she would be game if I told her the facts.

There did not seem to be anything immediate I could do about it. I could not drag the lady from her bed and run away with her cave man fashion, though I felt like it. I could only wait till next day without coming into conflict with established custom to a degree that would connect me with the police. So I sat there all night and drew on my future account with hell.

It seemed just then that there could be things even worse than war, or that if I couldn't have Sybyl, the more war the better, or that if I could have had her I might have faced the world tragedy with less of lostness.

There had been a few of us — congenital idiots apparently — who had thought the world growing saner and more democratic, really moving towards more far-reaching justice, hygiene, and comfort. These dreams were now proven to be of the pipe. We had been as the opium-drugged. We now awoke to reality — such a reality! The realisation that the dominating ideal of the world was still brute force and to find ourselves hurled back over night into the tooth and nail age. A civiliza-

115

tion still directed by the idea of material force, but negligibly leavened by the spiritual ideals of conservation and expansion had towered up to the skies, interdependent, delicate, intricate, sensitive, marvellous, multiple, yet to settle a grievance there was no better machinery than the days of the claw and the fang — force raised to the nth power of insane and menacing destruction by the wealth and fertility of modern invention.

Such an unintelligent mess!

It was so insane as to be almost laughable, but the insanity was so colossal, the hysterical delusions of the combatants so gigantic that to be mete it should have waked the laughter of cyclops tortured in hell.

CHAPTER 33
SYBYL REFUSES TO CONFIRM OR DENY

At nine next morning I appeared on Dearborn Street.

"Are you going to marry Bobby Hoyne?" I asked without preliminaries. I was to tackle this first and the matter of the war next.

"What made you think that?" she asked, crinkling up her nose and turning her head sideways with such intriguing sauciness that even a turtle of any virility would have been stirred. "How is your thigh bone and your collar bone and —"

"Damn my bones! Bobby is my authority. He speaks of being engaged."

"Tut! Tut! What an awful swear word! You should consult better authorities. Did Bobby say he was engaged to me, or I to him?"

"You little — you *little* — why you little *Tom cat*! What's the good of carrying on like that? Why do you prevaricate? Of course he said engaged to you."

"*Tom cat* that's delicious," she gurgled, but I was not to be turned aside.

116

"How the devil can he be engaged to you without your being engaged to him? Such silly quibbles!"

"You are cross. I'm not quibbling. I'm sticking to logical facts as if I had a man's power of reasoning," said she with inimitable Sybylness. But it was a changed Sybylness. Her girlishness seemed pinched and wan. That which had been so enchanting about her was her irrepressible — not so much joy, as merriment of life.

"I must know about Bobby. Do you approve of his looking upon the war as a grand adventure?"

"I envy him. He says it is evil working itself out and that explains the break down to him. He fits his environment. It seems that the ancient and honorable parrot brigade were right. 'Boys will be boys', and 'You can't change human nature'. There must be wars and rumors of wars for ever. What has always been must always be, was their room."

"They certainly have the bulge on us now," I admitted.

"Yes. It will be all right in a hundred years. In the evolution of the race this will be no more than the measles or whooping cough to a child, but it has wrung the cloth of life dry of everything that was worth while to me, and I still have to go on living for years and years. I haven't even climbed to thirty yet. What is the use of being in a world where one thinks differently from everyone else! Just think of the world taking the thing seriously and talking about the rights of belligerents. As if belligerents could have any rights except the care extended to maniacs. They should be fallen upon as soon as signs of military outbreak appear and be kept in straight jackets till they recover."

"But who could fall upon them unless a madder or more military militarist?"

She shrugged and was silent.

"Then what about Bobby? Can you uphold him in his idea of adventure?" I persisted.

"Adventure, that is just it! It is perverted love of adventure for which we have made no legitimate provision, which makes men glorify war. The poor little store clerk and the rich idler long equally for something tremendous to happen in their anaemic or bovine existence and they are duped by the hideous hag called war. They disguise her in false glory and set her to lilting music. Also, Bobby is not going to kill others. He is going to drive a car right out to the battle lines or run with a stretcher and help the wounded where the shells are falling. That will take as much courage as to be a soldier and I respect the courage which exposes itself to danger but does nothing to wipe out others."

"But Bobby," I persisted, "do you love him?"

"Love!" she scornfully exclaimed, and I recognised her cynicism as the refuge of the heart-sick. "It shows how little you can understand my idea of love that you mention it now. Love! Mothers of men! Men! Creatures through a form of demon-worship trained to be more deadly and bestial than the fiercest gorilla or cobra. Creatures to hide in filthy holes in the ground and kill other mothers' sons. Creatures who rush forth and spit babies and ravish women. Love! Women! Incubators for more cannon fodder! Other women can fancy themselves mothers of horoes if they like but I shall never be a candidate for any such doubtful glory. I will not contribute to a world of insane. I despise negative action but if that is all that is left me, well!" she shrugged her shoulders again.

"But if you marry Bobby?"

"But if I don't!" she retorted. "I am going with his party to see war at first hand and the deathless courage and the quickening spirit that penny-a-liners warble about. Imagine sitting down here on a cushion while all the rest of the world is otherwise engaged. Also my end of the business is practically dead. I have no contracts unfinished so I shall take a change. But surely, surely we shall wake some morning soon and see in the headlines that peace is declared.

She had no comfort to offer me. I had none to offer her though her heart was breaking, for in those days the people of benevolent ideals went down into hell and were scourged.

118

CHAPTER 34

Viewed from home, the war grew no less terrifying, but only more shockingly real. Home, youth, love, life, beauty, distance, wealth, art, culture, education — nothing could protect one from the anguish of that far-reaching calamity, which concerned every nation and every being on this globe.

A surprising realignment was taking place among old groups that had hitherto hunted in concert. Many who had seemed to be trivial conservative folk of negligible spiritual or mental register, who plodded along with second hand thoughts of approved patterns, now raised a clear strong voice in the din of a vast horror, while others who had figured as leaders and uplifters fell down as narrow unreasoning partisans of one side or the other — more unbalanced than the real belligerents.

The suspension of internationalism was a great social loss. Previous to the outbreak people had enjoyed each other through natural congeniality and found their national differences either interesting or amusing. Now, even in our blessed farraginous nation people had to remember whether their fellow citizens were British or German, Russian or Scandanavian, Latin or Oriental before they went into a friendly discussion on anything more fundamental than the weather.

I faced a new set of equations in regard to my love and to Sybyl. In those dark hours when I wanted her more than ever, I could not be sure how she and Bobby stood. A firm comradeship appeared to be ripening between them, which left me out in the cold. As a love offering my broken bones had sunk into oblivion and war sickness had so frayed my nerves that my temper was most unreliable. I returned to the charge again and again about Bobby but got little for my pains excepting whimsical perversity. She would admit no engagement on her side.

"Bobby engaged to me! You wait till I'm engaged to Bobby. Even then it might not be fatal. One man nearly

119

as good as you are was once engaged to me, yet I'm free! Thank God! They say any fool can get married but it takes a devilish clever woman to remain an old maid, so that is the distinction I covet. When a man becomes too vigorously engaged to me I change my geographical location and then he jilts me. I just love to be jilted. It relieves me of all responsibility and leaves the other fellow a friend for life." She pulled a wedding ring off her finger. "He had the ring all ready and then I moved, so he jilted me. He was so sorry for me that he sent me the ring as a souvenir. No doubt he remembers me as a poor little thing whose heart was broken, but that it couldn't be helped, he was so fascinating."

"That bluff wouldn't leave you free if you gave me a chance."

"That's why I'm careful not to give it. You are old-fashioned and come nearer to being a brave man in love. Your Aunt Pattie's training I expect. But oh, these Lily-Ann town dudes in Chicago's Loop with their soft girl-manicured fingers who come to me to supplement their second and fifth rate brains. They would run from an old cow or fall off a horse — too engrossed in looping 150 per cent profits in the Loop I suppose. If they can't get what they want first pop they sulk and run away from the game. Women have to flatter them and baby them all the time. They regard women much in the light of one of their eternal facial massages."

"Bobby's pretty sure about his theory of love," I interpolated.

"Yes he preaches the doctrine of loving everything from a cyclone to a flower. Wouldn't you like to be loved as a flower?" she asked archly.

"I'd consider myself in luck to be loved as a turnip — even as a caterpillar or katydid to get into your garden."

"It would seem that you had rooted yourself there like —"

"A hardy annual."

"I was going to say a perpetual bloomer — a very splendid bloomer with a refreshing perfume that wears well," she said, and flattery from her was an intoxicating beverage, though I had observed that she was never intoxicated by her own brows.

"Then let me be engaged to you," I said lightly. "You might as well have two engaged to you as one. 'If you can't be true to one or two, You're much better off with three' " I hummed.

"No", she said, suddenly wistful, "marriage contains such infinite possibilities of unhappiness, and I can be, oh, so unhappy."

"But think of the infinite possibilities of happiness if you could strike the right man."

"There is the man to be considered. He is entitled to his hundredth chance too, and perhaps would not get it with me."

"I know some of him who would be glad to chance it."

"Yes, it's a gamble to a man and he is so constituted that it doesn't ruin him if it goes on the rocks. Of course there are other times when I am not so serious about it when I think I might as well plunge into a matrimonial experiment for diversion. Supposing Bobby takes me first: He'll tire in a week and then I'll marry you." She was provoking again now.

"I'd rather be your last and final."

"Thank you, sir. You are a sweet thing to make such nice compliments. After experience you might regret not to have been the first and temporary. Seriously, what would you think of standing ready to comfort me when the fickle Bobby —"

"Not on your tintype! Bobby's a pretty smart duck. He'd know too well when he was in luck. The other way for me."

"You mightn't get tired and then I'd be stuck for ever with no chance of having Bobby."

"There you go. Bobby would be like the rest of us. He would find living with you like an exciting serial, too interesting to leave off. Bobby has developed a dangerous amount of discernment where you are concerned. Me first, Bobby second."

"No. Bobby first and you second. Bobby will let me

have some fun. I've never had any fun. I don't quarrel with him any more. I make allowances for him because he is a beautiful young nabob who has never had any discipline, and his personal possessions as well as attractiveness have tended to make him a spoiled darling. 'Unto him that hath shall be given'. The Lord has given him everything — health, wealth, breeding, and beauty. He thinks he's a young emperor, and so he is. He has the insolence of royalty and the right to his kingdom."

"All of which means that Bobby is first choice and I'm an also ran, so I had better take my hat," I murmured amiably.

"I think you had" she agreed, "for I see by your chin that you are going to propose again, and you're out of time."

"Am I out of tune?" I asked eagerly.

"I wont tell you, so there!" and she turned up her chin.

There was nothing for me but retreat. I was shut outside the concert hall, I, the music lover, while Bobby, the devotee of rag-time was inside in a seat of honor.

Oh, well!

I summoned self control. After being so worn down during the last year that I had to go away to get back into form I did not propose giving a full encore in the lemon proposition if I could help it.

CHAPTER 35

I decided to take up aviation seriously and go to France with the crowd to keep Hastings Howe and Bobby company. A couple more of the Howe crowd, Mr. and Mrs. Osborne Lewis, the well-known writers, had laid their plans to go in the same contingent as newspaper correspondents.

Asking Aunt Pattie to join us recalled my youth when the glory and patriotism of going to the Phillipines had consumed me. She had put the kibosh on that adventure with decision.

"You don't go!" she had said. I suppose my chin shewed sulky, as Sybyl describes it. I had sought to be defiant. Aunt Pattie had waxed sarcastic.

"Why, do you suppose I went to all the trouble of raising you? Nice troublesome object you were too — all through teething and well on till you were six or seven I never got a minute's rest with you. Always something the matter with you that you could just as well have done without, and my stars! to teach you to wear glasses! I had almost to keep you in my pocket for a year. Do you suppose I did all that so that you could go out there to butcher some other mother's child that she had just as much trouble with. No siree!"

I had disappeared with my tail between my legs, so to speak. That's where the foster mother has a child at a disadvantage. Had she been my real parent I could have sprung the old gag about not having asked her to bring me into the world, etc. That would not go gracefully with Aunt Pattie considering what I surmised in those days — surmises which had become certaities after the tenor of Aunt Pattie's latest refusal to be informative. It might very well have been that she also had not wished me to be brought into the world. The tactful thing had seemed not to bring upon myself the further reference to great obligations. That was the only time that Aunt Pattie ever mentioned them and it was in a good cause — her determination not to have the results of her raising efforts wasted in wasting the product of another woman's equally patient arduous tiresome specialised labour.

When it was put to her she was quite agreeable to go to Paris with the crowd only she did not approve of my being an aviator (even a professor of aviation) and helping towards the destruction of other people, whose fight was then none of the business of the United States. She agreed to help towards the fitting out of another motor ambulance and advised me to distinguish myself as a stretcher bearer. Her words were almost identical with Sybyl's about Bobby, "I shall rejoice in your bravery if you risk your life for others but I would shrink from you if you turn demented beast and murder them. The only role for a gentleman and an outsider is hospital service."

Sybyl was so much more riven than I that I forgot all about my own soul-sickness before hers. Sometimes I feared she could not live and continue to suffer as she did. She was totally unfit for brain work and confessed a longing for a charwoman's job to fatigue her physically so that she could not have so much capacity to suffer mentally. That was why she was glad of the opportunity to go to France as Nancy Howe's secretary. It was on that basis she discussed her plans and never let slip to outsiders that there was a Bobby in the case. When mentioned he was Mrs. Howe's brother.

The details of the ambulance scheme grew in interest and complications with the weeks. It looked as if it would take us all our time to get over there before the row ended. Some of us expected the first bite of frost to cool the madness, though by all accounts some of the belligerents had not yet awakened to the fact that there was a war, and they not those farthest from the scene of action.

Meanwhile the preparations for the big automobile race which was to precede our departure, went on with unimpaired enthusiasm. Bobby was a strong favorite with the fans and owing to his social ramifications got more than his share of publicity. I was letting things take their own course for the present without any of my overseeing and keeping away from Dearborn Street astonishingly.

However I did not escape from Bobby. I saw him once and sometimes oftener each day at The Caboodle as I could not dismiss him from among my tenants on the ground that he had defeated me in the field of romance. Also I had to hand it to him, to use the vernacular, in that he had stayed on the ground and pegged away while I had retreated. It was he who had shown that persistence for which I thought myself noted: and in her present reckless despair Sybyl was fit for some wild goose step with him, while I was not skilled with women so as to hawk my unique wares in a way to make her recognise me as her one and only fate.

After I cut down my peregrinations to Dearborn Street about seventy five per cent in number and fifty per cent in duration, Bobby ceased to regard me as either a rival or a nuisance, and discerned in me the old time repository of confidences and was quite free in discussing his joy of life. Soon the game of Bobby this and Bobby that on Dearborn Street turned to a siege of Sybyl thissing and Sybyl thatting on Ellis Avenue. I asked him how he had managed to capture her, for captured her he thought he had.

"Oh, I've figured to make myself useful to her, to stay right on the job and crowd every other toad off the plank, and also to hit up the pace and sweep her off the plank without giving either of us time to catch cold feet. Make yourself necessary to a woman, that's the thing," said Bobby with a grin of satisfaction.

"The proof of the recipe is in the results," I remarked.

He smiled indulgently. "I've quit scrapping with her. She's a little spoiled by her personal attractiveness. People have made her think she's some sort of a queen, and so she is. I'm just crazy about her myself!"

I sat squashed, looking at his imperial majesty. Evidently there had been common capitulation. While I had been away, royalty had recognised royalty and they had come to amicable adjustment over their common status. They had abandoned the struggle to establish individual supremacy and were happy in joint authority. Their past disagreements had been nothing more than the friction of a violent attraction.

Bobby shewed no disinclination to answer my questions. He regarded me as a young girl with lovers regards a spinster aunt.

"I don't tease the little creature any more," he

125

pursued expansively. "She has about seven brains mixed up in one, so I just go along and decide for her. She gets off a lot of bunk just to see how you'll take it but all she needs is some one to be very firm. I'll take care of her and she'll entertain me. That's a square deal. The real way to manage her is to make such a noise that she doesn't get time to think. If she does, it's fatal, she's much too quick for me, but stop the thinking business and she's done. Little four-flusher, got us all bluffed to keep off the grass, but I've got her number now. I just rush on with a whoop!"

"I see."

"She's the last word in the art of thrilling a fellow. Gee, I could head an expedition to the North Pole when she gets me all lit up. It will be some fun to take the nonsense out of her."

"The unfinished work of a life time," I assented, "but God how cut up she is over the war."

"Yes," he replied as pat as a primer, "but she will soon realise that it is evil working itself out. Great good will come of it. She will see that presently."

The spiritual leaven of which I had been rather contemptuous after all seemed to be working in Bobby. It had been a case where one basket for all the eggs had succeeded while we of many receptacles had been left unprovisioned. He no more nagged or hurried nor disputed about his creed but seemed to have gained from it much of poise and harmony. I even found myself prone to lean on his surety when all the other great spirits were groping in chaos. Any trail in an unknown jungle.

I invited him and Sybyl to various things in company so that I might observe them together and I took Miss Maguire to keep me in countenance. I first engineered an all-day pic-nic in the woods and thereby nearly threw Harold Brubaker into hysterics, which was a surprise to me, and a complete escape of his cat from the bag. Miss Maguire had been as demure as a little mouse.

Sybyl had changed. She had sobered and was prone to drop into long silences leaving the conversation to

126

others. I began to be satisfied with Bobby's attitude. He regarded her at such times with a tender light in his fine brown eyes which augured well for the future companionship and partnership which they seemed likely to weld out of the eternal duel. His tenderness too in putting her wraps about her and gathering up the knick-knacks which she was inclined to leave strewn in her path was quite unlike the late impatient Bobby. It was as if her evident suffering had called out something motherly in him which gave him a purpose and zest in life. A situation demanding better qualities than the ability to sign checks off-handedly had arisen and he had grown to meet it. The little Bobby-Boy of long ago who had buzzed around me in his attempts at self-expression, had grown up at last.

I saluted him. I wanted them to be happy. The feeling of relinquishment presupposed that Sybyl had been mine. That was it, a spiritual kinship over and above all others would hold its own place for ever between us. She would always be mine, no matter who won her.

In my conception of love there has always been the balm of understanding that it is more blessed to give than to receive. I could never spoil the splendid retreat of love by nagging possessiveness or stupid jealous exactions. When we are loved it is frequently a responsibility, if not a burden. It fills us with the necessity for self-examination. Do we deserve this tribute? Surely the lovers will discover us for the poor things we know ourselves to be, and what right have even lovers to make us run the risk of such embarrassment? We would be freer without such unsought tribute.

But ah, to love! The blessed creatures who can make that possible for us, who can irradiate our beings, they are of the angels and we seek nothing, not even to burden them with the knowledge of our passion, but only to glow with gratitude for the bliss they have given.

CHAPTER 36
WHOM THE GODS LOVE

"Unto him that hath", as Sybyl was accustomed to quote with reference to Bobby and I found myself using the same phrase, for he had everything, even a zest and belief in life and the faculty to grasp a philosophy — or a religion if that designation is preferred — which precluded soul-sickness and heart-break in the face of the present collapse.

His sister Nancy beamed when she spoke of him. She had been almost prostrated by the loss of two of her children. Then the war upset the benevolent social work she had taken up to occupy her mind so she too was glad to lean on Bobby's religion. His brother's vaticinal observation that he had a "hell of a lot in him" seemed to be vindicating the perspicacity of the author. He certainly was a lovable mortal and much to be envied. But in that I reckoned before all the figures were on the slate. For the fates were to cheat Bobby, or perhaps it was little Sybyl and myself they cheated once again, while to Bobby they tendered a royal gift.

It was the day of the 301 mile race at Elgin and all the veterans had gathered to the fray. Bobby was easily one of the most attractive as well as the most popular of the men there with his bright dark head and his blue dress, which offset his easy confidence and imperious bearing.

"Isn't he a peach!" enthused Sybyl. "With that belted suit and those big gauntlets, and shoes and socks to stun, he's almost as fine a bird as Dr. Devereux."

"Bobby sure can look some gorgeous when he is carrying all the dog he can get on," I agreed amiably.

Interest centered around him because he was a gentleman driver and had never been in a really big race pitted against seasoned warriors and winners of international trophies. Society was numerously represented and the newspapers had not neglected the story that he regarded this as a little practice preparatory to racing from

128

exploding bombs in France. His Brother Jim had come on from New York for the race and Hastings Howe and Nancy were there, as well as everyone who could get away from The Caboodle. Bobby had loaned his big green car to a contingent of them and I drove Sybyl and one or two others in my own machine. It was altogether a holiday.

Bobby had decided against his French machine in the last week and had gone back to his famous German Mercedes. Sybyl took half a mile with him before the race started just to say she had been in the car on the very day. She would have gone with him had that been permissable.

Bobby had lately settled down to employing, when addressing her, a tone which half petted and half teased and which was entirely indulgent.

"Now I am going to win," he said as we stood there during the final wait, "and the money goes to Nancy's French ambulance lay-out, and the cup, I know a head on which it would look well as a hat and lots nearer being a real hat than a tom tit's nest with a feather windmill on the back of it."

"All right!" said Sybyl "The cup is mine! I invite you to afternoon tea with me in a public place when I am wearing it."

"Good work! If you are game, so am I!" The sun in his eyes turned them to a splendid gold as he laughed at us with banter on his lips and the vivid light of love and life in every lineament. Each sound white tooth seemed to be a gem refracting high boyish glee as he stood there in the bright day dangling one of his big gauntlets in his firm shapely hands, and it is impossible to convey in words the glad joyousness of his laugh.

Time was called.

"Good-bye and good luck!" said Sybyl holding out her hand.

"Good bye!" he smiled, "Now you see me win, and you remember that you are going to wear the cup."

He went to get into position with his mechanician while we took our seats. Sybyl sat with me at a distance from Bobby's relatives and on the other side of her was Bobby's Christian Science teacher come all the way from New York for the event as Bobby's guest.

They were off at last into a record breaking event because so many of the cracks got far into the race without mishap. A Duesenburg car smashed a crank shaft in the first lap and was permanently out of commission. Another contestant's machine got on fire and caused some excitement but it was quickly extinguished and back in the race. Nothing seemed to happen to Bobby except that he called at the pit for gas and on again. The verdict of the bleachers at the end of the tenth lap was that Hoyne was running away with it. Towards the twentieth lap all the favorites were still well together and the rooters for the American cars nearly tore the grand stand down in their robust excitement. It grew more and more thrilling with the chief contestants keeping almost wheel to wheel.

We were badly placed for the glare and the machines soon became a blurred whizz to me, each with a tail a great deal bigger than a comet's, so I had to keep my eyes away from the course for most of the time. The roar of the grand stand and the bleachers brought my glances back from one of these vacations to see that a man in a Delage car had passed Bobby and then they went round for a lap or two hugging each other like bears. Tenser and tenser grew the struggle between the Mercedes and the Delage but it was in the twenty-eighth lap that the Delage wheel ahead of the Mercedes skidded and it was all over for ever with the grand race.

The women and men around me screamed, but there was not a sound out of Sybyl or Mrs. Roach on the other side of her. They flitted through the crowd and were on the way to Bobby before I had collected my wits sufficiently to run after them.

The mechanician had escaped with a severe shaking and no one else was mortally injured in the collision but our own precious Bobby. Neither his beauty nor his strength, nor his youth nor his bravery, nor his philosophy could intercede for him. The reaper had taken his own. There is nothing more to be said on the subject for ever.

The doctor, who reached him first, would not let any of the women come near. Hastings took Nancy away while Jim went with the beautiful form which never again would know our Bobby.

I put out my hand to Sybyl and with her fingers in mine we turned away.

CHAPTER 37

> Though one were strong as seven,
>   He too with death shall dwell,
> Nor wake with wings in heaven,
>   Nor weep for pains in hell;
> Though one were fair as roses,
>   His beauty clouds and closes;
> And well tho' love reposes,
>   In the end it is not well.

I took Sybyl home and left her with Dr. Margaret and Miss Maguire, whom I had caused to be called by telephone from Elgin while we were on our way. There was nothing any of us could do. She was not the wailing kind.

After leaving her I proceeded south along Michigan Avenue mechanically noting the diversity of makes among more than a double line of Loop automobiles parked side by side from Randolph Street to Twelfth. It had been a gorgeous day and the rays of the sinking sun fell full upon the western windows of The Caboodle transforming them to sheets of gold as I turned into the entrance court. All such details stood out with unforgettable clearness and seemed to accentuate rather than obscure a splendid figure laughing in the noon day sun as he toyed with a great gauntlet and waited for time to be called.

I went straight to Bobby's apartments to observe the

golden rule in small personal details by leaving all ship-shape there before going to Jim.

First I sought to remove any traces of a "romance" which some enterprising scribe might unearth to the confusion of Sybyl. From a key among the bunch which lay on the dresser I took one and opened Bobby's writing desk till I found what I had expected in a bundle of notes of every variety of size and thickness and kind of stationery, from expensively monogrammed hand-made paper to hotel advertisements and Manila office stuff. I next took down from a hook beside the dresser a big old watch he had had for years. I meant to ask Jim Hoyne later to let me keep it, and for the present I removed from inside the cover, the little picture of Sybyl at her most bewitching.

I took a good dozen of Bobby's own snapshots of her, which sad or serious, pert or alluring looked up or down from the bureau, the mantel, or the walls. He had snapped her many times in many poses — walking or standing, sitting or reclining, in fairy garments or wrapped in some of his own heavy furs. There was even one of her in my specs and "henpecking" me. Bobby of late had shown little jealousy of me. This had not been flattering. Evidently he had considered me in the grand-father class and quite out of the running. There were several of Bobby when Sybyl had been the snapper instead of the snapped, and one wherein he looked seraphic inscribed in her quaint writing full of wayward kick-ups: "Bobby dearest, darling duck!"

The mere inanimate things seemed to discount reality. It could not be that he would come no more to move among them!

Having left his apartments in order for his family to take possession, I proceeded cautiously to my own. I did not wish to meet any one and be interrogated about the accident. Safely in my own lair I put a match to one of the little notes and dropped the others one by one into the fireplace till only ashes remained. I felt this is what Bobby would have wished me to do for him. I knew that Sybyl could never bear to look at them again, and not all the wealth of the Loop could have tempted me to read a word.

It was done. No one could intrude and through misinterpreting the surrounding circumstances find false values in a delightful game of pitch and toss between two contestants when youth and sex glamor sang in the veins and the sun of life rode proudly aloft. I felt when time should have softened the pain, Sybyl would be glad to have the snapshots and to know that her letters had been carefully preserved and as tenderly cremated.

Poor little Sybyl! I wished that I might go to her and wrapping her close, close against my heart help her bear it through the lonely night, when the thunderous roar of the Loop dies down and all the big office floors in all the big buildings are locked and deserted.

I gathered up also the books of Bobby's new dogma that it should not be treated lightly. Not any creed can satisfy me nor serve me but the steady patience which awaits with open mind the unravelling of life's riddle — should there be one — for none of them can hold back the insistent reaper nor any more than guess what is behind the veil. But it would have been presumption on my part to feel that Bobby's creed had not triumphed for him.

"You are going to see me win," he had said to us. Perhaps we had.

Ah, me! Ah, me! He was so fair and strong!

I pulled out a big lumber drawer and carefully lifted the pictures of Bobby which in a moment of unworthiness I had torn from my walls. I should hang them up again where they could laugh down on me for as much of always as a man is permitted to enjoy or endure. Then, no! The gladness pictured there swept the agony of loss across me and I could not bear it.

Oh, that I could go to Bobby and tell him in some way that I was sorry, that he had proved himself under test much worthier than I! My past annoyance with him seemed so paltry in the empty silence where he had been used to come at night to tell me of the day's events. In the face of my royal advantage it seemed so mean.

133

After all I may not have had the advantage.

God, how that great silence beat back upon me in its baffling, impenetrable majesty! An hour or two since he had stood before me in all his beauty and strength, his voice surcharged with triumphant joy of life saying, "You are going to see me win."

Perhaps he had won. Perhaps he had!

So lately he had sat there in the big chair opposite mine: it could not be that communication with him was already irrevocably closed! The very chair seemed to have an expectant air. But that maddening silence! It was already as immensurable, as never-to-be-broken as that which has closed over those other young gladiators who tested their prowess in other arenas before other ladies false or fair, flippant or fascinating, the farthest memory of whom has been lost in a million years of dust.

So again, but with gripping tenderness this time, I gathered up the photographs of the big athlete, the laughing beauty (it was from Sybyl I acquired the habit of speaking of beauty regardless of sex), the interloping lover of later days. In his strength and his vivid joy of being he had passed like a wondrous dream in the night.

I looked long and long at the pictures till seeing went from my eyes and then I wrapped fine linen around them and put them out of sight.

I turned irresistibly to the old album where the little eagerfaced Bobby looked up at me as of old. Here he was real and enduring. This memory would not pass. Bobby-Boy had come back to stay with me.

CHAPTER 38
MARS AND MOLOCH

Those days were hard sledding for many of us.

Sybyl's disembodied-spirit effect intensified alarmingly. The shock of Bobby's passing told distressingly on us both. We never referred to it. I think we were restrained by like sentiments. We felt we would be qualifying as weakly sentimental dubs to make a noise over the sudden extinguishing of just one splendid creature who left no helpless dependents, when the plains of Europe were being strewn for hundreds of miles with other women's sons, husbands, sweet-hearts, just as beautiful, just as potential, just as keen to live as Bobby had been.

In those days a man felt he had better be secretive or apologetic about subscribing to a baby saving campaign, or a tuberculosis hospital, for why take trouble and expense to raise more babies just to be sacrificed to Mars and Moloch? Why be so sickly soft and sentimental as to try and save a few weaklings when in Europe millions and millions of the mental and physical flower of half a dozen nations were using every device of modern science, every piece of strategy, and straining every nerve to slaughter and mutilate each other in the most terrible way?

The statesmen of Europe had been forced by their own frankenstein of military preparedness to revert to the methods of tribesmen, with the result that all the world suffered from beyond Kerguelen to the Behring Sea, from Madagascar to Maine. The spiritual devastation was staggering. We reeled in a world denuded of sanity and brotherly love, where all the trails of the soul were being obliterated by a reversion to that which would have disgraced the Saurian age. We stood helpless because no people in the world has yet evolved en masse beyond the materialism which in this Armageddon had but reached its apogee. It was only by accident that the conflagration had started in Central Europe instead of elsewhere: it would be miraculous if the United States and other neutral countries could fend off the furious contagion.

We could only look on and suffer unless we were money-lenders or munitions manufacturers, in which case we could make billions, while in a mighty tract of country which can be made to flow with milk and honey, able-bodied men begged for honest work that they might have food and shelter, and the bread lines lengthened in every big city from New York to San Francisco. For society will not give ear to the idealists. It shrinks in fear or boredom from them, as madmen, and follows with blind idolatory the so-called practical people, regardless of where their machinations and mismanagements lead the world. Humanity has yet to go inching upward through tedious aeons of evolution before it will slough off the superstition that its gods — Mars and Moloch — demand the masses served whole as a sacrifice.

It was Miss Maguire, astutely penetrating, who took me aside and confided that she thought it less the shock of Bobby's sudden death than the war that was killing Sybyl by inches. The former, she said was after all a thing that time was softening every day, but the war was a grim torture offering no respite while it lasted.

Miss Maguire, one of the most practical people in the universe, had her own philosophy on the war and she was a good business woman with regard to philosophies as to other things. Hers were for week-day use. She did not allow them to lie idle and become a liability instead of an asset. She discussed the war with me.

"It doesn't seem to me that dying of a broken heart on account of the war will do any good, or even stop it. To grieve till we are useless doesn't help those poor fools over there. The best gift we can make to Europe is to keep America out of the mess so that there will be one sound, flourishing place of refuge when it is all over. And we shall have to keep our heads and go along as well as we know how. There will be more than we all can do working double shift to clean up when this stops."

"Admirable!"

"Of course I could make myself as sick as anyone; it isn't that I have no heart, but sympathy that makes people ill isn't any use."

"Quite true!"

"Miss Penelo needs to be diverted and business is almost at a standstill so you must do something for her.

You are the only person who has any influence with her."

I gazed at little Miss Maguire so demure and so sure, to see if she were flattering me. Such words were too sweet to be true. Influence with the little squirrel! I was a door mat, a faithful dog, an everything or anything, but influence with her, never!

"Oh yes," contended Miss Maguire, "if you neglect her she droops. The way to get at her is through her affections. A person she loves can make her do anything."

"Then it's a cinch she doesn't love me."

"You shouldn't be trying to get ahead of her, that just makes her perverse, let her alone and the next minute she will be hanging around you waiting direction."

"Miss Maguire," said I, brightening perceptibly, "you are a natural psychopathist. You would be worth millions as the wife of some great artist. Get ahead of her ladyship! I couldn't in a thousand years!"

Clever little Miss Maguire, as gentle as a dove and as cunning as a stage manager. She laughed complacently regarding her protegee, "You shouldn't key her up unnecessarily. What she needs is a little stupidity and quiet."

"Ah ha! That is where I might qualify!"

Miss Maguire was covered with blushes and said she did not mean it that way. So serious was she to impress upon me what she did mean that I inveigled her to dinner with me at the Blackstone.

Upon her instigation I started out the next night with Sybyl to see what the average citizen's notion of a "good time" would do for us. We did not expect of it spiritual or mental relief. We sought nothing higher than a counter irritant. Said I, "Such as you and I are only freaks and cold-blooded unvirile neurotics who give evidence of the decline of the race, according to the conservatives, so let us mingle with the great wholesome crowd of real people and not put on any airs. Events

137

have proved the majority to be the practical people and such as we are no better than dotty pipe dreamers."

We bestowed our patronage on the popular plays which had the full houses and long runs and dozens of automobiles waiting in the street, and the well-dressed, over-fed, sleek, smug, hearty, respectable people filling the main floors. How they laughed! How popular were the popular plays! And Sybyl and I! Well, we stood half a dozen of them. Then, ye gods! we turned sadly from the theatre.

"I've changed my mind," said I. "War is all right for people like that. War or any similar disposition of them is good enough. They are only a very low form of animal life."

"Much below the vultures and the wolves, for *they* only kill when they are hungry."

It was unavailing. We could not enjoy what was a delight to the great so-called sensible, normal, average world that believed in war and was afraid of the franchise for women and the eight hour day for labour. It was not their fault, nor ours, but merely that the brand was on us. We could not be born again and become as other men. We had no fellowship with the general public and were thrown back on ourselves and a few other fellow sufferers.

But a change was also overcoming me. I had been wont to regard myself as a man of higher sensibilities. Love I had held in high account. But a lowering of spiritual fibre seemed to be taking place in me. My finely tempered desire was changing to something unleashed. I realised a hardening determination to possess Sybyl hit or miss, whether she wanted me or not, and though she should shrink from me it would only whet my desire. I wanted her sick or well, willing or rebellious, by fair means or foul, now or later, and I felt capable of cheating without qualm if only it would throw her into my power. Was it the universal lowering of ideals that made me reckless; was I too reverting to the abysmal, or was it merely that hitherto my emotions

138

had not been stirred to the dregs? Were all men, myself not excepted, beasts at the core?

Not that I betrayed this to Sybyl. Her sway over me was too strong. I still acted as I had been wont to but I was a whited sepulchre and the very touch of her little hand on my arm sent wild devils careering through me.

I wondered about myself just a little dismayed. Was it a passing phase or had I but lately come into my own? I felt less contemptuous of my fellow men and their common confidences of their adventures in the swine pens of lust.

CHAPTER 39
ADVICE FROM MISS MAGUIRE

One day after Sybyl and I had essayed the "good time" receipt to drive away painful reflection, Miss Maguire gave a faint hint for me to appear secretly in her private office. Immediately I suspected her of some scheme for the expansion of her business in which I should carry out suggestions so skilfully presented that I should think them my own. In all probability she had in mind some opulent gink with literary ambitions whom she intended I should bring to her parlour, where she could be trusted to proceed in such an unobtrusive, soft-voiced, blue-eyed way, that, as my special bell boy might express it, "He couldn't have no kick coming because he wouldn't know what had happened him till it had." But no, Miss Maguire was going to let business slide for once.

"Your style of entertaining Miss Penelo doesn't seem to be making her any happier," she remarked, and far be it from me to contradict one who is of infallible wisdom. "You should have had her won by now."

"I should," I said, convicted yet unashamed, for I was growing inured to my hopeless suit. So long as no one else was winning I had something to be thankful for.

"You haven't given up the struggle yet, have you?" she pursued, her cheeks deliciously pink at the realization of her temerity in jumping into my affairs.

"She's a wilful little squirrel," I observed.

"That's because she was raised in some far away place with lots of men. They always spoil a little girl. She does everything I want her to very gently."

I'd like to see the creature who would not do what Miss Maguire willed for him. He'd surely be some wily and too astute to accomplish anything but puzzles in this world where it is the persistent boob who best succeeds.

"You see I might — I might," Miss Maguire grew adorably fussed, so I took up the strain.

"Ah! Ha! I believe that young pumpernickle of a Brubaker who took a duck fit the day I had you at the pic-nic —"

"Oh, I wouldn't like anything said about it. It is quite indefinite." Miss Maguire cleared her throat.

"Oh quite, a mere nebulous idea to be kept in the confines of my bosom."

"Yes."

I proceeded to tease Miss Maguire a little. "Like your distinguished partner you don't think all men so worthless that it is unsafe to fall in love with them or marry them."

"It depends upon the training. If they have been well trained and marry before they get into bad habits and their wife knows how to keep them up to the mark, I think some of them are all right. It depends upon the women, first their mothers and sisters and then their wives."

Just like young Brubaker's luck to get himself taken care of by a fine young woman like that while I went capering after a little minx who expected a man to sit upright on his own back bone and keep her out of mischief as well. Three cheers for Edna Mary Maguire! Here was a worthy American woman who had the right idea in recognising that the goodness of men is the business of women. Here was one promulgating no hard

and unattainable ideal about self-restraint and instinctive fastidiousness and being good owing to a sense of
innate refinement.

"Miss Maguire," said I, "I would that there were two
of you and that one of them would marry me."

"Oh," laughed the fair Edna, smothered in the
loveliest blushes. "It is very kind of you to talk like
that, but the girl you want is the most wonderful I
know. I could never come up to her."

"I have given up hoping," I said.

"That's where you are wrong. Never give up till the
goose is cooked and eaten. You can see for yourself how
it is. People you thought were going to marry so-and-so
married some one else altogether at the last minute.
Keep right on. Don't be afraid to blow your horn. It
pays to advertise, even in courting. In fact most courting
is nothing but advertising with no delivery of the goods.
In case I should change my way of life before very long
— I am telling you this in confidence as a friend, and I
don't want it known, but I should like to go in for the
law and in that case Miss Penelo must have some one to
care for her."

"You would leave this business?"

"I am thinking of selling out and going to South
America for a year to look round. I think connections
there are going to be worth something and I know a
little Spanish."

So, ho! Miss Edna was really springing a business
proposition on me after all! She wanted me to take part
of her stock in trade off her hands. As I had been trying
to burst up the business to that extent ever since I had
become acquainted with it, this was heaping coals of
fire on my head.

"Now, this is just between friends," she repeated.
"We can forget it if we want to, but I had an idea that
Miss Penelo — well, that you appreciate her as much as I
do — and I want her to be happy again. She used to be
like a sunbeam last year."

This might have savoured of parental interference
from some, but not from Miss Maguire with her sweet

141

little voice and her utterances made in such a hesitant suggestive fashion that their real import did not strike home till later. Besides it was like a glass of ice water to the thirsty to hear that Sybyl had a predilection for me.

"Of course if I am making a great mistake, you must forgive me out of friendship and I would be delighted to take Miss Penelo to South America with us, but I don't know how she and Mr. Brubaker would get on —"

"Wouldn't get on at all," I said with conviction.

"I could very easily take her. Her ability would be an asset anywhere but I haven't put the idea into her head. It just breaks my heart to think of being without her. I really do not know how to break the news to her. I have been hoping she would come to tell me something first." Miss Maguire's blue eyes filled with tears to think of Sybyl bereft of her dove-like care.

"You promise me Edna Mary Maguire, if you are a friend at all, not to suggest that she could go to South America with you."

"Very well, but I want to know why you wait so long. No two people in all the world could be more suited. There is no one to say you mustn't."

To the end of the information on the outside door should have been added, "Miss Maguire, specialist in match making." I said so. She laughed merrily.

"Miss Penelo would kill me if she knew I talked to you like this. I couldn't do it only I look upon you as a *real* friend, why couldn't you?"

"That's what I wonder myself," I replied, throwing away pretence under Miss Maguire's kind and coaxing little way. "You would be a wax woman not to see what I've wanted ever since I started coming here, but there's nothing doing with her ladyship."

"Perhaps you don't bring matters to a head."

"I've put a head on them the size of a cattle pumpkin. I've said everything and then some, but I don't get any farther."

"Perhaps she is too sure of you and does not like to

give up her liberty. If you went away for a while it might help."

I recalled vividly and sadly the results of going away. "No, going away would not help. She never tries to keep people tied to her. She would simply think I had forgotten her and wipe me off the slate if I went away."

"Teach her to dance," said Miss Maguire. I was delighted with the idea. With Miss Maguire as an avowed accomplice I felt that victory had grown more probable.

CHAPTER 40
LAYING THE TRAIL

Love affairs wait for no man. He has to run after them. I found the chase as strenuous as the real estate business.

I invited Miss Maguire and Miss Penelo to take dinner with me the following evening at Midway Gardens, as it offered a bear pit for dancing in the middle of the terraced arena. I also had the presence of mind to invite Harold Brubaker on this occasion.

An ostrich dinner was billed that evening. Sybyl said it was a waste to use ostriches for food as they grew such lovely feathers and if we waited till they were too old for feathering hats they would be too tough for anything but a sausage machine to masticate. As this was my first meeting with ostriches gastronomically, I cannot be sure whether that was what ailed this beast, but after a while the orchestra struck up a gay tune and a young woman with little on, accompanied by the kind of man that dances at cabarets, came out and gave a sort of can-can, the chief feature of which seemed to be how much roughness they could achieve short of bursting their clothes or breaking their legs. The performance was loudly applauded.

I arose and asked Miss Maguire to dance. We led the ball. Miss Maguire was a good dancer and dressed prettily. I took it for granted that Brubaker would dance with Sybyl, but he left her with a man and wife with whom he was acquainted at a table near by while he trod a measure with the daughter. As soon as he was safely on the floor Sybyl left the father and mother and went back to her own table. Miss Maguire and I returned to her and I invited her to dance. Her sudden distress was a surprise. Could it be possible that her chin was quivering and her eyes dewy with tears. She was as disgruntled as a child of nine or ten. Nothing could move her so it fell out that I had to take Brubaker's partner while he re-captured his own lady fair. When we returned from the second dance Sybyl had recovered and was her own merry self.

"I have a wooden leg. It is a sore point with me. I did not know there was dancing here for the common people or I should not have come."

We had several dances after that but Miss Maguire soon very tactfully grew weary and suggested going home. I took them all in my limousine. I dropped Brubaker at The Caboodle as he had a series of night letters to get off, next I deposited Miss Maguire on the West Side, after which I was to go North with Sybyl.

"You offer to teach her to dance," said Miss Maguire as I escorted her up the steps to her apartment building.

Sybyl was silent in the car. "Would you like to learn to dance?" I ventured.

"Don't talk about dancing," she exclaimed with emotion.

"Is it distasteful to you?"

"Distasteful! I'd give my hair to be able to do the simplest two-step or waltz."

"You don't mean to say that you can't dance at all, do you?"

"Not one single step!"

"I thought you could dance like a streak by the way you trip about."

"I'm not a cripple," she flashed. "I should be able to dance like the wind as my natural right, yet not a single step can I do."

"But why?" I amazedly inquired.

"There was little opportunity for it where I grew up and my family did not believe in it."

"Why don't you go to dancing school?"

"I've often thought of that, but then I'd feel ashamed."

"Thank the Lord God of heaven and earth!" I exclaimed, "That I have found something to faze you at last. You are human after all."

"And then," she continued, now that her tongue was loosened, "with whom would I dance? Dancing men belong to the magazine cover girls. If you don't learn social capers when young, it is all up a tree."

"Supposing I jump in and teach you to dance?"

"It would be lovely," she said politely but without enthusiasm. "Do you like to dance? I never heard you say that you could."

"I went to dancing class when I was so small that when gloves were forced on me I held each finger out straight as if it were wooden. Up till ten years ago I used to dance a blue streak. At school I was practically out of the sports I loved best because I could never be sure of seeing the ball. If you only know how I envied the foot ball heroes when all the girls fanned after them and never could distinguish me from a basket of chips."

"Like me with dancing. I understand."

"There were times when I thought of jumping in the Lake and all the rest of it. But I struck a way of coming out even. I became an expert dancer. I made it a business to dance with all the girls, the awkward ones as well as the belles, and gee whizz, I soon had the athletic ginks jealous and depreciating me as a jumping dolled-up sissy. My success took away all the soreness of my incapacity to shine in the more doughty sports. But I got tired of it after a while. All my running mates took a girl each and dropped out of the giddy throng and I no longer needed to rival them in anything but scraping in the dollars. The rosebuds of today look upon me as an antique. I was wishing the other day that I had some one to learn the new dances with me. The secret is that they have the latitude of *vers libre* and each person has his own style in them, and a special partner is really necessary. You now can dance with the one partner as many times as you like in one evening, unless it is a very intimate ball. Suppose we learn the new dances together."

"It would be nice," she said indifferently, "but I don't even know the old ones."

My spirits were rather dashed, but after a day's brooding on it I decided to teach her to dance if I had to kidnap her and take her out of town to some barn or jail to do it. In preparation I went to my old friend Mme. Daggot on Michigan Boulevard. She was one of the girls I used to dance with who had married a football hero, who could neither dance with her nor support her. Now she was supporting her children by running a fashionable class in the new dances and advertising the fact in the street cars with a picture of her face, which myself, I considered zero in advertising. But she was A1 on her feet and I devoted several hours that week to becoming proficient in scrambling and posturing and striding around the floor in the several variations of an invigorating walk to music then coming in fashion under the mantle of dancing, wherein the man in the case, from the vantage of untramelled limbs and walking forward, pushed the lady involved backwards around the ring.

The Caboodle had a splendid gymnasium occupying a whole floor in which we could hold dances or stags or public meetings whensoever the spirit disturbed us. Of what avail to be the proprietor, manager, and chief steward all in one of one's residence if a man could not graft for some favours, so I gave notice that the gymnasium was mine for a couple of hours on certain afternoons. There were not many people to interfere in any case. We were a working population sheltering there as the place was strictly barred against women. They were forbidden in any private apartment and this included even sisters and mothers, who, as in the case of more distant relatives, had to be entertained in the public parlors. I was called Grandma Grundy for my iron rules, but it was necessary. I had found out that chaperones could not always be depended upon, they could be hired. I was acting on experience gained in a yacht club, which I used to frequent, where the wives of members had eventually to be barred because even a Reno divorce rate could not have kept pace with the change in personnel of the wives.

Aunt Pattie was one of the rare exceptions and we could not debar her. All and any of my enterprises were an open book to her. By right of office as my foster mother she was the chief superintendent of my performances. Besides I was an affectionate cuss and there would have been something missing if she were not interested in my undertakings. No matter how high I climbed there was always one above me and that was Aunt Pattie.

I could not call upon her in this instance as she was out of town so I turned to our housekeeper, she who looked after the sheets and chambermaids and such, who was a lady in reduced circumstances and who wore the seal of Aunt Pattie's approval on her brow. She was a Scotswoman — one of the guid old sort with a dignified finish no longer indispensable in this generation. Her part in the play was to look into the gym. occasionally to show that all was correct while I taught an unimpeachable young lady to dance.

CHAPTER 41
THE DANCE IS THE THING

Having laid the trail I telephoned Sybyl. She was much easier to undermine by this means as she could be got to promise things over the wire before she thought, and then one had her, as she had a peccadillo about keeping her word.

"I should love it," she replied enthusiastically.
"So should I. I've long laboured with a phenomenal desire to teach you the grizzly bear hug."
"But could we go where no one would see us?"
"Yes, there's a little ball room at the place where I work. Can you come this afternoon?"
"Yes, if you'll really, actually teach me to dance."
I pranced down instanter in the car. I was in a gray business suit, very natty, according to my idea. I had had extra seances with the barber and manicurist, so as to be prepared for the best, and never since the days when rosebud belles had smiled upon me for dances had I been so particular about the foundations of my toilet. I had instructed Sybyl to put on a wide skirt and when she was divested of her wraps she wheeled about like a replica of Pavlova in a maze of blue accordion pleats and on her feet were slippers of silk adorned with glittering buckles.

I set the trusty gramophone pumping out a two-step and there was my dear, my dove, my ardently desired, my tantalisingly elusive, skipping readily into my embrace, her pretty arms outstretched, the expression of an eager child on her face. I wanted to whoop for triumph. Any favour that Edna Maguire should have thought fit to ask in that hour would have been willingly granted. Blessed be the philanderer who invented the device of dancing in couples. Lovers owe him a glorious monument.

It proved to be true that Sybyl couldn't dance a step and she was half paralysed with self-consciousness and physical timidity and the fear of being a bother to me. She was too nervous to try at all under the inspection of Mrs. McCorkle and when that estimable matron appeared would stop dead, mendaciously asserting that she was tired. So I ran Mrs. Mac in, and in spite of her cackles and girth found she was quite a waltzer in the top-spinning fashion followed by the Britishers.

We sat down for a rest between the acts and soon Mrs. Mac and Sybyl were such cronies that I was chary of interrupting the conversation. The subject which brought them together was short bread — real Scottish short bread. Mrs. Mac promised Sybyl some of her own baking which she pronounced "kuiken". Mrs. Mac had a broad accent which tinctured even her laugh. I think she would have been willing to let me subvert the rules and entertain Sybyl where I pleased. I was enchanted with Mrs. McCorkle.

What a surprisingly gentle and unsophisticated little creature I found my lady love in this heavenly physical contact — as alight and soft as a child, as frail as a flower. Like the unpractised she was quickly dizzied and exhausted, but the dance was the thing with her — the dance and the dance only. She took it with a stern seriousness I had never seen her exhibit towards serious questions, as if health and livelihood and happiness depended upon it.

As soon as she emerged from her shyness so that her natural suppleness and activity got into play we had a great time and at the end of half an hour I was swinging her around like the cabaret gentleman. I had him for precedent. A slight colour came to her cheeks and she had her teeth shut on her lower lip in the ardour of counting. Woe if I did not give full value to a step, for in the beginning dancing has to be done by rule of thumb. I held her little right hand in mine, and her left, she should have placed lightly on my shoulder, so say the etiquette books, but she was scarcely tall enough for that and clutched the muscle of my arm like the drowning. I determined not to instruct her in this detail till we were to make a public appearance and the public appearance I meant to delay as long as possible.

I admit unblushingly that I took advantage of her innocence of the dance to crush her little form in my arms, "I'm afraid you'll slip if I am not careful till you get used to balancing on the floor," I explained, not very logically, as I was swinging her above the boards, but she did not protest. She simply repeated, "One, two, three and then a hop, that's right, isn't it? Yes, don't let me break my leg or arm, I'm afraid I might as this is too much joy to be true. It seems as if something must surely come to stop it."

She was light as a feather and gentle as a dove. At the end of an hour I retired for a fresh collar and two or three early homecomers looked in and asked what I was up to.

"Times are not so good," I said. "I'm trying to earn a few dollars on the side as a dancing master."

"I'll give you a few dollars above your price to let me take your place," said Brubaker, but I shooed him off with a deadly threat. He was beginning to know too much and it was only my knowledge of his affairs which kept him silent about mine.

"This place will be vacant for another hour are you too tired —"

"Please keep on if it is not too much trouble. I might never get another chance."

"Another chance! I'm going to teach you to dance or know why. All these other fellows are clever, or fascinating, or pretty, or good talkers, but the only thing I am is persistent and I've set out to teach you to dance. You don't escape from me till you are the finished product."

"And perhaps after, I shan't wish to," said she giving me the downward sweep of her lashes.

"Now Sybyl, you mustn't coquette with me and lead me astray if you don't mean it."

"All right, but if you will really teach me to dance, I'll write you a lot of advertisements out of office hours."

"Give me one hundred dollars worth of work for a three dollar lesson, I guess. It's a good thing you have Miss Maguire to take care of you."

It was with great regret that the hour came for ending the first lesson and I returned my precious pupil to Miss Maguire. She was very quiet returning to the office but she had the most contented expression I had seen on her face for months. She burst upon Miss Maguire without ceremony and that attractive young woman received her with a motherly smile. "Dancing is lovely! Just as lovely as I knew it would be, and I can

150

very nearly dance already. At least I can do a little, can't I?" She turned deprecatingly to me for confirmation. "You could go to a ball now if you only had a little more self-confidence. If you really never danced till today you are a peacherino," I hastened to assure her.

She got up and between the desk and wall shewed Miss Maguire the steps she had acquired. "It is lovely, and he is going to keep on till I can really dance, isn't he a duck-a-down-dilly?"

She had the fever. It was refreshing to see her with a whole-hearted enthusiasm, and to think that it should have come through such a simple, mundane thing as the opportunity to dance! The eager desire of that child for play was pathetic.

Miss Maguire looked at me behind Sybyl's back as she capered back and forth counting, "One, two, three, four, turn," and one of her blue eyes danced in a wink — yes, the dainty and maidenly Miss Maguire actually winked at me. I wunk back at her. "The device is the thing, "I observed oracularly.

CHAPTER 42
ON WITH THE DANCE

When we had devoted about half a dozen afternoons to the terpsichorian art I suggested that Sybyl had progressed far enough for a public appearance. She clung to me in a way to delight even a practised philanderer and said that she could not possibly dance with any one but me. This was highly gratifying. She had scampered over me like a chipmunk for ages and it was sweet indeed to have her humble and clinging.

We put the matter before Miss Maguire to whom were known all the resources of life, social and otherwise, in the city. She suggested public dancing places because there one need only dance with one's special partner and gain courage under the mantle of the crowd.

"Mr. Brubaker and I should be glad to make up a party," she said with a becoming blush.

Congratulations to Brubaker. She was going to be the making of that fellow, and hadn't he the devil's own luck to be taken in hand by such a business-like and handsome young woman who would guarantee that he ran his life as it should be without the worry of affinities or pestiferations such as the unguarded man is likely to encounter in Chicago's Loop!

Sybyl was a little afraid that a public dancing place was not quite proper. She was most unconventional in some ways and unbelievably Victorian in others. However, the presence of Miss Maguire reassured her and during several weeks, for at least three nights out of the seven, we pranced and capered at some Dreamland Pavilion or patronised a theatre which provided dancing between the acts and where the floor was grand, the music first class, and the crowd so large and orderly that Sybyl could not but lose self-consciousness in it. She was quick to adopt the most gracefully conventional poses and her taste was to be relied upon. No more did she clutch my arm like a canary bird on its perch, which was a loss to me but I could not keep her unsophisticated and mingle with the world of dancers.

I never met such a devotee of the dance. She found it a sensuously intellectual exercise to disport the body to melody and rhythm. To her it was a sexless art, the partner only a part of its furniture. I heard her telling Brubaker that she would like solo dancing so that she would not have to be dependent on another.

It might have been all that to me when I was younger, if I had not been so industrious in getting on a level socially with the fellows who had things showered on them through their athletic prowess. Now I admit it was a form of delightful dalliance, a set of manoeuvres to bring me into contact with my beloved who squirrelled away from me every time I tried to imprison her. The manoeuvres were unexpectedly successful. She was totally unconscious of anything but following a social art, besides, she had so much to learn that it employed

152

her mentally and exercised her physically to exhaustion. I took advantage of her. I was no longer the high Sir Galahad with regard to a woman's downy innocence such as walked through old time novels. I enjoyed myself greedily, quieting my scruples — my scruples did not long remain. I banished them with the thought that what Sybyl did not realise could not harm her.

She danced with her whole being, such a fairy, divine, ecstatic partner as a man never had. I taught her every new step as it developed and being her only partner, excepting for an occasional scamper with Brubaker, she danced as the other half of myself, responding to my every gesture, following, and sometimes anticipating me with the surety with which a musician with a perfect ear follows the conductor. I never had such a joy since my teens and early twenties and it was comforting to find that intoxication was not diminished but deepened and broadened as a rich and ripening wine beside some new and acrid vintage new pressed.

When she grew to be at home on the floor, I broached the matter of giving a party for her.

"I don't want you to give me a party," she said perversely, the softly-rounded chin mutinous. "That's why I wish I could dance by myself. I didn't like putting you to all this trouble but I've explained that I don't want to marry you or be a pest —"

"You surely have, *ad infinitum* and ad break my heartum. It has been one of the drawbacks of teaching you but it is a sorrow I am growing used to. I just wanted you to oblige me by being an excuse for a party. I'm literally crazy for a party. I must have a girl to hang a party on. I couldn't hang it on any other fellow's girl and if I hung it on any unattached girl but you she would think I was dippy on her. If you let me give a party with you as the excuse, I promise I shall not make it the excuse to propose. When is your birthday?"

"It's on the way."

"If you never had an eighteenth birthday dance, let me give you one now."

"It seems wicked to be comfortable and dancing here when our fellows in Europe —"

"Now dearie, we've gone over this before. Religion has failed, philosophies are buried beneath the lava of eruption. It will take decades and the good optimistic livers of the very young at heart to revamp them for future use; so for the present we must armour ourselves in sophistries. The Lord in his wisdom permitted this spectacle. He knows why. We didn't bring on the thing. We did not choose that we should sit here amid material comfort while our fellows are wallowing in the mud and dismembering each other in Europe. We are not making a fortune out of war munitions while pretending to be too holy to fight. We are even derided feminists and anti-militarists. Why should we pity the war-smitten? They would pity us if they knew our hearts because we cannot discern the glory of the cause. Had we been there, I, a maddened beast with a bayonet and a bomb, you a maiden of invaded territory, I suppose — but here we are, not there. Let us accept the situation philosophically. Through all the ages there have been the victims of disasters and those who escaped. Regarding those who escaped, would you not have had the number larger rather than smaller if you could have willed it?"

"Yes, oh yes!"

"Then we have as much right to be the fortunate as the victimised, and as it is all a chance, take the good fortune that the magi have apportioned us. Come, let us dance. Keep sane so that we shall be ready and fit to help when our chance comes."

She arose at my bidding, but her feet lagged and her eyes were heavy with unshed tears. A certain undertow of sadness in her like the mellow lower tones of a violin, I accepted as in key with my own — it would be an empty soul which had not its wells of sadness, but this acute grief was a different thing.

I resolved to call Aunt Pattie to the rescue. It was time to offer her some information in any case and enlist her in this the greatest of my affairs. I was sure that she and Sybyl would get on well together and I looked forward to her being on my side.

After Bobby's death we had let drop our plan of going to France. Since Bobby was no longer with us to make an adventure of the undertaking, his sister Nancy felt that there was more to be done at home and Sybyl never referred to it at all. The funds and materials collected had been sent to augument the work of Tony Hastings and his mother.

In view of Aunt Pattie's willingness to go to France with me, I was invaded by a notion of inviting her to come and live with me at The Caboodle. I think also that in the strange times which had fallen upon the world, disrupting all complacent habits of thought, I had the small boy's desire to get back to mother's skirts.

My invitation was disgracefully casual. I hardly expected her to accept it, as she might very well have been disinclined to move from where she was, but her voice broke with emotion and she confessed it was the dream of her life. I think she had expected to do so upon the erection of The Caboodle. What a crude brute I had been! But I hereby plead that it was not all thoughtlessness. I had not realised that she would want to live with me, but I came to see that if she had been tender and brave enough to rescue me from some person or place and rear me, that she probably had grown to have an uncommon interest in me."

I wanted to have a great housewarming in honour of her advent but she specially requested that I defer it till some time later. When I became urgent she said she had her reasons and I was so well trained that I did not longer insist.

Nevertheless she had a royal welcome spontaneously extended. She had more bouquets than a debutante and during the first dinner at which she appeared as an inmate her fellow inmates arose in a body and marched around her table singing college roundelays with gusto.

Aunt Pattie was touched to tears. Many of the young fellows, after the example set by Brubaker, kissed her.

I gave her time to be cosily established beside her own hot water radiator and then one night I made my confession. She listened with characteristic astute attention, seeing through me like an angel with a flaming sword as she had ever done since as a near-sighted kidlet I had blubbered out some defeat or felony before her. I should as lief have tried to deceive St. Peter as Aunt Pattie.

"I wondered if you were never going to tell me," she remarked rather dryly. "I was afraid you would entirely spoil your chances before you came to me."

"How did you know?" I asked blankly.

"Oh, your flying, and your letter about your mother, and the general lunacy of your actions and bearing this long time."

I shut my head and let her take the lead.

"Is this to be the girl?" she inquired with a twinkle in her eyes. "Have I got to abdicate or will she marry me too, do you think?"

"I don't think you had better look upon it as so sure. I've been trying to make her *the* girl for over a year now: we're real good pals, but I sometimes think it is going to stick at that for ever."

"Humph!" she grunted. "I don't think you know how to go about it. Over a year! Pshaw! A year in which I could have been enjoying her if she's the right sort, and a year in which I could have been learning to endure her if she is obnoxious. Why haven't you brought her to my notice before?"

"I don't think she'd come. She always says there is not a living soul in the world she wants to see except on business."

"Sounds too sociable for anything."

"She is radiantly sociable if you meet her unawares."

"Order the coupé and I'll go and call upon her unawares right now. If she will not condescend to meet me as a social equal perhaps I may have the honor of employing her. I guess you are making a mess of the whole thing. It's the fakers who are artists in capturing the best girls. Get me my coat. I'm glad it's come at last. I was afraid you were going to wait till you were in your dotage and take up with some snip."

"I warn you that Sybyl is more on the flutter-budget than the elephant order."

It was not long before I was packing Aunt Pattie into one of the bird cages which they have for elevators in the Concord Building. I couldn't guess how Sybyl would act but Aunt Pattie was a real sport.

Sybyl received us in the reception room. She held out both hands to Aunt Pattie looking her directly in the eyes with distinct approval. She usually approved of old ladies. She said she did not see why she should like old nincompoops just because they were old, but that very few old ladies were nincompoops because they had usually endured enough to make them interesting. Aunt Pattie was full of fire which appealed to Sybyl and they were immediately on the best of terms.

"I came to see you because my nephew tells me you are too haughty — too much of a snob to come and see others, that you do not condescend to waste time on them."

"Your nephew is a rail — spelt backwards," said Sybyl, with the utmost *sang froid*. "I haven't time to see people really. Earning my living is about all I can manage, but I think it is lovely of you to come and see me."

"She'll have to work tonight to make up for lost time," said I.

"I wish he would think that sometimes when *he* is wasting my time," said Sybyl, "but men always think they are so interesting."

"Yes, they're a sorry lot, and getting worse," laughed Aunt Pattie.

I presently put her in her electric and pretended business so that I could return and find out how Sybyl had liked her.

"She's great," said she. "Right up-to-date".

"She trained me. Otherwise, how did you think I could have put up with your views?"

Aunt Pattie was equally pleased with Sybyl. "I'm glad my boy you had the sense to pick her as a friend. Men usually like the inferiors of our sex. She's a relief to meet. There are only two sorts of young people with regard to us old folks. Those who look upon one as a piece of old china to be respected, (how I do loathe to be *respected*), but never spoken to like a real live person, and the others who look upon one as a back number and a fool and something to be used for their convenience and then scrapped. Your little Sybyl treated me as if I were one woman and she another — just two women, nothing more or less. I am going to see all I want of that girl," and when Aunt Pattie desired a thing she usually took it.

CHAPTER 44
AUNT PATTIE GIVES A PARTY

Aunt Pattie was assured that I was too slow to capture the imagination of a girl famished for romance and adventure as she diagnosed Sybyl. Aunt Pattie undertook matters herself on my behalf. She seemed to be leagues more attractive to Sybyl than I and following their first meeting they were frequently together. Aunt Pattie even prevailed upon Sybyl to come and spend weekends with her, but it was precious little good to me as they retired to their own apartments early after dinner and did not have the grace to invite me with them. It was a case of love at first sight and I couldn't get a word in sideways.

"I'm going to give a party for Sybyl," Aunt Pattie announced at the beginning of December. "I've always wished I had a little girl. A girl makes a better toy."

I put forth my notion of an eighteenth birthday party for her.

"Good! When is her birthday?"

"The twentieth of December."

"Mine is on the twenty-first. I'll make it my eightieth and get it done with and celebrate them both with a Christmas revel."

Aunt Pattie's was the twenty-first of June, but I never batted an eye-lash. Two birthdays in one year were none too many for a lady of Aunt Pattie's zip, even if she had not yet celebrated her seventieth anniversary.

"I shall kidnap Sybyl for the event and save all that argument with her."

I expostulated that Sybyl was an imperious and independent little sausage and it might be dangerous to interfere with her liberty. "Nonsense!" ejaculated Aunt Pattie, "I'm surprised at your lack of initiative. It positively invites disaster. She's a childish little creature with a lot of whimsical ideas that are very amusing. She needs a person with a firm will to lay down a scheme of life for her. The proof of this pudding is in the eating. I never can stand any woman around me who sets up her will against mine, but I should like to have Sybyl Penelo with me constantly. She would give me something to do and gad, how I love those who can entertain me! They are the salt of life. I feel more and more that the only real labour of life is to be entertained. Just let our little Sybyl think you sympathise with her notions, which are quite harmless, do not force her to go against her ante-diluvian Victorian conscience and she would live with you at peace — a delight to the world's end. Imagine her brains being wasted to bolster up the like of Swinbank Dummer Dummer-Jones, when we could have been enjoying her for ourselves if you had had any enterprise. Her partner, that young woman —"

"Miss Maguire," I prompted.

"Yes, Miss Maguire has had the insight to recognise what the girl is worth and I'm going to help Miss Maguire all I can for the fun of seeing her become one

159

of the most successful people in the Loop, but I want the Sybyl girl for my own personal possession."

"If you had preposed to her as often as I have, you would know that —"

"If I had proposed to her even once or twice," retorted Aunt Pattie, "I'd have something to show for making a fool of myself. That's why I'm going on deck now."

Being the ordinary average fellow, I did not waste time on resistance. The average American man characteristically never bucks up against his women if they are competent. He would as soon think of struggling against some incontrovertible fact of nature. One of my familiars has thus expressed it: "I never think of bucking against women if their minds are set. I've got too much sense to get in the way of a cyclone. I find it safest to go with it."

Aunt Pattie was more cyclonic in her effects than many, though she had a quiet precision as to method. So after adjuring her not to make a complete blithering billy goat of me in the eyes of my love, I prepared to move in the same direction as the greater force. Miss Maguire was also cycloning with us, if her unobtrusive persistence could be called that, and with her and Aunt Pattie in cahoots it seemed that all I need do was to encourage nature to take its course. I saw the finish of Sybyl and was glad.

I enquired as to the details of the Christmas venture. As I had not exhibited any mental intelligence in my campaign Aunt Pattie had decided that if necessary I could lend physical aid in hers.

As the time approached she connived with Miss Maguire, and Sybyl walked into the trap of inviting Aunt Pattie to afternoon tea by way of celebrating Christmas eve. I was included in the invitation. This was our chance. As we came out of Harrow's, whither we had repaired, the limousine was waiting and we offered to take Sybyl home. She stepped in taking a seat between Aunt Pattie and me, when Aunt Pattie laconically informed her that she was going to stay at The

Caboodle till Monday morning. Christmas fell on Friday that year.

Sybyl of course protested. There was one excuse after another ending with that of clothes.

"I feel so uncomfortable. If only I had some clothes!"

"You are too self-conscious for any use." Aunt Pattie was severe. "If you picked up a friend and took her off to Christmas would you care about her dress so long as she was clean and comfortable?"

"No."

"Then you see, you only think of yourself and you are like a doll or toy now. You don't care about my pleasure."

Sybyl laughed. "You are very clever. You can beat me at my own game."

"When folks have had their own way all their life it might be dangerous to cross them on their eightieth birthday."

"I've never had anything I wanted in my life," said Sybyl wistfully.

"Serves you right, if you think you are going to live and die unto yourself," said Aunt Pattie. Sybyl then turned her glances on me? They were freighted with disdain.

"I believe this is his idea and he hadn't the pluck to carry it out by himself." And while she talked like that she stretched out her hand under cover of the carriage robe and the darkness and gave my large paw a pat which set my being on fire.

"No, he hasn't daring enough for anything like this. I did it myself with my little hatchet. He merely has to do what I tell him or I'll cut him off with a dollar with a hole in it."

Sybyl kept her subjugating lashes down a little longer and then it was too much for her sense of humour. The smiles began to ripple her cheeks. "I am glad you are doing this with me," she twinkled to Aunt Pattie. "You are bringing it on yourself so you can't blame me. And it's a real adventure, a surprise!"

161

There were other surprises in store for her. One was an outfit of Christmas red from heel to crown, shoes, hose, and frock. There was even a red necklet, bangle, and ornament for the hair. A red bouquet with holly as the chief motif had been left for me to provide.

One of the fellows who went home for the holidays had left vacant his suite next to Aunt Pattie's and it had been prepared for Sybyl's occupancy, with the smell of tobacco vacuumed and aired out under Mrs. McCorkle's good old British thoroughness. Everything that her little heart could possibly desire had been provided and she entered into the spirit of Aunt Pattie's party delightfully.

It is surprising how many people are lonely at Christmas time. There were a score or two of them in my hotel, some who could not get away and others who had no homes or relatives available. Some had their sisters or mothers come to them — special concession on my part in honor of the season with Mrs. McCorkle as censor and Aunt Pattie as chaperone.

Of course Dr. Margaret Hengist and Miss Maguire were at the party. They were among a select score or so that we had up to dine first, Aunt Pattie presiding in a very genial mood and Miss Antoinette Toby — one of North Side Society's inimitables — to keep the ball rolling. Sybyl was very quiet for her.

The Christmas tree was at the end of the dining room and Mrs. McCorkle appointed herself as chief dispenser of presents assisted by a little girl all the way from Maine to stay with her uncle, her only male relative, and her genuine uncle, as Mrs. McCorkle gave what was equivalent to an affidavit to that effect.

Sybyl complained that she had been taken unawares so that she had no presents for others, but Aunt Pattie gave her another lecture on the snobbishness of selfishness which kept her quiet. Her presents were many and her pretty self-conscious thanks were enough to reward a man for giving away something really useful which he needed himself. A bottle of prefume from young Phipps Toby, brother of Antoinette, gave her pronounced joy.

162

She opened it at once and sprinkled it about.

"You could have swum in it long ago if I had guessed you like it," I said.

"It was denied me when young on the grounds of vulgarity," said she in explanation and Aunt Pattie twinkled right under our noses at the proof of her contention about childishness.

The Christmas tree finished we proceeded to the gymnasium for dancing; and the birthday cakes were to be cut at midnight.

CHAPTER 45
AUNT PATTIE INTERROGATES

As we entered the gymnasium two guests appeared, one bearing eighty roses for Aunt Pattie, the other eighteen for Sybyl. Aunt Pattie was pleased with hers and insisted they should have been ninety, but she took me aside and said it was a scandalous extravagance, that the money should have gone to the Belgian Relief Fund. I expalined that I had bought the roses at wholesale price and at a bargain at that. I asked her to remember that the poor and the Belgians had all the charity societies and millionaire philanthropists in search of diversion to look after them but that Sybyl had no one and this was for her. Whereupon Aunt Pattie quit her talk of extravagance.

No doubt women have some sort of little garments which they have decided are sufficient protection but when they appear in a cobweb or two they seem quite ethereal. Sybyl had such a diaphanous air dolled up in a kind of gauzy red stuff tied together with a big sash that I was afraid that if I did not handle her very gently she would be a replica of "September Morn", and now that she had dropped all high brow and head cracking dissertations on "causes" and had taken to dancing in the most enthusiastic way, she appeared positively infantile.

She was in demand among the male caperers from the start and soon had her programme crammed, with nothing saved for me.

I had not come forward in a hurry partly because I had been sure that the little minx would have held at least two or three rounds for me, and partly because I did not want to be a drag on her because she was my pupil and I had insisted upon the party. I had wished her to feel free. She had.

"What dances have you saved for me," I asked her after a time.

"I didn't know you wanted any," she said with apparent concern. "You did not ask for any."

"Didn't know I wanted any!" I said ratherly blankly, "What do you suppose I taught you to dance for if it wasn't for this supreme occasion?"

"But you never asked me and all the others did," she persisted.

"But good gracious, didn't I think all your dances were mine, and that you would have to ask my permission to give one or two to these other fellows!"

"Well, I thought the reason you were so desperate for a party was so that you could foist me upon the public and get rid of me." There was mischief in her eyes now.

"Sybyl, you're a fibber, a consummate black-hearted little rail spelt backwards, and these fellows are thieves — horse thieves and bandits and they deserve the fate of a horse thief. If I catch you dancing with any one of them more than twice, tomorrow he is homeless. No more does he find a refuge under this bachelor roof and should be attempt to, Mrs. McCorkle, acting upon my instructions, shall poison him," and so saying I caught her in my arms and strode into the dance with her in spite of young Phipps Toby who was waiting to devour her.

"It's my dance!" said he.

"Yes it is," said Sybyl, struggling to be free and I was afraid of that tulle rucked gown giving way and my having to provide her with a pair of pyjamas to carry on.

"Shoo little boy!" I said to young Phipps, "You go and dance with Mrs. McCorkle or tomorrow I eject you from this roof."

"I'll dance with you just as soon as I can," said Sybyl to Phipps, giving me a delicious glance, "I am now over come by force but as soon as I escape from this cannibal and heathen and Hottentot —"

"He's no gentleman," said Phipps with a grin. "He wants a closed session all the time. He knows he hasn't a chance without," and in spite of a waiting list I whisked Sybyl off into a little room near by and said, "Now madam, give an account of yourself."

"They'll be sending after me!"

"I don't care if they arrest you. Possession is nine points of the law."

"I like to be possessed," said she with cool impudence; "that is if I'm possessed by some one by whom I like to be possessed," she added, subjugating me with her lashes.

"What did you mean by not keeping me one single, blooming, goddarned dance?"

"Just what I said."

"Then you have nothing to forgive in my carrying you off like this."

"Does one need to forgive what she enjoys?" she said with one of her pulse-quickening glances out of the corner of her eyes.

"See here, you are the damfisticatedest quintessence of a pestiferous jube-jube. You are not a woman at all. You are a wraith, a mind without a body, a snare and a will-o'-the-wisp and I'd be ashamed to be taking up the space of a real flesh and blood woman with legitimate human emotions if I were you. Why didn't you save me a dance, you heartless, cold-blooded, impossible, cruel, ungrateful —" She giggled merrily. To substitute opprobrious names as terms of endearment always vastly entertained her.

"*Ungrateful*," she emphasised the word. "I was trying to be grateful. I am so glad you taught me to dance, but because you were so good natured I did not want to saddle you always."

"You have an extraordinary way of being grateful. It is much too spiritual and intangible for me."

"Do let me run back to the ball room. It is such bad form to be out here and all those beautiful, lovely, irresistible young men waiting to dance with me on my eighteenth birthday — somewhat delayed."

"If I let you go, what will you do to make reparation? I've a good mind to shut you up out of the party for the whole of the night. Sybyl!" I moved towards her on an uncontrolled impulse.

"That's not fair," said she. "You are going to propose as surely as anything. I can see it in your chin, and you promised me once that you wouldn't get mushy or anything if I'd come to a party."

"I was only joshing. I wouldn't propose to you any more to save my life. I couldn't be hired to propose to you. An earthquake or the war couldn't make me propose to you."

Then the little squirrel stood up before me and said, "How much will you bet me that I can't make you propose to me tonight?"

"Well, now you know that that bet is won and it isn't acting fair as a real human being, you are falling back on the ancient and immoral weapon of feminine charm."

She fled towards the door. "I'm not going to propose to you; I'll keep my promise," I hastened to assure her. "But what are you going to do to make it all right with me for not saving me a dance?"

"When the ball is finished, if you'll turn on the gramophone, I'll give you all the dances you like before I go to bed."

"That is the best news, I've heard tonight, and what about the mistletoe?" I asked as I let her go in peace.

"I'll tell you by-and-bye." She tilted her chin over her shoulder in the doorway.

She was highly delighted with her success and the rare colour came to her cheeks with the exercise. Between

166

the acts she kept closely to Aunt Pattie and explained the new steps in a corner as I had explained them to herself just a matter of weeks earlier.

I took refuge with Mrs. McCorkle who was as great a belle as Sybyl and less fickle, as she had saved me three dances. Aunt Pattie and I had addressed a very formal invitation to her which she had accepted like royalty. She was firmly harnessed in a black satin gown and her British respectability shone forth like the glow on a well-scoured copper kettle. She wore my orchids on her bosom. She had received numerous floral offerings but had decided on mine because it had arrived first.

The interest of the ball for me was the end, and I engineered the cake cutting sharply at twelve o'clock as I didn't want to wear Aunt Pattie out on her premature eithtieth birthday so that our festivities would have to be curtailed. She and Sybyl each slashed at their cakes at once and then followed a few tommy rot speeches, compliments, and the expression of amiable flub dub, a little mild punch and Aunt Pattie so thoroughly and graciously dismissing everyone that only Sybyl and I were left.

Aunt Pattie sought a word with me apart. "You ask her to marry you tonight and insist upon a definite answer. If she refuses as if she meant it, I'll find out the reason why and try my hand at the job."

"I don't want to frighten her off altogether."

"As you don't seem to have coaxed her on to any extent, I don't think you had better worry."

"But I promised her I wouldn't propose if she came to a party," I muttered lamely.

Aunt Pattie stopped and gazed at me as if smitten with breath shortage. "She talks to you like that and yet — really my boy your understanding of women is so limited that I have fears for your common sanity."

"I don't think that what she says matters," I ventured, "she'd say anything to anybody." Aunt Pattie waved her hand and went towards the door.

Seeing that I wanted the right to kiss her in private as often as the spirit moved me I had not teased her under the mistletoe as the others had done all evening long regardless of age or length of acquaintance, but when I had taken Aunt Pattie to the door I came back to her.

"Sybyl, a very merry Christmas! What about those dances?"

"Yours, sir! Yours, with pleasure!"

But I saw she was tired and I led her to a seat. She did not resist. "I wanted to kiss you under the mistletoe, you don't know how much; but I don't want to plague you unless you care for me enough to give me the right to kiss you always. Are you never going to? Are you going to keep me waiting for ever and ever with life at low water compared with what it might be if only you would make it so? You know how I feel towards you. Once more, will you be my little wife?"

"Oh, as for that silly mistletoe business," she remarked, "I think that a nuisance. Why shouldn't I kiss *you* under the mistletoe, just for a novelty?"

"It's a free country and I'm sure I shall be more than delighted."

"All right. Sit down under it where I can reach you, and you've got to shut your eyes, and if you move so much as a finger I'll loathe you for ever and ever."

Far from my intention was it to mar such an adventure. She placed a chair. I took it. She promised great efficiency.

"Such a horrible, little pig's bristle tooth brush," she observed of my moustache. She was not the least flustered. I was no longer responsible for my actions. She could have asked for my kingdom.

"I detest moustaches," she continued. "In the first place, they are monstrositios of hideosity and in the second they're so dirty — unhygienic I suppose is the right word. You couldn't expect anyone but a slave or hero to kiss you."

"Go on," said I, "I admit that you are a martyr."

"Aren't you ashamed to have coarse, ugly hair on your face like a wild gorilla? Would you like to kiss me if I had a nasty tooth brush on my upper lip?"

"Surely. I'd like to kiss you if you had a gopher trap

there. I'll cut off my moustache if you'll make a habit of kissing me." I was wont to think Samson a chump and deserving of what befel him for allowing any woman to interfere with his hair, but I am more sympathetic now. Sybyl could have ordered me to shave my head and I would have been willing to do so for favours it was hers to give.

"Oh no! I don't want you to cut if off. If you were mine I might, but if you like it, it is your business. Now will you kindly hold your head up so that I can get at you with as little as possible of the tooth brush effect. It's at least very small, not one of the weeping willow walrus species, thank heaven."

I did as directed. I would have worn a hoop skirt had she demanded it for the ceremony. I was hers to do what she willed. She willed to put her roseleaf lips to mine, though it could scarcely have been called a kiss. It was like one of those unfinished kisses that an infant gives. I scarcely dared to breathe lest I should frighten her away.

"It's not so bad," she announced complacently, "I don't know why men make such a fuss about kissing. It prickled a bit. I think if you will hold your head high it might be more comfortable. I'll try again."

Would I hold my head that way! I should have been glad to stand on it for such an experiment.

She put her arms around me this time and I ventured to put mine gently around her. There, I was clasping the little form which always seemed as if it would melt in my grasp? It was not fluttering like a frightened bird but was as quiet — alas, as quiet and unconcerned as a bird at rest on an inanimate object, while my heart kept time to my desire.

"You know," said she, "I can't tell you what a darling I think you have been to teach me to dance. Now I can listen to gay music without the tears of envy choking me. I do so thank you. You are so *dear!*"

She took off my glasses and patted my eyes for being sleepy without their aid. She told me my hair was lovely because it stuck out from my head so nicely and yet was so soft to the touch, and, "Your chin is dear. It tells your every emotion. It very nearly has a dimple. You see the Potter promised you a dimple, but he forgot and was just going away when he saw the disappointed look in your eyes, so he turned back and said, 'oh, that dear little boy, I forgot his dimple!' and the clay was nearly dry but he stuck his finger in it and that's why it's a dimple — almost. It wrinkles up in the sweetest way if you are glad and when your feelings are hurt it is too adorable for anything." I was grinning like a shark, sheerly fatuous under her caresses. She rubbed her cheek against mine in the gentlest way, I half expected it to dissolve like a ghost. God, what I should have liked to do with her and tell her!

She rubbed her finger along my lower teeth assuring me they lapped over like the bricks around a flower bed. "You know dear heart, you must not propose to me any more because it hurts me right through so that I cannot live when I have to refuse you. I love you ever so dearly as a friend but now I shall never marry. We will not dwell upon the reasons. To discuss them would only hurt us both too deeply with what should-have-beens. You must keep away from me if you cannot be only just a dear, dear friend. Or I shall go away to another country."

Then she stooped and kissed me fair on the lips as serenely as a mother with a child. She looked so unstirred, so remote, did she know what she was doing to a man, and he deliriously in love with her? I wondered and again I wondered. She was a puzzle to plague a man, a magnet to —

"You are so dear," she repeated, and then she was flitting like a butterfly, but I thrust out my hand, roughly I fear in spite of that cobwebby gown, "I can't let you go like that. You must say good-bye and if you love me, I don't understand —"

She was unresisting as I wrapped her in my arms, her stillness, her passivity chilled my heart. It was a wraith I clasped not a warm pulsating woman.

"I love you," she repeated with perfect composure,

170

"I am growing so fond of you that it gets more and more insupportable to think of life without you, but I am never going to marry. The war has finally decided me and I have finished experimenting. It is interesting, but the evidence it uncovers makes me so sad."

"Is there anything the matter with me? Why do you say you care for me and still refuse me?"

"Dear heart, you must not keep on worrying me. It only hurts. Let me go. I thank you for asking me to marry you. That is the grandest Christmas gift I shall ever have. I shall remember this night all my life, when I am old and lonely. Kiss me! Kiss me hard!" she said with sudden emotion, "Kiss me so that I shall have it to remember always when I'm old and lonely and there are no more kisses, no more lovers and presents, only weariness and melancholy!"

I held her close, close against my heart, intoxicated to do her bidding, striving to warm that soft sadness from her eyes, but she presently slipped from my grasp, the wraith again, and was gone. Just as I seemed to grasp her she always fled to a farther vantage ground.

A thought that I struggled against admitting was that her heart might have been buried with Bobby. If so I should need to give her more time to forget, but if it were my parentage — what the devil was my parentage!!

I sat there in an emotional stew half painful, half uplifting till Aunt Pattie presently came and found me.

"Where is the girl? It is nearly an hour since I left you here together."

"She left me a long time ago," I said.

"Has she accepted you?"

"No."

"Did you ask her?"

"Yes, and she has made me promise not to ask her again because it hurts her."

"And you, you poor babe in the wood, I suppose you'd do what she says."

"I don't think it dignified to torment her for ever?"

"No wonder she hasn't accepted you. I'll have to propose myself, for *I* mean to have her whether you do

171

or not. I'm disgusted with you." Aunt Pattie marched off. She turned back after a few steps. "A woman likes a man who is daring in love. He can't be too daring if he is attractive. You are free and honorable. Why don't you kidnap the little hussy, if you want her? I bet that would so capture her fancy that she would be as infatuated with you as if she were the Silly-Sally sort."

"I'm not so sure of her liking me, and I'd be afraid of hurting her."

Aunt Pattie snorted. "That little wisp of a thing! I could almost take her under one arm myself." I realised the truth of the promise that all is mind, for if Sybyl had taken a notion to kidnap me she could have done so with a thimble for a carriage and a butterfly for a charger.

"Why has she refused you?" she asked. I should have liked to escape my distinguished foster mother then, but she had me well trained.

"I guess she doesn't care for me. She doesn't give that as the reason, but girls always pretend they love a fellow and would marry him only for something. Only the very young ones say straight out that they hate a man."

"Is there any reason why she should not marry? Had she a husband in that past life about which she says nothing?"

"She told me once that there was no reason on earth why she shouldn't marry if she so desired, and I believe her."

"What theory have you for her refusal?"

"I have two."

"Well, the first?"

"I think perhaps she cremated her heart with Bobby Hoyne."

"Bobby Hoyne! You don't mean Bobby-Boy Hoyne of the twostep and tango brigade!" ejaculated Aunt Pattie incredulously. "The last fellow in the world she could be bothered —"

"Oh, I'm not so sure! You didn't see Bobby this last year. He came on wonderfully, took to C.S. and to using his skull contents — and you never can tell what kind of a fellow that kind of a woman will fancy."

"Nonsense! I'll find out! Even if she had married him, widows love again. You had another theory?"

"Yes. My uncertain origin. She has the old country point of view in that. I guess her lineage is straight from William the Conqueror, Henry Eighth, or some such staple progenitor. You notice she never fails to ask what and where are the fathers and mothers and uncles and cousins of each person she meets. She likes you, but I'm only some waif you picked up and she doesn't know what breed I may be."

"Hum," said Aunt Pattie, "I shall make it my business to find out. Have you any theory about your parentage?" She eyed me sharply as she put the question.

"I guess I've got the hang of it pretty well," I said laconically.

"Oh, you have, have you? Then who are you, may I ask?"

"I guess it was no mystery to the Pater. I suppose I'm the result of a chivalrous affair with some poor fool who didn't know the ropes, and you came to the rescue and raised me. I wouldn't care so much if I could only be sure that my mother was a fair sort of an individual. In blue moments I have imagined her as some defective or worthless creature. Can you tell me who my mother was? I have never liked to intrude upon you for details, but I should be glad to know once for all."

Aunt Pattie swayed in her seat. I wished I had kept silent. It had then been a tragedy to her as I often imagined.

"I'm sorry. Forgive me for mentioning it. It is of no importance," I said seeking to support her, but she drew up quickly remarking, "I almost toppled off my chair, I did not know the edge was so near. Let us talk this out."

Being wound up I kept on like a child saying a piece at a school concert. "It was very brave and decent of you Aunt Pattie. I never have forgotten it for an instant.

It is not a thing a fellow enjoys brooding on. Only for that I think I should have seized upon Sybyl long ago."

"Do you mean to tell me that this doubt about your parentage has been a drawback to you?"

"Off and on it has. If my mother had been a janitor's wife I should not have cared so long as there had been a decent marriage."

Aunt Pattie looked at me strangely.

"There is a lot of talk about environment being more than heredity in the life of a child," she said, "but I think that neither heredity nor anything else counts. A man is according to his superstitions. If the superstitions he has imbibed when young are happy and strong, he will be a happy and clean-minded man. If they have been dark they cripple his soul for ever. You evidently have labored under a dire superstition about the rites which should precede parentage and it has wounded you. I wish you had come to me long ago."

I did not remind her that she had effectually extinguished my goings to her on the subject and instead I ventured, "Do you know who my mother was?"

"Yes, I know her — none better."

"Well the, was she, was she all right?"

"That depends on what you consider all right."

"Well, was she, was she one of the — well, what is called a *bad* woman?"

"Stars alive!" exclaimed Aunt Pattie. "You are getting on towards forty and have been suspecting that all this time. I never did approve of secrecy. There was no need of secrecy in this case excepting for the feelings of some one else. My husband was not your father, so you have been misjudging him. My husband was ten times the man your father ever knew how to be. Many a time I have wished you were the son of my dear husband. He was a brave man and a gentleman. I am going to ask Sybyl why she will not marry you — it is some silly thing connected with her theories I think. If it is the memory of Bobby Hoyne, that is nothing. If it is your parentage which is making her balk, I shall tell her what it is and find out the truth. You had better not go to bed, the girl may want you later."

"May I not know the worst and get it over," I asked, but Aunt Pattie said, "No! I would rather speak to Sybyl first," and she disappeared.

Sybyl was to learn what I had guessed at wrongly all my life. Would it make any difference? Had I hope or was it to be over for all time?

I did not know for months what happened as I record it here, then I heard the story first from Sybyl and later from Aunt Pattie herself.

CHAPTER 46

Who is the happy husband? He,
Who scanning his unwedded life,
Thanks Heaven, with a conscience free,
'Twas faithful to his future wife.

Aunt Pattie went to Sybyl's room and found her combing her perfumed tresses preparatory to retiring.

"Come to my room," said she, "I want to talk to you and I'll get into bed. I'm not young enough for a whole night's debauchery any more."

Sybyl did as commanded and when Aunt Pattie was comfortably lying down curled herself in a big chair drawn up beside the bed.

"Why wont you marry my boy?" was the first question, just like that.

"I, oh, I —" stammered Sybyl taken completely unawares by the directness of the onslaught.

"Does the memory of Bobby Hoyne stand in the way?"

Sybyl had time now to gain her quick self-control which was almost self-subterfuge.

"No," said she analytical and detached. "At first I should never have thought of him because of his

175

reputation with women, but then I nearly married him because he was so self-sure and decided and I was all at sea and unhappy and reckless because of the war. It seemed that I might as well do one thing as another but — dear Bobby — 'Unto him that hath'. He has the best of it now."

"Fudge! We don't know about that," said Aunt Pattie. "My boy has certainly been persistent".

"Persistent, but not decided and overwhelming and determined to —"

"Oh! But surely persistence is as wearing as the cave man racket?"

"Yes, but it gives me time to get my thoughts straight."

"And then?"

"I've decided not to marry at all."

"Why?"

"That is a tedious story. Please don't discuss it. It has nothing to do with your nephew. He is a dear. I should be glad to marry him if things were different."

"What things?"

"Men."

"What differences would you like chickabid, short of reconstructing the crazy contraptions from the ground up? Come and snuggle up here and tell me all about it."

"I mean if they weren't such ravening creatures."

"Some of them are not. When you've lived as long as I have you'll be astonished by the virtue that individual men display. It is more noteworthy than women's achievements because they have not such good stock-in-trade to start from."

"Oh yes, there are perfectly saintly men, though I don't care so much for the ascetic type. There are also clean, healthy athletes, conspicuous for strength and virility, yet unspoiled of woman, but I fear they are not for me."

"Indeed!"

"I know all the lectures on the other side. Have in fact adduced them myself. I was wavering once or twice lately, I was so lonely, but now I know I cannot overcome my sex fastidiousness. In the feast of love women can sit down to a banquet of soiled and broken meats or go hungry. I prefer to go hungry."

"Some of the best and ablest men — the finest God ever put breath into, have strayed in red paths in their youth and then have turned out better than those who never yielded to temptation. Have you ever thought what it must be to a man to have every channel of thought teaching him that without indulgence he is not a man, is not 'virile', is set apart from his fellows? There is a fixed routine there for every man to go through. He is usually plunged into it with the terrific force of a marching regiment before he has had any time to think for himself and only one per cent of people have any capacity to think for themselves in any case."

"I have considered all that. If they turned from it with sickness and shame as soon as they realized what it means, I could forgive them and understand. So many men have asked me to marry them and when I put that to them, they never offer any defence that I would make me forgive them. The best ones go out like the men in the Bible. The others uphold themselves with the cruellest and most degraded sophistries — that nature cannot be denied, you know all the silly old talk about their precious natures? Well, I am free to choose and I don't want their natures, that is all. Loneliness is ghastly to me. I should prefer death tonight to the long lonely years I see ahead, but I prefer loneliness to what the economic dependence of women has made of love — the cruelty to my sister women, the degradation and danger to myself."

Aunt Pattie nodded and was silent.

"I have a deathless grudge against men and their brutal commerce which has defiled even love. They have spoiled the most wonderful thing in the world — the birthright of every normal man and woman. Swine!"

"Is that why you have refused my boy?"

"It is why I am never going to marry."

"Did he turn and go out without defence?"

"I never let him get to that. That's what I do now. I

177

am very fond of him, he is perhaps better than ninety per cent of men. I did not want the hurt of the same old story. It always makes me ill. And what's the good. Men seemingly can be so lovable and still have to their credit a cowardliness and uncleanliness which is revolting to me. After much analysis I knew I could not subsist on dirty bread, no, though I must go hungry all my life. I have tested it in my imagination and if I can not get a thing right in my imagination I have found that it will not come right in reality. I have tried to accept the standards which content other women and men but I cannot. That wonderful emotion, passion, the flame of love's fire is always extinguished by the thought of what other women of another class have had from my lover. I could not take joy in a thing offered some as an honour and which comes to others as a vice and a negation of all true womanhood. The two fields cannot be kept separate as men have pretended to suit their indulgence. The sin and shame of lust which buys at a bargain in the market place because of hunger and subjectism and ignorance leaves its miry footprints and debris and disease in the palace of love. Men cannot defeat their own science of mathematics. Women would not attempt to do so. I do not want my garden of love to be either an untidy lumber room or a harem."

After a silence of some minutes Aunt Pattie remarked, "You just refused my boy on general principles, you did not make sure?"

"I don't suppose there is any doubt."

"If he had never defiled the banquet of love, would you accept him?"

"Rather! It would be paradise really to be able to let one's self go in love and not always have it turn to icy disgust when one is keyed to fulfilment."

"You did not give him any definite reason."

"No, as I said it is less painful not to. I don't suppose he cares very much. Men don't, do you think? They make a terrible noise for about a week if a girl rejects them, but that is because of their lack of self-control, and then off they go after the next candle-light. And it is the same whether they win or lose. Their over-indulged fancy endures for a day and declines."

"That is not so if you look after a man."

"Oh yes! Watch the dear little pet and guard him and plague him and never let him off a string. I don't want that way of earning my living. I am getting tired of working in the Loop but I'd rather keep on there than start in being the keeper of a man," she teased her chin with great wilfulness. "Besides, I despise an animal who can't be clean and honest owing to inner fastidiousness and spirituality instead of by reason of the keeper who sets watch over him and wheedles and bullies and flatters and deceives him into being decent. I can be decent by myself, why can't a man? He has such superior intelligence to help him too."

"Your idea of men has been warped by these fools with full purses and empty brains that have been knocking about you. Most of them should be in asylums, but the useful men of the world really have a quite human intelligence. Do you know why my boy thinks you have refused him?"

"What does he think?"

"Well, you see, he is only my adopted son. There is some doubt as to his origin and he thinks that is why you don't fancy him. He is afraid to grasp his happiness owing to one set of superstitions and you repulse yours on account of another. You really are a well-mated pair of lunatics."

"He's very childish to think that. I've aired my views plainly enough for him to guess why I'm not taking a husband."

"But as that reason doesn't exist in his case, he wouldn't think of it."

"I guess it exists alright, though every wife and mother thinks her precious gosling miraculously exempt from the general infection."

"Does the obscurity of his birth cut any ice with you?"

"Not a bit. He has been reared by you since he was an infant. He has had the environment and opportunities

179

of a gentleman, he is not the child of a lunatic is he."

"He comes of clean stock."

Aunt Pattie drew the girl down on the bed beside her, "This night I am going to tell you something that only one or two of my girlhood friends knew and they are dead. I want to tell it to you because my boy loves you, he loves you consumingly and if he can trust you that way I guess I can trust his choice. I have never seen him love like this before. If it was one of my other nephews I should advise you to go ahead and give him a wholesome jolt, but with my boy it is different. He will never get over it if he cannot win you. He is a good man. You will never find another like him. What are you going to do with him?"

"Don't make it harder for me."

"It needn't be hard for either of you if you only loved him and were content to trust life and the ever present good in people instead of getting all balled up in some silly superstitious notions. My boy thinks he is the son of my husband and some creature he betrayed, but it is not so."

"Who is he really, Aunt Pattie?"

"He is my own child."

"Yours! Oh, I am so glad!" Aunt Pattie folded her in a warm embrace. "I am so glad!" she repeated. "Why doesn't he know you are his mother. It seems too good to be true."

"That is the secret. My husband was the usual good match. He had not broken the laws as men deem them worthy of keeping — so that my father or brother would forbid him coming to the house. He managed his profligacy according to masculine etiquette. He never injured 'good' girls, as men assure us so fluently." She smoothed the silken tresses straying across the bed and drew the girlish form even closer, "I know it all, my sweet! You have suffered no hell that I haven't gone through, and the hells were darker and lonelier in my day. Well, my husband's machinations had all been upon the previously exploited and in their turn they worked retribution — and the innocent suffer with the guilty.

After ten childless years, years of longing, I came into a small fortune and took the law into my own hands. I determined to have a child. I told my husband and went abroad leaving him to do his durndest."

"And did he?"

"He went about his business and thought it over and kept his mouth shut, which alone shows he was an unusual man. I was abroad for over a year. I meant to stay there. I told him he could get a divorce or do what he liked. I was so happy with my baby that I cared for nothing else. When the child was about four months old and I was progressing in my study of the Italian language —" the old lady grunted humourously — "my husband came over to see me. He questioned me very closely and when he found that no lover had left the United States with me nor visited me, he made me an offer. It was a matter of pride with him I believe. He said that if I stayed abroad till the boy was a year old and kept his origin a secret, why then he would adopt him. If I would be satisfied with that one child he would make him his heir or make me his heir and let me do as I liked with my son. I saw that he had suffered as few men have it in them to suffer, and suffering had ennobled him."

"Oh, Aunt Pattie! How wonderful!"

"He told me that he loved me, that he had sinned while a coarse young brute trained to nothing else. He was shamed to have robbed me of motherhood and if I could forgive him and live with him on my own terms he would strive to be the dearest friend and protector woman ever had, and that he would respect my secret and love my child as his own. It was something of a wrench never to have let my darling know I am his mother, but I was willing to the terms then. In that absence I found out that I loved my husband, though my desire for a child had proved stronger for a time. By contrast with other people I was struck with his courage and generosity. As life advanced I proved that the human partnership called marriage does not rest on a single quality alone in either party, that it is mostly a

181

grand compromise. I should like to tell my son even now, but I am not sure how he would take it — if he would forgive me. How do you feel, you girl that he loves, you girl of his own generation, while I have to look on as a back number, a thing that has been put on file perhaps never to be called for again by anyone but Gabriel?"

"Oh, tell me more, it is like a book! How did it turn out?"

"He was a man of great force of character and strength of purpose. He kept to his bargain and we had a grand life together. As the years went on we grew closer friends and lovers. We eliminated the past and built always on the present."

"And the other man."

"Oh, he was nothing but an incident. He died long ago. Lots of married women are irregular. More men than ever dream of it are deceived, and deserve to be — it helps to even the score. Fortunately the boy is nondescript in appearance, neither very like me nor his father's family."

"How splendid!" exclaimed Sybyl. "It is the desire of dozens of women I know to go forth boldly and have a child when they think fit, but they have not the pluck that you had. Also of course they are not independent, but it is a growing thought in the heart of women and that makes your son seem very precious. He is certainly of royal birth."

"And royal upbringing. I determined that no son of mine should wallow in primrose paths because of ignorance. I put it to him scientifically and from the viewpoint of independent women, but I doubt if women have the final influence in this matter. Their point of view is held in contempt because it would mean a self control which to men's hot-house fancy seems unnatural. His foster father also gave him the facts of the case. He said he was not going to have the youngster shut out of paradise when it came because some shyster had persuaded him to sell his right to it for a string of beads or a cup of rum in the long ago."

"But even that doesn't prove anything. I know several men who said their fathers taught them the truth but that it made no difference. Boys are so afraid of being laughed at that they go with the mob."

"My boy did not," maintained the mother. "Have you found him going with the mob in his philosophy of life?"

"He speaks fair, but men can pick up any jargon to please a woman while their desire is burning, and besides they are the most wonderful spinners of theories and they never think of bringing practice at all parallel. Look at the war!"

"You have fixed up a philosophy as a shield against disappointment. It is the resource of the sensitive, the reaction of the abnormally idealistic, but you are overdoing it. There are more men walking around today even on Dearborn Street than you ever suspect who have your own ideal of love. You are going to get fooled by not being easy enough as a subject of foolery."

"If I could only believe!"

"Why not go and find out!"

"I have cultivated an indifference and to be waked up to hope again only to be disappointed would be too painful. I would rather remain in my precent twilight state."

"You're a coward! You haven't the courage to believe!"

"You certainly have the right to say that after your own courage. I shall go and ask him if it is true and if it is, I hope he will propose to me just once more."

"Yes, go at once. He is waiting for you. And I think you might even propose to him now after all the chances he has given you. You owe him that."

"Perhaps I do," said the girl buttoning her negligée. Aunt Pattie held her tightly a moment, "And what of my secret, child?"

"If he accepts me I shall tell it to him on our wedding night."

CHAPTER 47
HEART OF MY DESIRE

I tried to read all sorts of things without success. I tried to play solitaire, which Sybyl considers the pastime of fools. I tried to do some accounts. I tried to write a letter. What would I not have given to walk it off! But Aunt Pattie had told me to hold myself in readiness. Each sound or motion in the corridor approaching my door sent my heart into my throat. But she did not come. It grew very late. The small hours enlarged. Sybyl by this surely knew that about my parentage which I did not know myself. It had made a difference. Did it mean no hope, or fresh hope?

The clock chased the hours and hope died down. I guessed it was all over. Oh, well!

Hush! Yes, that was a delicate knock. Never have I awaited a knock like that one. I leapt to the door and opened it wide.

"May I come in and talk to you?" I stood almost paralysed. She was such a little girl in the loose silken gown with her long hair flowing. She said she could always read my innermost thoughts in my chin. She could. I wished that I could do the same with hers. I could when she let me see her eyes but the lids were drooping now giving me nothing but that divinely intriguing line of the long lashes sweeping the cheek. All the house but us was at rest. Regardless of Mesdames McCorkle and Grundy I shut the door and had her with me.

Instead of saying anything she played with her long tresses, slipping around her, electric with life, heavily perfumed from young Toby's Christmas present. She looked at me appealingly, tremulously as if she were going to weep.

"Don't you just love attar of roses," she said playing with the spun snare. I buried my face in it — a heaven of perfume and silk. I was the one who was cool now because I saw that she was seeking to chatter as a subterfuge to cover her agitation. The pulsation of her throat showed that tears would have been easier than speech. My heart melted with tenderness. Here at last she was overwhelmed by emotion. She was the most emotional creature I knew but nearly always she played with her emotions as a juggler with his swords. Now they drove her tumultuously.

"What is it dearest?" I asked to steady her.

"I have come to ask you a question."

"Yes."

"And on your honor as a man, your oath as a human being you will tell me the truth?" I shall never forget her eyes as she looked at me then. Good God if I should have had to answer that question as men usually do!

I said, "If I can my darling. You can depend on me. I have never lied to you in any grave particular."

One appealing look from her eyes dewy with apprehension, starlike with hope. How deliciously undone she was.

"I want to know what are your ideas of morals for men."

I was completely nonplussed by the question. I had, I fancy been expecting her to ask forgiveness for some imaginary thing — probably for a heart divided with one who had gone. But this!!! It was so funny that I had a to do to keep from a broad laugh, for it was nothing amusing to her. I knew her views upside down and inside out and there had always existed between us the great frankness of cleanliness. There were no subjects we had to pass charily owing to prudery or because the glass of our houses betrayed skeletons. Why then had she not been equally conversant with my ideals? No man can tell in cold words the girl he loves as tenderly as I loved her, that he is a saint, that he has observed the same laws of cleanliness as she. In the first place, to the decent man — and there are more of him even in Chicago's Loop than the Y.M.C.A. can swear to — it does not seem so unusual as to warrant mention. He does not feel called to talk about it any more than he would advertise the fact that his training had been such that he knew how many baths to take per diem or per week, and how many sets of clean linen to account for within the same time limit. And that is where he loses out, for the other kind of fellow constantly blows the horn of his "virility" and parades his slavery to "human nature", and there are so many of him that he has it all his own way in bluffing women that he is the only real man around.

"My idea of morals for men," I gasped, "my dear child, they are just the same as yours. I have always been in perfect accord with you and upheld you. You knew that. What do you mean? I have always tried to be a thoroughly moral man."

"What do you mean by that?"

"I mean the same as you mean if you should tell me that you are a chaste woman. I have never admitted the double standard as anything but a mathematical imposs-ibility and a silly excuse to cover a disgusting lack of self-control in men. No one but self-indulgent conquerors talking to slaves, drivelling sychophants, or cowards, would think of promulgating such a theory for a minute."

"You don't mean it! It can't be true!"

"Yes it is. Of course it is? There is nothing queer about it. Lots of fellows keep the law. I have any number of friends of my own age and order —"

"And not married when they were sixteen?"

"They are not married at all — the ones I refer to."

She stood silent with her head against the door. I was at a loss to know whether it was my move or hers.

"Will you please propose to me again some day?" she said in a voice that was lower than a whisper but love carried it right into my heart. Her face was ashen white.

"Will I propose!" I had difficulty to restrain myself from shouting at the top of my voice. "Will I propose! You try me, my little pet, I propose right here and now and shall never stop if you can give me any hope at all."

She made a shy gesture in my direction. I wrapped her close.

"I want you to hold me tighter and tigher and closer

and closer and kiss me and kiss me till I cannot breathe, and never let me go."

This was no elusive ghost. She had come to me a hot-hearted throbbing woman turning my being to a flame of wild delight. Oh, little heart of my desire!

I gathered her to me. I carried her around the room in exuberance of joy. All suddenly my strength had become as that of giant. The pain and sorrow and sadness of the world vanished. I could see as in a vision that such things were mere phantoms, erroneous figments of imagination blurring but not injuring the original design. Grand shapes towered in a rosy mist. Joy and beauty triumphed. My love! My love! The great illusion had claimed me with never a stain nor shadow on it.

"That was why I never meant to marry except as an experiment and I have grown weary of experiments, because they only prove the worst to be true. Why did you not tell me long ago?"

"Why, my precious! How could you doubt me? I have never doubted you."

She laughed deliciously, quite at ease through her sense of humour. "It's only women who can put on airs when doubted in that line."

"And do you mean that you might have been mine a year ago —"

She nodded her head, her eyes grown misty and tender.

"The joy of finding love after all, of knowing that I am not to go lonely to my grave. All those long years ahead — now you will be there with me!"

"We shall take them together."

"You've got to love me hard and fast to make up for lost time and get all the pent up love into the years. You'll be there in the night when the phantoms come, those grey ghosts of the futility of life and the pain and the sadness and the sin and the shame, and no way out? And the fear, the horrid fear of death — nasty repulsive death which has to be plunged through some day, and old age, creeping down the hill an object of repulsion, no more youth or love or beauty."

"Yes dear, we shall take it all together, I understand *absolutely*. There will be joys too. I'll hold you tight when the phantoms come. They come to me too."

"I feel that I am not deserving of you," she said with divine humility. "I was growing so careless about my soul. I was letting its lights of love grow dim and befogged and untrimmed. I was letting the weeds creep into the garden and the seeds sown by the voluptuaries and profit seekers were taking root. You ought to have the most lovely woman ever born. You should not be wasted on me. I would be willing to give you up —"

This giving me up business did not suit me at all. Here she was melting into the chest again, ready to relinquish me to live in the spirit rather than in the everyday world.

"Life can never be as grim again after knowing that love untainted invited me to the feast. Just to have known that fills me with a happy content."

I strove against this wraith-like quality which I could see taking her from me like something too ethereal for the physical manifestations of love.

"Sybyl, mia, Life would never forgive you if you did not accept her invitation and sit down and eat at the banquet of love. Just to have appreciated the invitation, the opportunity, in not enough for Life. She demands fruition — fulfilment."

"Oh yes, but I'm telling you."

"And I'm telling you that I'm going to eat you," I retorted, suiting the action to the word. "Oh, my pretty little dear, my heart quails with fear from the torrent of my pent up love. I am in danger of loving you to death. It will hardly be safe for me to have you for my very own. Can I curb the brute in me?"

"The brute in you!" the incredulity in her voice was a caress.

"No man knows till he has been put to the supreme test."

She laughed warmly and right down on earth. "I'm

188

not afraid, and if I'm not, you need not be. If a woman has evolved above a dishcloth and the man above a minotaur, the woman keeps the keys."

Strange old-wife wisdom which comes from those who are innocent enough to believe. I was comforted and reassured.

"Fears!" she laughed joyously. "You couldn't be anything but an angel with the woman you love — with any woman. It is a simple law of nature. Only the man who has defiled the god in the core of him can be a beast."

"I thought you may have been afraid of the uncertainty of my parentage. That was all that has kept me from running off with you long ago."

"There was nothing very uncertain about it. The fact of your being here vouched that some sister woman suffered the great travail that you might be and also vouched that she or others have tended you with that long, patient, minute, tenderness which has produced such a sensitive, affectionate, splendid creature. You know," she tilted her head thoughtfully, "the only thing which is going to count some day in a man or a maid's birth will be that they are royal beings because some woman decided that they should be."

"And you didn't mind the uncertainty of mine."

"There wasn't much uncertainty," she laughed roguishly, "Miss Maguire told me long ago what was popular history and Aunt Pattie has just confirmed it. Only you were uninformed after all, and only Aunt Pattie imagines it a secret."

Dear me, why had I not thought of consulting the encyclopaedic Miss Maguire.

"Well, what is my origin," I asked.

"It is wonderful! Too wonderful for anything. You don't dream how you happen to be here. It makes you a thousand times more precious."

"Ah, Sybyl tell me?" My heart went thumping.

"It is a fairy story."

"Tell me girl, tell me at once."

"Some day."
"When?"
"On our wedding day."

CHAPTER 48
A LETTER FROM MY LOVE

Another characteristic, or shall I say habit, of Sybyl's
was never to be satisfied with a conversation, flirtation,
argument, or dispute as it was left by the participant.
On going home she would often send a supplementary
note by special delivery. She was recklessly extravagant
with postage stamps. While so fluent in some ways she
was curiously shy of expressing tenderness in person,
but she would impetuously write what were entrancingly intimate confessions. No niggardly caution about
the possible consequences of her epistles falling into the
hands of the unscrupulous or those lacking nicety,
deterred her. She might never have had letters from
other admirers for all she said about them — one rare
exception had been the blow struck by Bobby — and
evidently she leant upon a similar code in others.
    Upon whispering in my ear that the secret of my
birth was a glad one she fled to her own apartments, but
she did not retire. Instead she wrote a letter which shall
be precious to me for as long as our love shall last. She
put it under my door where I found it in the dawn when
I arose from a sleepless waiting to make my toilet. It
was fragrant from the attar of roses and in her own
handwriting — the first she had written to me that way,
as she averred she would rather walk by hand than write
in such an antiquated fashion.

> Dearest One,
> It was beyond me to convey to you just now how much I love
> you. The surprise and joy were too overpowering and I always
> become flippant for fear of becoming mushy.

It cannot actually be true!

It must be a heavenly dream that will melt with this glorious Christmas eve!

I cannot wait till morning when you must tell it to me all over again, and over and over again, a thousand, thousand times till the dream becomes a glorious reality.

I want to tell you of all the ways that I love you, the whys — all of which would have died without flowering if it had not been for you.

I love you first of all for your angel gentleness, but that I have often told you; and because you are tall and broad and straight, and for the way your head is put on, and for the proud graceful lines of your shoulders, but that you know; and because you are not a bit self-conscious and not a bit ego-tistical, and because you talk very little and because I can buzz all around you and over you while you are mobilising your mental artillery to begin; and because you are so restful, and because I shall be able to impose upon you in every direction. I could never feel safe with a man that I could not impose upon; but you are so easy to impose upon that I am almost scared that I shall impose upon you too much: but here, this is a bargain. I shall always be honest about it and tell you when I am hen-pecking you and bam-boozling you so that you will be able to take it for what it is worth, and not be entirely eliminated.

I love to see you rising out of a crowd. You could never be hidden under a bushel or in a clothes basket. And I love you because I can make fun of you and because you are like a sheltering rock in the wilderness, and most of all because you persisted and knew what you wanted and never relinquished pursuit, and because, and because, and because.

I want you to understand how grateful I am to you because I can love you and let down the bars so that the pent up flood in my heart can for once go wide like a sweeping torrent in the spring.

I shall get up early so that you can tell it to me all over again and swear again what I never thought could be true. Life for me was staleing horribly and becoming an empty terror but you have turned it to wonder. I feel now that it is a mighty mosaic with a terrific pattern made up of us, one by one. If we can be part of the pattern in the centre with its gold and its colors, instead of the grey background, how beyond realis-ation, but glorious even to be the background and when one had expected nothing but to be one of the discarded atoms.

That honied letter flooded me with a tenderness that was paradise. Her sweet generosity and warmth had unlocked all that was good in me. Here were no inhibitions, no stipulations, nothing but a full-hearted surrender. She had let in a flood of sunlight to disperse uneasy dreams. All fears of an eruption of the devouring brute which had threatened in me of late months fled like a dragon mist shape when the sun appears. A feeling of holiness pervaded me. All was peace, rest, serenity. The fret and fume, the lust of desire denied transformed into glory in sight of the goal of fulfilment.

Patience had won. The little squirrel nestled close on my shoulder at last.

CHAPTER 49
A LETTER TO MY LOVE

I was for announcing the engagement right away, and having the marriage follow without delay, but the lady, she said nay, and gave such seductive reasons that I was enraptured to await her pleasure.

She insisted that it was such a miracle to be in love at last, to have been given the opportunity, that she could not endure the breath of common knowledge to blow on her treasure yet. She wanted its full wonder undimmed by the interest, knowledge, or curiosity of any soul. Just a little while, pled she.

Then came the most glorious week of my life.

I set the jeweller to design an exquisite setting for that letter so that it should not be worn to tatters with perusal and re-perusal. I knew it by heart but still it seemed that in some intoxication I must be imagining phrases until I got out the perfumed document and verified them with my eyes.

I felt braver and prouder than any man in the Loop or out of it. It seemed that mere ordinary mortals must note the splendid estate which rested on me and be filled with envy. I was consumedly, hilarously, flamboyantly, shamelessly happy. When I saw young fools in love I pitied them that in their immaturity they were rubbing the nap off something which could only blossom fully in maturity. I looked at the men of my years, blasé in their chains and was sorry for them that they had eaten their cake so long ago and had now to jog along on corn beef and cabbage, whilst I at the flood tide years sat at the feast of the Gods. And Sybyl, suffused with a new softness and warmth now turned all her wit and vivacity to the expression of her love FOR ME!

I saw her in the morning, sometimes in the afternoon, and every night. I called her on the 'phone as many as five times a day, and each morning came the little note written after we had parted to add the finishing touches, which, in the joy of the hour, she had neglected. Nothing could be more transporting, not even announcing the engagement. I came into the office with a jaunty air which had no cloud upon it, for had she not capitulated, was she not my promised wife, yes, *wife,* and she a woman of her word. I was content with this secret. Like the boy with the dark lantern, it was enough to fill the most phlegmatic with incandescent thrills to know of its existence.

It was towards the end of the week that she announced, "I'm going to marry you on one condition."

"Madam! You have promised to marry me on any number of conditions. One more will not signify."

"Good boy! I want the suite at The Caboodle that I had the night I accepted you."

"A most flattering sentiment. You are wlecome to all the suites you can use my Precious, but we are not going to live at the old Caboodle at all. I am going to build a little nest especially for you."

"No you don't!" said she merrily. "No little nest — horrid little cage for me, isolated and immured! I'm going to live in the house of bachelors! That's the reason I'm marrying you."

"I shall no longer be a bachelor." I bowed to her.

"Yes, but you'll have to continue to be a sort of janitor or *maitre d'hotel.*"

"I like the frank way you tabulate my status."

I sat down weak with a premonition of my end. I was not going to take my bride to The Caboodle to be under the curious eyes of all those fellows. I wanted to build something special.

"If I bring a wife there every other mugwump will want to do likewise and as soon as that happens —"

"— Yes, it would become the private family hotel where Popper pays the board while the females of the species over-run the premises. Never would a man be seen there again excepting the janitor and elevator men. Far be it from me to wreak such a calamity on such an abode. You see, it is this way —" and when Sybyl began her whimsical explanations and unreasonable reasoning, it was so entertaining that it was taking a mean advantage of me.

"You see I was reared by men and any taste acquired in youth sticks. I have been trained in many of the mental habits of men — that's why I'm not at all weak or deluded about them —"

"No, you certainly are not so that it could be noticed any."

"Yes, they are no mystery to me, but through habit I like them around. I am more interested in the things they are interested in than in the teeterisations of the idle middle-class wife and mother — heaven save me from her when she is truly womanly and sits around a boarding house all day and has no civic activity. I don't care if she is the sacred producer of cannon fodder. I can talk with less restraint to men than women and the older I grow the more I find myself reverting to habits acquired in my youthful environment. Yes, I've made up my mind. That's where I shall live, far from the madding sphere of woman. It is a rare opportunity to meet men, as, except by chance we have no meeting ground that is ordinarily and comfortably available for men and women. There is supposed to be a great deal of freedom for girls in this country. The Latin is bulgy-eyed when he sees it in operation, but it is not freedom for platonic association. American society is composed so that men's and women's lives have a great gulf between. Father lives in one hemisphere and makes money, some of which mother spends in the other. The American girl is free in that her parents don't watch her all the time like Italian duennas, but that is all the freedom she has and it only lasts till marriage. After marriage the country farmer puritan ideal prevails — couples are unrelievedly yoked. They must never look at another. No wonder so many are driven to divorce."

I let her prattle on. If she would only be meek and self-effacing in a man's establishment it might have been all right. But that was not Sybyl's attitude by long chalks.

"You needn't be afraid of women invading the place excepting as transient guests," she continued. "I don't want the only place where I can study the male of the species, spoiled. I'll help you to keep it intact as a museum of men. I asked the men on Christmas Eve if they would like me as a roomer and they said they would be enraptured, but that I should need to get around you."

"You'll never do that. I am going to have a home of my own."

"All right you can live in it by yourself, and I'll hang out at The Caboodle.

"I don't want other people gaping at my domestic felicity."

"No little private bird cage for me, sitting up on a perch and cogitating upon the mats and meals and so on! No young man! I give you back your freedom. You can wed Mrs. McCorkle."

"Sybyl," I protested, "I'm jealous. Can't you have a little mercy. I want you all to myself. All those darned fools would be falling in love with you."

"What matter so long as I didn't reciprocate. Do you suppose when it has taken me all these years to fall in love once, that I'm going to make a continual orgy of it now! Are you expecting to have such a demoralising effect upon me that I'll fall in love once a day. I wish I might. I've always been envious of the fickle."

195

"It isn't a bit of use your talking all that bunk just to put me off the trail. I wont have you there among those fellows. It would spoil the morale."

"Well, you see I'm not the simple cow-like person that could ruminate continually in the dull pastures of unalloyed domesticity."

The simple cow-like person my lady surely is not. Her husband will never have a chance to moon around and whine that he is unappreciated and misunderstood. He will be too busy trying to keep up with and shoo off the fellows hanging around trying to tell her, no matter what kind of a man she has that she is wasted on such a goop."

"Well, that's settled," she said.

"Yes, I'm going to build a nice little house."

"Not for me. I'm not going to be kept in a tame hen coop to sit and wait for you coming home at night with no entertainment but a matinee or a woman's club lecture or some futile fancy work. No siree! I must have something to counteract the evil effects of matrimony."

I was really huffed. "Of course if that's the way you look at it and if you don't care enough for me —"

"If I don't care enough for you therefore to become a tiresome empty-pate — cockadoodle!" said she.

She had been so tractable since the engagement that I began to feel sure of her and was tempted to exercise a little authority.

"You must allow a man to have some judgment in these things. I am sure you have always found me a reasonable man."

"Yes indeed, you are a perfect duck, but let us submit it to arbitration — Aunt Pattie?"

"No siree!" said I, "Aunt Pattie is worse than yourself. Miss Maguire. She's the most sensible person in town."

"No ma'am! I believe you give Miss Maguire a bonus to uphold you in everything."

"I think this is too much, the first trifling thing I ask," I assumed an injured tone.

"Young man, you are free!" said she.

I arose and flounded out, if a being without flounces can be said to use that form of protest. As a sedative I tried the movies, but it didn't act. I went home and flung myself into a chair in Aunt Pattie's room. She addressed me. I replied with absent-minded grunts. Presently with her eyes twinkling she laid down her paper.

"The little girl been entertaining you," said she.

"If you like to put it that way. She has made up her mind to live at The Caboodle.

"Where else would you have her live?"

"I wanted to build for her."

"Some little nest and put her in like a toy, but you see she is not the sitting-hen type."

"I don't know what to do. By the simple process of marrying her I've come to the conclusion that Solomon had nothing on me in the variety of his harem. By the simple process, did I say — I meant by the complex, devious, strenuous, apparently impossible process which I have been struggling with night and day for half eternity, it seems to me."

"Too bad when there are feather-heads without end to be won without any trouble at all! I don't think you show much cunning in capturing your seventeen different women in one. And think when you win, you will never be bored by marital sameness. Of course she wants to live at The Caboodle. Perhaps if you humor her in this one thing there will be a time when of her own accord she will want the separate nest."

"Humor her in ONE thing! And I wouldn't have it ready then"

"Well, of course, if this house is the essence of matrimony!"

"I think she must be your daughter," I grumbled.

"I hope she soon will be if you have any sense."

"I don't want her among all these men. She really is a flirt."

"You are surely sly enough to know that the puritan in her will keep the unconquerable coquette from letting innocent mischief develop into malice. I have taken her number long ago and am quite satisfied."

I flounced off from Aunt Patty. I was quite sulky, but the jeweler sent home that contraption for the letter and I had to frame it and read it and thus was conquered. If she could be generous, so could I. I sat me down with a good fountain pen.

> My One and Only, my First, Last, and All-the-Time,
> Of course no place could come up to The Caboodle. I am overjoyed that you prefer it. If in addition to the proper place to live you entertain principles about the economic independence of married women and would like to run the shoe-shining parlor in the basement, or indeed if you would like to set up such a business just outside the front door on the pavement, I'm sure it can be arranged. I shall never put anything in your way of this manner of self-support, should be one of your patrons, and should take pleasure in recommending you to others.

I felt much relieved after this was despatched by special. I looked for some squib in return but here again was an occasion when she did not act in line with expectation.

CHAPTER 50
THE NAME OF TWIDDLE

One morning the indefatigable Press reported that Lord and Lady Twiddle were in our midst. The name was no more Twiddle than Tweeser, if one went by the spelling. This is a simp. spelling rendition of the way it sounded when pronounced in the English fashion which makes irreverent hash of so many proper names. It is as near to Lord Twiddle's cognomen as the other names in these yarns are near to the originals should you find the owners walking on Dearborn Street or otherwise cavorting in the Loop.

Aunt Pattie was pouring cream on her cereal and up she bobbed, grabbed the paper, and took a rise out of me by announceing that she was great friends with the Lord and Lady, that she had met them on the plane of irrigation and congeniality in Egypt. They had frequented the same hotels in Algiers and Rome and she had been to one of their country places in Great Britain.

"I would telephone them," said she, "only it would be useless. They wouldn't understand a word, and we'd all be exhausted by the campaign."

She hurried through breakfast to write a letter which she despatched by me with orders to get it and some flowers to them and tell them she was completely at their service and would follow without delay.

"It is strange that they did not let me know of their arrival," she commented. "But they do not know our mail system. They think it is like London where one can get a letter inside an hour or two." As she spoke, I spied a letter among her pile which looked like the Twiddles and she opened it. It had been mailed the day before. "Go at once," repeated Aunt Pattie, "while I go upstairs and dress."

I was kept waiting among a roomful of reporters who were alert to write the things which the papers always print about Englishmen. His Lordship gave out that he was over about irrigation schemes though the papers hinted his mission was munitions, and both sets of papers, pro-Ally or pro-German were alert to make the most of it.

"What's the bloomin', blawated Hinglishman 'ere for?" said one reporter. My average countryman always uses these expressions to indicate an Englishman. Such international pleasantries will continue till we are much more cultured and cosmopolitan than we are today. It is at best no worse than the English idea that we all, regardless of caste or clique, pick our teeth and trim our nails in public, chew gum and rush the cuspidor.

"His Royal Highness is interested in irrigation," remarked one reporter.

"Let's ask him what he thinks of a "dry" Chicago," added a third.

The attendant said his lordship was engaged with an

old personal friend and presently the door opened and the friend came out. As I live, it was Sybyl, looking as happy as a spring day, with the two distinguished visitors escorting her to the elevators, with British tenacity attempting to keep up private household courtesies in a big hotel.

I wondered if my poor sight were playing me a trick, but Sybyl dispelled all doubt by introducing me as the nephew of their old friend Mrs. Pattie Cavarley. I doffed my hat and was for executing my errand and escaping with proverbial native celerity, but Lady Twiddle would have none of it. She asked Sybyl to take me into the inner room while she and her hubby met the reporters. Sybyl and I disappeared into a feast of kisses as if famished by lengthy separation while Lord Twiddle and his Lady won the hearts of the press by their courtesy and stately cordiality of demeanor.

"What are you doing with these people?" I asked of Sybyl. "I always suspected you of being something in disguise. Are you their run-a-way child or what?"

"Not *their* run-away child."

"You have grossly deceived an honest man."

"An honest man! For years posing as a waiter — a respectable useful waiter and you turn out to be —"

"— one of the criminal rich."

"Presactly!"

We had little time for recrimination about our past before Lord and Lady Twiddle re-entered.

"Well, well!" exclaimed his Lordship, "To think we should find Sybbie here, and this is the nephew of our dear friend Mrs. Cavarley, I am glad to hear that she is in such excellent health."

"Sybbie hasn't changed an atom," purred her Ladyship.

"Not a bit!" chuckled Lord Twiddle. "Wait till I shew you. She presented me with this," He indicated a bunch of American Beauties. "She tells me this is your leading rose and that bouquets of them are always presented to prima donnas. I can't sing a note — not a jolly note. I

200

make a beastly noise like a steam calliope when I attempt to join in song. That is a joke! Ha! Ha!"

His wife exhibited a bouquet of violets. "Sybyl says lady-loves receive violets every morning in the States."

"My love, I must make a note of that," said the old gentleman with a charm which was inspiring to one on the brink of matrimony.

"She is just the same dear quaint little mad-cap that she was long ago. We are devoted to her," continued Lady Twiddle.

Sybyl beamed riotously. "You know when His Excellency — I always call him His Excellency —"

"Yes, when I was —"

At this juncture Sybyl sprang up and clapped a hand on the dignified mouth of Lord Twiddle with as much assurance as she would have flipped my ear and exclaimed, "Oh, your Excellency, not a word about my past. Not one word! As a gentleman, on your honor, you've got to keep it secret. No one knows who or what I am or where I came from. If you told, my mysteriousness would all be gone."

"Just the same little Sybyl as of yore," smiled Lady Twiddle. "You are a most ridiculous child. You haven't settled down at all!"

"Well Sybbie, what else do you want me to do for you while we're here?" proceeded her friend.

"Lord Twiddle is such a dear," explained Sybyl to me. "He does things for one in the true English fashion. I could send him out to buy a penny worth of nothing done up in brown paper."

"And that," said the gentleman with a deliciously modulated laugh, "is the true test of affinity."

"And a man's right to live," said I.

"The high right of service," added her Ladyship. But the attendant came in and announced Mrs. Pattie Cavarley at that moment and our chatter dropped hurriedly to make way for more important matters.

Three days later Aunt Pattie commanded my presence in her apartments. Having made my bow and betaken myself to my favorite chair she told me that

Sybyl wished to announce our engagement. I refrained from fool observations. So long as she had decided that we were to marry I was content. I had learned that when I wished to know what Sybyl and I were likeliest to do, the best fortune teller was Aunt Pattie. Sybyl pranced out from behind a screen in such a state of enthusiasm that she could not wait for Aunt Pattie's explanation.

"Aunt Pattie is going to give a great party when the Twiddles come back from California, at which Lady Twiddle will announce my engagement. Won't that just be grrrrrand!"

"You snob, scraping to these English nobobs like that."

"You don't know the joy of seeing some one who knows all about me when I was a youngster; and so many people have tried to exploit me and treat me carelessly because I had no visible protectors and was merely self-supporting, that I thought just for once I should like to have some one vouch that I too come from the protected class of women and could have been a petted parasite if my inclinations ran that way."

"Such associates! Is that the fell secret of your past?"

"Yes, and that I escaped from the home, thank God! Ran right away out into the world"

"You can't make the announcement without mentioning my name can you?" I inquired, feeling like going on a joy jag.

"You don't mind, do you?" she asked archly, her little impertinent nose tilted.

"My anxiety was that I might be left out. What have I got to do? Bow down while the titled gent hits me with his sword or his spats or anything?"

"Don't be silly. You can go out for the evening if you like. The importance of this party is me. ME!" Aunt Pattie nodded approvingly.

"Why this sudden egotism of the female of the species? Have I to be gotten up in a Mother Hubbard?"

"I think you had better take the evening off."

"But if the Tweedledees announce the engagement,

when shall I be able to announce the marriage?" I asked.

"Yes, that's the only drawback. If I announce the engagement I suppose I shall really have to get married. Perhaps we'll just have a party."

"Fraidy cat — little fraidy cat, not game to get married!"

"I'm game enough to get married. It's the long stale staying married that scares me. I suppose I'll either have to marry or remain single!"

Knowing her strong leanings towards remaining single, I hastened to say, "Let's announce the engagement at any rate. Think how swagger it will sound in the English accent."

She looked at me with her most impudent expression and her chin tilted so that I got a great expanse of eyelash — a piece of coquetry which always tempts me to clutch her tight and dishevel her with kisses till she has not a speck of spic-and-spannes nor dignity nor assurance left about her.

CHAPTER 51
MISS MAGUIRE EVACULATES

Then came the dog days after Christmas when January has been beaten back to the arctic, and weak-minded February tries to capitulate with the calendar by coming out in the sheeps' wool of spring. It was that desolate swamp of weeks when there is nothing like fall or Christmas to work up to, when spring and summer vacations are still a long way distant, a dreary stretch to those chained by circumstances to one spot in the United States and which always drives the wasters to Florida and California, Egypt or the Riviera.

They weren't going to Europe or Egypt this year. They were hearkening to the See-America-first patriots whose megaphone was loud in the land. A few of them were following the new sport of being heroines and heroes by activities in war areas, but many of them thought too much of their well-massaged skins for even this and were going to Coronado Beach and the Panama World's Fair. More of them were staying at home and meeting the financial dullness as best they could and trying with might and main to keep out of the ranks of the bankrupt.

The war at that date has receded for a time from American interest. It had shrunk from glaring headlines covering most of the front page of newspapers to one headline on the front page while the remainder of the information, manufactured or authentic, had crept back to obscure columns. As a news item, the winning or losing of a few yards of trenches had grown monotonous and local scandals, legislation, and elections were taking their usual prominence. Humanity had grown used to war. We no longer regarded it with dizzy unbelief as a ghastly nightmare from which the world would blessedly awake some morning. The world, to its incalculable deterioration had accepted it as the everyday routine. Lots of the commoner clay had given up worrying about it, if indeed they had ever regarded it as a matter concerning them at all. "Pure Americans" untravelled, and provincial in the wholesomest sense, were inclined to dismiss it as a European distemper like kings and castles and caste. To others of us it had grown beyond thought and we could only feel in a dull way about it. Idealist and business man alike now realised that it was no overnight eruption, no one case of bubonic or cholera to be nipped in the bud by our superior facilities for hygiene, but a cataclysmic subversion of civilization.

The folk whose text is "business is business" were having a colossal innings. They throve and fattened — some of them on bloated army contracts and rake-offs between "friends", and the world went very well with them. Not a ripple disturbed the seas of reaction. And the dreamers and fools — there have never been enough of them to be dangerous.

There was in the magnitude of the European debacle — all the able-bodied men living like rats in sewers, alert for opportunities to kill, while the old gentleman sat at home and edged them on and vapoured of glory — a wild magnificence of paranoia that was spell binding, whereas in the neutrality, smug or timid, of the countries still at peace, there was little more than the craftiness of vultures who foresee an unprecedented harvest. At first when the propstick of Central European trade and industry was knocked away we had whimpered with fear and discomfort, but now like a child that is offered a stick of candy, we were starting to glow at the prosperity which must inevitably be ours out of the misfortune and madness of others.

A few perennial souls were whispering the word peace and thereby affording a satisfying butt for the buffoon jokes of the multitude. The world had so thoroughly accepted the disease of war that those who talked of peace were as completely ridiculous as if they had sought to discredit the rotation of the seasons. Aunt Pattie and I had dipped into our jeans to send a working woman to The Hague as a member of a peace excursion. Well-to-do uplifters always insist upon a member of the working class if possible to give local color to their entertainments.

Sybyl wilted before my eyes. Work was slack, she was thrown back upon herself and withdrew more and more from me. I was for marrying and taking her right away, as the announcement of the engagement in the delicious accents of the Twiddles had been an unqualified social success, but she said she did not want to marry at all now. I was goop enough to argue with her.

Calling at Dearborn Street one day to continue the argument I found she had gone home long before office closing hours. Why had she gone home? Lieutenant Yellow-Hair returned and asked me to go into Miss Penelo's room as Miss Maguire also wished to see me. But she was engaged. Would I please wait, as it was most important.

Lieutenant Yellow-Hair stopped and hesitated, her

alabaster complexion more eatable than ever. I was overcome anew by her beauty and virginal superiority, and by a certain human air about her which made me feel less of a worm than I usually did in her presence. She looked at me, blushed, started to laugh and say something, thought better of it and, with a missish air, retreated. What could be the matter?

The plot thickened presently when Miss Maguire came in as super-blushingly as a peony, and so hesitant that I put my hand on my handkerchief to be ready for any emergency.

"Where's your partner?" I asked. Miss Maguire became even more rosy, if that were possible.

"She's gone home." Miss Maguire looked positively guilty. The tears sprang to her eyes. Her voice entirely gave way at last.

"Nothing up with Miss Penelo, is there?"

"Oh, no, not a thing. She's just a little upset." Miss Maguire really wept. I rose to comfort her, finding her a scrumptious little quail, but personally administered comfort scared her into normality.

"Sit down and I'll tell you all about it," said she. There followed the story of affairs on Dearborn Street. Lieutenant Yellow-Hair had made public her engagement and had given warning that she was leaving to "get her things ready". This the explanation of that young lady's manner. Miss Maguire, seeing the times, had a satisfactory offer for the reduced business and she and Harold Brubaker were going off to South America.

"And you," she said, "should marry Miss Penelo at once and take care of her. That child is really ill. I have never seen anything like the way she frets over things that are all right for a set of old professors in conventions, but a young person wants something happy and bright."

Congratulations were in order. I was jubilant as Sybyl's last excuse for delay was now removed. I put away anxiety over her absence to render unto the bride-to-be the things that were hers.

"Three cheers for Brubaker," said I, "and Miss

Maguire, I envy him so that if he falls short let me hear of it. I'll make it a personal proposition. I'll give a great shivoo at The Caboodle in honor of the event, and it shan't be a stag, as I want you at it."

Oh, to see her blushes, as her taper fingers took refuge in the little frilly pockets of the little frilly apron as I so distinctly remembered them doing on the first day I saw her.

"And you, Miss Maguire," I continued hilariously, "as I have said before, I would that you were two and that I could have one of you. Why did you not inculcate Miss Penelo with your ideas?"

"Don't you worry. She will achieve the same results as I by different methods."

I did all I could bar standing on my head to express my delight and sense of brotherly affection for Miss Maguire, discussed preliminaries of a big party at The Caboodle, wondered what the deuce I'd get her for a wedding present and then hastened to Sybyl. Dr. Margaret came to me in the parlor.

"I have put her to bed," said she. "Look here young man, why don't you marry that girl and take her away where she will not have sight or sound of the things that are on her mind or she is due for a serious breakdown."

Dr. Margaret took me up to her suite which adjoined Sybyl's, and where I had first learned of her existence, and finding that the patient had not obeyed orders, allowed me to see her. I found her in a highly nervous state and weeping bitterly for the loss of Miss Maguire.

She said that life was totally spoilt. That she couldn't possibly live without Miss Maguire. She insisted that she herself had no more intelligence than a beetle. She had no idea of making a living excepting with a partner like Miss Maguire who stage-managed her talents and secured the work. She had held up so as to throw no shade on Miss Maguire's happiness but now she did not care. And that beast of a Brubaker, she wished he had broken his neck years ago. He was a scatterbrained thing and not half good enough for Miss Maguire.

I assured her that she did not have to earn her living,

which of course made her mountainously sure that she must. I assured her that she had me, but she brushed me aside. She could never marry now. She was too unhappy. Marriage was for the happy. It would be incogitable to marry a man and make him miserable. "I can never do the kind of work again that I have been doing. How am I to put in my life?"

I advised taking a day at a time.

"For the first time in my life I understand and have sympathy for the people who rush to Coney Islands and movies and even those who rattle dice in a box all day like they do in the barbers' shops. I even can understand now why men take to drink, and I used to despise them so because they had no resources within themselves."

"You had a little castle of retreat, but it will rise again."

"I want the hollow unintellectual entertainment to pass the time and keep me occupied till it is time for sleep, and I want some one there in the morning when I have to wake again to the day-mare of realities. The old reactionaries are right. Human society is only a different form of a lot of sharks around the carcass of a whale — the biggest and boldest shark gets most of the meat — and survives. The old clap trap about the survival of the fittest — the greediest and coarsest is right. We go back to first principles, cutting each other's throats for food and warmth, the society we had imagined to be evolving crumbled at the first touch of materialistic reality. Our ideals were the vapourings of abnormality. Now we go back to normality and I have no place in such a normality."

"Let us cut away from it all," I said. "Let us go sailing and sailing away from these people who have come to be nothing but contraptions, who think and eat and love and die by science and introspection. We'll go to far and primitive places where only the faintest echo of the war can come. We'll live with the people and grow things."

"Eat grass like Nebuchadnezzar," she smiled.

"Yes, we'll go far from the track and accumulate a fund of primordial experiences."

"We'd have to be married," she sighed.

I could see rising that coldness which the male rampant awakened in her and hastened to forestall it.

"Not necessarily. We'll take Aunt Pattie to look after you."

We should climb up on those high sweet planteaux of humanhood undisturbed by the overkeyed emotionalism of sex till she was healthy again and able to eat of all breads of life, finding each good in its just proportion, even the bread of lovers baked in the pure flame of passion. I could wait. I had patience — and self-control. I had never been a follower of the popular schools of manhood.

Dr. Margaret came in and rescued me. I reached for my hat and hiked for Aunt Pattie. I was fortunate to find her home. I flung myself into a chair and maintained silence.

"Why don't you marry her and get that part of it over," she remarked after a time.

"Seems to have changed her mind about being married at all."

"Sounds as if she is nervous," said Aunt Pattie with a tonic twinkle in her eyes.

"She seems very frail and weary."

"Always will when the source of her emotions is unhappy for she feeds on the spirit, but she is essentially sound and she will soon be herself again. What are you going to do?"

"I suggested going around the world."

"And she?"

"Says she would fade away at the thought of a honeymoon."

A smile flickered about Aunt Pattie's lips. "She may go with me."

"It all depends on you. Will you take her away and let me butt in on the trip? She needs to get back to mother earth and grub there and raise flowers and chickens. Dr. Devereux is right about that, and for once

Sybyl agrees. She says animals are so superior to men."

"They are," promptly agreed Aunt Pattie; "I was thinking myself that I was beginning to get enough of the heat out of me to go back to the children and the flowers."

"Aunt Pattie," I pled rather unsmoothly, "will you take her in hand."

"Is she so very, very dear, my boy?"

"Just about the only thing that ever happened, I guess."

"Hu-u-um! It is one chance in a million when it is so with a man, and it is the right woman. I believe our little stranger is the right woman. We'll take a sea voyage first. I think I'm old enough to traipse around the unknown places now. No bandit would think me worth eloping with. I was always going as you know, but I became immersed in the new movements. Now the war has made them unseaworthy. It will be a long time before they are water tight again and I shall be glad of a complete change. You can be Sinbad, I'll be the old Lady of the Sea and Sybyl can be the Mermaid when she feels disposed."

Aunt Pattie and I loved the sea. She was one of the toughest salts I knew.

"Sybyl is surely ill with it all."

"So are the rest of us, though not in such poignant degree. For myself, I am old and withered, and because I have suffered more than the young, I know more. I have dared more and experienced more. I know that the sun will regain his brightness and souls leap again for joy. If not in this generation well then in the one after, and when you come to my time of life, a longer perspective gives more patience. Things do not seem so tragically worthwhile. The fall of an idol, the dispersing of an ideal does not cut so deeply. The very old and the very young do not feel this debacle to be so tremendous. The old have had their love life, or have missed it for all time. The very young still feel sure of their birthright, and things may in a way adjust themselves for them. It is those of delicate sensibilities and advanced beliefs between the ages of twenty-five and forty-five, I should say, who are most crushed. You were rejoicing in a rapidly improving society — largely the structure of your imaginations, in which the love-life as an example, was to be so much broader and wholesomer and more satisfying, not "sicklied o'er" with such frowsy sentimentality, such coarse indulgence on the part of men, such parrot-minded dissembling and hypocrisy on the part of women — and then the deluge! There is a horrifying recrudescence of all the worst elements of a materialistic civilization resting on brute force. And no recovery in your time. Poor children, I understand, but you have each other."

Aunt Pattie regarded a milk-white Lake Michigan contemplatively for some moments and then spoke dreamily as if addressing the Anti-Humming Club for the Adolescent high-brows.

"My children, fret not yourselves so egotistically because of evil. Life seems a patternless chaotic mess. No wonder the gambling instinct is one of the most ineradicable in all peoples. Life is the arch gambler with us. Only one in a great many has the gifts of the gods in either beauty, health, wealth, love, or happiness. You and Sybyl seem to be offered this millionth chance of happiness. You are well favored; you have health, you have no bread and butter problem, and now, chief of all, love has come to you, and there is no obstacle. Rise up to meet the royal chance which life has given you. Go bravely, the two of you, let come what will. If reverses should come, take them intrepidly. Do not be too unhappy because of the sorrow of others. Each and all of us have to drink the cup of life to the very dregs, to find in some cases that the dregs are not so bitter as our anticipation. We have to take the sin and the shame, and the pain and the defeat of life with the beauty and blessing, the joy and radiance, and on the whole find it good. We have to leave our minds open, my boy, and not be downcast because the best and greatest of us are paltry insects with minds to match. This war, after all, has smashed only our immediate insect calculations, by which we squirm to make two and two come out as four, and each Jack find his Jill. The guiding power would seem to care not a jot how the story ends or whether it drops in the middle, or never gets farther than the beginning, but to keep time with some mightier wheels of rhythm and harmony, the knowledge of which is still shut from us."

Aunt Pattie was silent for a long time, her beautiful hands with finger tips approaching Miss Maguire's in symmetry, lying quite still in her lap.

"Where is the voyage to be?" she asked presently.

"Bermuda or Jamaica, I should think would be the safest route these days, or the Southern Pacific. Britannia's cubs seem to have mopped up the seas in that direction."

"Sybyl a good sailor?"

"One of the worst, she says."

"Fine! let us take a slow boat and potter around Jamaica and Panama, perhaps go and see the exhibition all on the water. We could put in April and May in Florida. Those people want to throw back the lease of Meadow Lark Farm." This was an old farm house in Connecticut overlooking the Sound, which my foster father had maintained for summer occupancy and always filled with guests. It was a dreamy old-fashioned place made new by steam heat, electric light, and hot water and certain cunning enlargements.

"I think the trip down the coast will be plenty for her," continued Aunt Pattie. "I hope we have rough weather. I think I'll take back the lease of Meadow Lark and tell the gardener to get ready for us this summer."

I could have hugged Aunt Pattie. "You are a conjurer," I said.

"Not at all, merely an old woman with a little experience. I have seen a good many bored children in my day and some genuinely weary. That's what is the matter with your little friend. Like other people in this world she is suffering from too much spurious efficiency. She has been using her brain too exclusively till the wheels run round like lightning and wear her to the ground. She

212

is like one of those air plants which grow without earth but which eventually die if they don't get some substantial nourishment. Take her back to the earth to play. Give her a little spade and bucket and turn her loose on the beach. Free her from worry. Don't bother her with love till she is ready. Beware of that my boy. We'll fill the house with a regulation crowd. She'll enjoy them as an antidote for perhaps a few weeks. Then, if the war has not swallowed us too they will have palled upon her. You do the work of the trip and leave Sybyl and me nothing but to enjoy ourselves. Your commission is not to rock the boat."

CHAPTER 52
THE SEDUCTIVE SEED CATALOGUE

I acted bravely on this receipt though the temptation was to be on Sybyl's doorstep again next morning. Discipline had its reward. When I arrived home the next afternoon, there were voices in Aunt Pattie's apartment. I stopped on the threshold and heard my foster mother droning in soothing tones, "Yes, we'll go sailing and sailing, and then digging and digging. We'll have a garden of our own with roses and violets —"

"— and sweet Williams, and pomegranate, and a magnolia tree, and jessamine, and Japanese honeysuckle, and passion flowers, and little English daisies, and anemones, and gillie flowers, and wall flowers, and cowslips, and ribbon grass, and sweet scented thyme, and the sweet scented verbena tree. Violets white and blue and double and single, and La France roses by the front gate, and the real old cabbage roses, and the moss roses with their heavenly perfume. And did you ever smell a loquat blossom when the night dew is on it?"

"I didn't know it had a perfume," said I, unable longer to resist such allurements.

"Some people don't know that pansies and ranunculi have a perfume."

"I don't believe you could dig up a mosquito to save your life and I'm just sick of your trimness. I'd like for once to see you with your hair all awry and your face dirty — just dirty."

"You never see a person with any other sort of face in Chicago," she retorted. "I actually have to go to a masseuse to clean my pores every once in a while after the soot has clogged them."

"But I mean nice mud dirt, and fat — Sybyl Penelo how I should laugh to see you fat and with pink in your cheeks. I believe I'd really fall in love with you at last if you were fat and untidy."

"Nearly time," she chuckled. And to Aunt Pattie, "Couldn't we grow a tree somewhere?"

"We'll grow a whole raft of trees. We'll give up the riddle of the universe. We've been suffering an exaggeration of egotism to think we could solve it and we are sick in our souls as well as our tummies from the resultant indigestion. We'll let the Lord mind his own business for a while. He doesn't seem to have appreciated our efforts as he should and I think we've already done enough to get us by St. Peter in case the old superstitions are correct. We'll go and play with nature and calm ourselves. We'll swear off the anguish of purposeful action. For a violet to have bloomed, a butterfly to have flitted in the sunshine, for a child to have gladdened us by its laughter and lisping words, is enough. For us to have worked and suffered and enjoyed and loved is an all-sufficient purpose of existence."

"I don't think I want sweet peas in my garden," pursued Sybyl. "They are ragged without being graceful and their perfume is sickly."

"Well," I interposed, "we'll have my lady's garden and everything you like shall be there and Aunt Pattie and I will take the culls in our garden. What can we have besides sweet peas?"

"You can have the peonies and nasturtums. I want the larkspurs and snapdragons, but I shan't be mean. I'll

214

give you lots out of my garden. I'm sure they will love you better than they will me and if some of your things should want to grow in my garden, I couldn't be inhospitable to them."

I could see that where her garden and ours began or ended would soon be lost in flowers, and I saw also that the sickness of her soul was not very deep when the recognition of flowers as our little brothers and sisters was still so vividly alive.

"You can have the lilies of the valley," she offered, "but I want the pansies — yards and yards of them, and a canopy of wistaria. Haven't you any seed catalogues? Seed catalogs and dictionaries are the most fascinating of all literature. I never can pry myself loose from either. After reading a seed catalogue for a couple of hours I have a whole flower and vegetable garden in full bloom in my imagination. It is so refreshing."

"We'll take a cargo of seed catalogues on our voyage around the world and wrest their innermost secrets from them so as to be ready for achievements vast and dazzling as soon as we return."

"All right, that's settled. I'm all ready to go," I remarked injudiciously.

"OH, the thought of marriage spoils it all. You'll be for ever buzzing in my ear about how you love me and kissing me and persecuting me all the time. I don't want to be loved or married. I want to be let alone."

"I'm the person you should marry," said Aunt Pattie promptly. "I shan't be buzzing in your ear that I love you. In fact I don't care whether I love you or not. I find you agreeable and entertaining."

"I wish I could marry you."

"We'll go on a long honeymoon together which will be as good."

"And I'll be little Tommy Taggy-Tail and come along in the rear."

"You wouldn't come far enough in the rear."

"He would if I were in control," said Aunt Pattie. "He would be useful to buy tickets and make out routes and find out when to catch boats and trains."

"You are an optimist if you think you can control him. It's more than I can and I don't feel like being squelched any more at present."

"I think it is I that am entitled to look upon myself as squelched," I contended; "all spread out in the mud like Sir Walter's coat waiting to be stepped on, and being stepped on too, till I'm out of sight."

"Too bad if you prefer to be fawned upon," said Aunt Pattie.

I recognised it was time for me to remove myself without that last word which men so deeply covet. Aunt Pattie talked to me about it later.

"If you don't have the judgment when to leave alone a frazzled child with nerves all on end, you had better remain an old bachelor."

"Well, she said," I protested.

"That is enough, my boy," said Aunt Pattie. "If you are going to begin that 'she said' business, you are in the wrong pew with that partner. There are many large cow-like soothing women to be had who would never necessitate the 'she said' lay. Leave her alone when you are bewildered. Let the comedy book be closed and begin reading at the next page that is opened, even if it slightly disconnects the thread of the story."

"What do you really think of her," I said. "Does she care for me?"

"I'm entirely satisfied with her. I demand some entertainment in life which she is designed to contribute. Don't you be such a callow youngster as to irritate her. Don't pursue her too closely while she is fagged. Leave the courtship to me and the seed catalogues. I'll see that you are represented in some capacity, even if I have to develop sciatica and have you to lift me around. But let her alone. Don't tease her. Sex is always a disturbing element, divinely stimulating to the fit but it can be very wearying and repulsive to the frazzled."

After a while she fell asleep — under my roof. In repose her face had a parched appearance. She was inexpressibly dear to me. I wanted her as a lover in the fulness of life and patience was a tedious necessity.

That supreme selfishness, the ego of the individual consumed me and I wanted my love, my mate, in spite of the fearsome carnage with its broken, starved, and violated bodies where hate and lust brayed loud in Europe. It made not one atom of difference in the driving urge for the fulness of life, and could I have had my woman I could have forgotten every horror near and far enthroned in the kingdom of my own emotions.

CHAPTER 53
THE PIRATE'S BRIDE

Thus it was settled.

We married Miss Maguire and Harold Brubaker, with great *éclat*, gave Lieutenant Yellow-Hair a fitting send off, entrusted The Caboodle to Mrs. McCorkle and young Phipps Toby, forsook the reconstruction of the universe, and were at liberty to reconstrue ourselves.

An acquaintance financially strapped was glad to let me have his boat and picked crew of blond Scandinavians, and thus after all it was the pirate act that was to secure Sybyl to me.

"We'll take aboard our privateering barque a cargo of seed catalogues — soothing, satisfying, and stimulating," said Aunt Pattie with a delicious chuckle. "And we'll devote ourselves to them to the exclusion of all mental gymnastics, and in a week, if Sybyl happens to be a good sailor, the monotony will so whet her curiosity that she'll begin to wonder if we have forgotten about marrying her: and if she is a bad sailor, she'll be ready to come to terms to get on dry land again. Either way, once aboard the lugger and the girl is ours. We can be married in Jamaica, so you had better have all papers and passports ship-shape."

So we steered our little barque of dreams away from the big harbors where its tiny toot was drowned amid the bellow of the mighty engines of those whose spiritual ways were not as ours. We set our milk-white sail without relinquishing one jot the hope one day to bring it into port again higher up the stream of progress. Notwithstanding the present rout we were assured that time was on our side — but such a long time that it entitled us for a space to empty our hands of the old tasks, to shut our hearts against impossible fancies and take to the high seas and the far seas without the qualms of moral deserters. We fled from a people sickened and spiritually debauched by all the demoralisation of war *sans* its chastisement, to remain in exile till the abatement of the carnival of blood or till some new development might sweep our nation also into the vortex and constitute a recall.

Being a law-abiding pirate crew, in lieu of the Bully Roger we tacked to the mast head some lines which ran in our memory:

Not all the joy of life is lost,
   Not all its savour glad and keen,
There still are seas I've never crossed,
   There still are lands I've never seen.

We set our faces south towards the great sun where the seas are indigo and the blossoms have rich fragrance and gorgeous hue. Since the high gods of chance had singled us out for favors, premeditatedly and systematically we shut from our sympathies for a time the suffering of others, while we clutched at a little of joy and love and laughter and beauty which should continue — who knows what a day may bring forth?

We were entitled to our gambler's luck with clear conscience for we were among the weak impractical fools and dreamers. As Sybyl said of herself, she was weary of working to support unpopular causes. Now we had been put to flight. We, the inconceivable fools who had thought to change human nature, well merited the raucous derision which screamed at us from every ruling source the world around. Our arrant tom-foolery

218

exposed beyond peradventure of doubt, nay more than that, frantically suppressed as actively mischievous, we were silenced, defeated.

So to up-anchor without a backward glance and leave to the victors their far-reaching victories. They who have worked their will according to their pattern, it is for them to carry on.

In other days, through all the days unceasingly, other weavers of sweet dreams shall have their being and out of the struggle, belief, and hope of their fancies leave human society just a little better for the great masses who persecuted and derided them at the direction of their masters. Thus up and up through the aeons — to perfection or Nirvana: who has more than a faint whisper of proven knowledge of what lies in the Great Silence?

The sun will hold his pageant in the west for a million million evenings, the birds carol their music at dawn. Lovers will for ever stray beside the sea or rivers in the perfumed dusk, finding life good, even as we, so long since dust. The listening hearts will ever thrill to the imperative siren song of truth and beauty and brother-hood, and always and for aye will be other listening hearts to beat as those which broke in August 1914.